Leslie

From:
Donna

My granddaughter is on the cover!

Dancing
in the
Rain

Monica Eldridge

Dancing in the Rain

Copyright 2014 by Monica Eldridge

Published By Monica Eldridge

www.monicaeldridge.com

Ebook edition created 2014

All rights reserved. No part of this publication may be produced without written permission of the publisher.

This book is a work of fiction. Names, characters, places, events, businesses, and dialogues are either products of the author's imagination or used fictitiously. Any resemblance to actual persons, living or dead, are entirely coincidental.

Scripture Quotations are from the King James Version of the Bible.

To my husband
The man who taught me how to
Dance in the Rain

I Love You

A time to weep,
and a time to laugh;
a time to mourn, and a time to dance;
Ecclesiastes 3:4

PROLOGUE

July 1908
Asheville, North Carolina

BELLA COULDN'T SEE FOR THE heavy sheets of rain dimming her vision. Her legs had grown tired from the uphill climb, and the ray of light before her had become smaller and smaller.

Something inside Bella called out to the silver lining, but it didn't hearken unto her bidding. Instead, its form continued to fade. And then, like a vapor, it was gone.

The immense darkness enclosed around Bella. The droplets of rain coursing down her forehead burned her eyes like a molten fire as her bare feet splashed into the deep puddles of water in rhythm with the echoing thunder. A bright flash of lightning illuminated her surroundings, but nothing was as it should have been.

The house was gone.

The trees had been uprooted.

And she was alone.

For a moment Bella wondered if her feet was even on the ground or had everything around her been turned upside down?

Bella's spine stiffened as she arose from her pillow. Her insides quaked when the thunder rattled the window. She took a deep breath and fell back onto the sack that was running thin on goose feathers. Her palm reached over and rested on her sister's side. Relief flooded through her veins.

It was only a nightmare.

Finally, after deep, even breaths, Bella's heart had begun to calm a bit. Careful not to wake Ashlynn, she eased herself up from the bed and took cautious steps toward the window. She grasped the threadbare curtain and pulled it back slightly.

Chills ran along her spine when she was greeted with bright flash of lightning. Her fingertips rested against the cool glass, but the window prevented her from reaching out and feeling the droplets of rain bounce in her palm.

Childlike giggles filled her ears as Bella caught a glimpse of the shadowy figures dancing in the rain. "Papa," Bella whispered.

He didn't answer. But it was him. So strong and masculine and much younger. And the child, it was her. Her blonde pigtails danced when she threw her head back, her mouth open wide catching the raindrops on her tongue. Papa took her into his arms, nuzzling her neck, and together they collapsed onto the ground, their laughter filling the air.

"Papa! Don't Go!" Bella whispered so loudly she surely thought Ashlynn would awaken. Grabbing handfuls of her nightgown, she fled from her bedroom and darted through the kitchen and out the door.

Once she was outside she called out. "Papa!"

Sobs erupted from the deepest parts of her soul when he was

nowhere to be found. "Papa!" Bella's feet turned her form in a slow circle. "Papa!" Hot tears ran down her cheeks mixing with the coolness of the rain.

"Papa." She whispered just before she collapsed to the sodden earth.

"Bella! Wake up!" Ruth Ann shook her sleeping body without mercy. "Wake up, Bella! Yer not gonna b'lieve this!"

"Huh? Mama?" Bella groaned as she struggled to arise from her bed.

"Look!" Ruth Ann shook a piece of paper in her face. "Read this!"

Bella rubbed her eyes trying hard to focus on the words that seemed to be running together.

Dear Miss Bella Westbrook,

I am very sorry to hear of the unfortunate death of your father. I asked your Uncle Morton of what use I could be to the family during their time of loss and suffering. He suggested I offer you a position, and I thought the idea was grand. So, yes, that would be the purpose of this letter. I am presenting to you an opportunity to be employed at Biltmore House.

Do be aware you will be expected to board at the Manor, and you will be granted one day a week free from duties and half a day every other Sunday. Your wages will consist of twenty five dollars a month for your services. If the offer doesn't disappoint you, I wish to send a carriage for you soon.

In Regards,
Edith Stuyvesant Dresser Vanderbilt

Bella's heart skipped a beat. Edith Vanderbilt was offering her a job? Now she must be dreaming. Surely she would awaken at any given moment.

"Where's yer suitcase?" Ruth Ann's voice boomed.

"What? I don't even have a suitcase, Mama. You know that." Bella said as she swung her legs over the edge of her bed. "Where's Ashlynn?"

"She's eatin' her breakfast."

"What time is it?" Bella yawned.

"Only a few hours till noon."

"What?! I'm late!" Bella hurried to the chair where she had laid the brown gingham dress.

Ruth Ann stepped toward Bella and jerked the dress from her hands. "Yer gonna reply to this!" she demanded as she shook the letter in Bella's face.

Bella flinched. "Mama, you know I can't leave Ashlynn for any length of time at all." Her Mama's eyes grew dark, but Bella allowed it to intimidate her none at all. "The exercises are too critical at this point. I can't afford to leave her for any amount of money."

"I said yer goin', Bella."

Bella stepped back toward the bed. Since her Papa died less than a week ago, Mama had not been the same. Well, neither had she. The same bitter anger showed through each of them equally.

"I can continue to milk cows for a living," Bella challenged.

Ruth Ann propped her fist onto her hip. "You can't call that little work ya do at Sawyers a job!"

Bella's brow lifted involuntarily. "At least they keep us in milk."

"Oh, what about the flour? And the meal? Or maybe you can sleep on that worn out bed the rest of yer life!"

Bella gritted her teeth as she tried to keep herself in check. Just when she was about to suggest her Mama find a job of her own, an unstable figure made itself visible.

Ashlynn.

Due to the cruel disease at the age of five, Polio had almost conquered her sister's life. Since the ending result left Ashlynn's left side almost paralyzed, Bella had an undying hunger to see the handicapped child move with ease and heaven sent grace.

For her sixteenth birthday, Papa had given Bella the gift of her dreams, *The Philosophy of Physiotherapy*. The book had taught Bella all she needed to know about the ins and outs of thorough physical therapy. Together she and Ashlynn had traveled miles. Muscle strength had been blooming in season and out of season, and Bella couldn't imagine walking away from her sister now. Especially since they had come so far.

"You would be a beautiful maid, Bella," Ashlynn said.

Bella studied her sister of almost twelve years. Her bright blond hair was much like hers used to be. Instead of having chocolate eyes though, Ashlynn's were as blue as the summer sky.

"I'm not supposed to be a maid, Ashlynn." Bella smiled sympathetically. "My purpose is to milk cows and relieve your tense muscles."

"Yer to do what yer mother says, and I say yer goin'," Ruth Ann clarified.

Bella couldn't stop the sudden urge to run. If she hadn't still been in her nightdress, she most certainly wouldn't be standing in her room. She took the dress from her Mama and stepped past her.

"Where ya goin'?" Ruth Ann asked.

"Your room," Bella answered without giving a second glance.

"Hurry it up!" Ruth Ann's voice boomed. "You have a letter to write!"

Bella hated being rebellious. Really, she did. But as her feet drew near the *one* she longed to talk to, she couldn't help but smile knowing her Mama must be in a frenzy by now. Especially if she stormed into her own room where Bella was supposed to be getting dressed and found the window open and the curtain blowing in the wind.

The pebbles dug into the soles of her feet as she approached the grave whose marker read, *Walter Westbrook March 1869 - July 1908*. Her jaw tightened when she noticed the rose was still lying in the heart of the mound of dirt, although its petals had wilted underneath the force of Mother Nature's tears, followed by the scorching of the sun.

It didn't seem possible. Walter Westbrook had walked the beams countless times without flaw, but this time the skilled carpenter lost a balance he could not regain. His body plummeted to the ground, some thirty odd feet, leaving a lifeless future for his wife and two daughters.

Bella dove to her knees. "Why did you go, Papa?" she broke and heaved from the deepest parts of her soul. Life was never going to be the same again. The sun would never shine as brightly as it did before. The stars would not twinkle like diamonds. The ache in her chest would never die.

"I really don't want to leave home. I'd rather stay close to Ashlynn," Bella whimpered as her finger wrote in the fresh dirt. "I know you understand me, Papa, but I also realize that I should see to their needs as well."

Thunder rolled in the distance. Bella observed the clouds as they grew darker while she inhaled the heavy scent of a distant summer rain. Once she released the frustration that had mounted inside, she muttered, "I'll take care of them."

A steady drizzle of rain started to beat upon Bella, but she didn't care. Let it rain. Let it pour. It really didn't matter anymore.

The rain meant nothing like it did once before. Bella used to find delight in a cloudy day because Papa never failed to take her hands into his and dance in the rain until she felt faint. But that was yesteryear and life called for much more than anticipated.

Bella was hardly the frail little eight year old girl that Papa would take by the hands and twirl her about until she was dizzy. Instead, she had grown into a lovely young woman of almost twenty years, with a thick honey coated braid that laid lusciously across her shoulder and piercing brown eyes strong enough to freeze any man in his footsteps.

And just how life had gotten her to this place, Bella would never know. The only thing she felt certain was no matter how hard it rained, there wasn't a storm strong enough to put a bounce back into those feet of hers.

CHAPTER ONE

August 1908
Asheville, North Carolina

CLICK!
The clasps fastened the suitcase closed. It held very little, not that Bella had much to take along with her anyhow. A marred, hand held looking glass, still clear enough to judge the position of her braid. A brown gingham dress. An aged photograph of her Mama and Papa on their wedding day. A dried up four leaf clover found by Ashlynn. And her book.

The Philosophy of Physiotherapy.

Not that Bella would have a need for reference to her most favorite book. But when spare time arose, she would be studying the next step to Ashlynn's physical progress.

Bella inhaled the same familiar scent of the cottage where she had grown up, sort of like a cedar freshly hewn down. She tucked the woodsy scent away in her heart knowing that a longing for home would find it's aching way back to her. Taking a last look around her tiny room, Bella gripped the handle of the borrowed suitcase and walked out.

Bella stepped into the kitchen and found her Mama and Ashlynn seated at the tiny table eating boiled eggs and toast. Steam danced above the fresh brewed coffee, a perfect invitation to the breakfast table.

"Good morning," Bella said as she sat the suitcase by the door.

"Good morning," they said in unison.

Bella pulled out a chair and sat down. Only then did she notice there was no milk. "Where's the milk?" Bella asked as she made a grab for the last egg.

"Don't have any," Ruth Ann answered as she stuffed her mouth with toast.

Bella's eyebrows drew together. She had just gone to Sawyers' Dairy yesterday and gotten a fresh jar, not to mention that it was the fourth time this week that the milk jar had been found empty. Bella wondered where it could be going. Even when Papa was alive, they didn't drink milk that fast.

"Who is drinking it as quickly as I am bringing it home?" Bella asked.

"Fluffy," Ashlynn answered as she brought the napkin to her mouth.

"Fluffy?" Bella looked from her Mama and then to Ashlynn. "You've been giving the cat our milk?"

Bella didn't receive a reply from either of them. Instead of enjoying her breakfast at the table, Bella grabbed her egg and strode for the door.

"Where you goin'?" her Mama called out.

"To get more milk," Bella replied as solemnly as possible. She had to make certain her Mama and Ashlynn had everything they needed before she left for Biltmore Estate.

"You got time, Bella?!" Her Mama called over her shoulder. "Yer Uncle Morton won't like it if yer late!"

"I have until noon, Mama." The door was almost together when Ashlynn called out Bella's name. Bella peeked her head inside, "Yes?"

"Do you mind to get me a stamp?" Ashlynn asked.

Bella knew why Ashlynn wanted a stamp. She had promised to write to her and keep her informed on her progress. Bella awarded Ashlynn with a warm smile, "Of course."

The streets were crowded with pedestrians and carriages. The clip clop of the horses' hooves echoed without restraint. Friendly manners passed from person to person, warm smiles and waving hellos.

Bella spotted Mr. McGee, the town's banker. Jolly as always. And there was Miss Vivian, the dog lady, with a trail of five dogs nipping at her heels. There was Mr. Potter, the shoemaker. Oh, and there was Mrs. Hurley, the best baker in town.

And then there was the Post Office.

An uneasy churning began to thrive in the pits of Bella's stomach. Just one more day for a long, long time. Facing Rudy Moyers was one of the last things Bella had on her list before she left for Biltmore House. No, to be certain, the task wasn't on her list at all. His name suited him just fine. He was rude. He offered unwelcome opinions, and he looked at Bella as if she were a steamy pork chop.

Bella entered the tiny Post Office only to find it as crowded as the streets. That was good in a sense considering Rudy would have little time to scrutinize her. She fell in line and waited for her turn. It wasn't long before she heard the annoying sound of Rudy's voice. "Well, well. If Bella didn't drop by to bid me farewell."

Bella glared at him, "All I need is a stamp."

Her boldness affected him none at all. He stood there unmoving, his skinny arms folded across his narrow chest. "So you plan on writing me from the mansion?" a quirky line formed on his freckled forehead as he drew his eyebrows together.

"In your dreams, Rudy."

Finally, after a few remarks from customers behind Bella, Rudy placed the stamp on the counter. "That'd be ten cents, Bella."

She knew something wasn't right. The last time Bella bought stamps, they were only two cents each. If the price had increased since then, Bella felt sure she would have heard of it. "Ten cents, Rudy?" Bella questioned him with a scrutinizing glare.

"Would you like for me to make it one quarter?"

"You can't do that!" Bella protested.

"Who says I can't?" Rudy leaned toward Bella with a hint of mockery in his eyes.

"Me."

Bella turned at the sound of a very masculine voice.

"I've got it," the man said as his big arm reached a shiny, silver dime across her shoulder, landing it right smack in the middle of the counter.

Bella was tempted to grab the dime and hand it back to the man, but his massive size stalled the action. "Thank you," she said weakly as her nervous fingers moved aside the bangs that had gently fallen about her brow.

"Not a problem." The man's disarming smile made her melt inside, topped off with a flutter-fly in her chest. She truly didn't mind him scrutinizing her like he was at the moment. Bella felt a scorching heat swiftly rising to her cheeks as she blindly reached for the stamp. Thankfully, she was right on target. She politely sidestepped the gorgeous man and took her leave without giving a thought to offer him the two cents she had in her pocket.

The man stepped forward.

"Darby," Rudy said without removing his folded arms.

"Rudy," Darby's deep voice sounded, "Why don't you start picking on somebody your own gender?"

Bella held the jar of milk in one hand and the stamp in the other; yet the stamp seemed to beckon her attention most. Still feeling quite flustered at what had taken place, Bella silently chided herself for acting so childish. "Why didn't I just take it like a woman?" she whispered.

Relief swept over Bella when she realized her Uncle Morton had not yet come. She hurried inside the tiny cottage, finding Ashlynn in the midst of an exercise. Placing the jar of milk onto the table, as well as the stamp and two pennies, Bella rushed to her sister's side giving aide to the struggling limb. "Where is

Mama?" Bella asked trying not to show her irritation as she slowly lifted Ashlynn's left leg.

"Hanging clothes on the line," Ashlynn answered.

"She told me she would help you while I am away. Ashlynn, you mustn't discontinue these exercises or we will lose all we have worked for."

"I won't. Besides, I want to be walking like you on my birthday." Glittery hope shined vibrantly from those blue eyes. She really believed it was possible, but that only left three months.

Bella swallowed the lump in her throat. "I hope you are." She gently worked Ashlynn's left arm, massaging the muscle, praying it would come to strength.

"I will be twelve in November." A bright smile plastered on Ashlynn's face. "You know what I want besides walking pretty?"

"What?" Bella asked.

"You. You being happy like you used to be." Ashlynn's smile was gone, overtaken by a sad countenance.

Bella smiled. "I am happy," she said. "I'm happy I have you and Mama."

"Just sad 'cause you don't have Papa?"

"Oh, I miss him something terrible, but I often wonder if he is not one of the stars shining down on me." A weak smile formed on her rose petal lips.

"I'd say he's real proud you're goin' to work at Biltmore House. Any Papa would be proud'a that."

Bella laid Ashlynn's arm to rest. "I'm sure he is."

"Bella! Yer Uncle Morton's here!" Mama's voice shouted from the porch.

Bella's hand slid up the side of her sister's face. Her thumb found Ashlynn's brow. "I'm going to miss you." Bella placed her lips onto her sister's forehead and embraced her.

Ashlynn sighed, "I'll miss you more."

"Oh, Ashlynn." Bella was doing this for her sister and her Mama. A keeping of the promise made to her Papa that she would see to it that they were provided for. But why couldn't she escape the nagging feeling that she was getting the better end of the deal and they were the ones being left out? It wasn't like Bella prayed for this to happen because she didn't. Even God knew that she would have rather stayed behind and tried working two jobs, three if need be, just to make sure Ashlynn was exercising properly.

Bella stepped onto the porch, Ashlynn limping close behind. A sad smile formed on her face, "Bye, Mama." She allowed the suitcase to fall to the wooden porch, her arms embracing the one who had enforced her decision to work at Biltmore.

"Bye, Bella. Go on. Yer Uncle is waiting."

Bella held her tears in check when she gave Ashlynn one last hug. "Keep exercising, sister." She smoothed away the blond strands of Ashlynn's hair that had fallen about her brow. "I love you," she whispered.

"I love you, too, sissy."

Bella took the suitcase and ran toward the carriage. "I love you, Mama!" she called out once she was seated. All she received in return was the waving of her Mama's handkerchief. Passing through the stone archway had been a bit exhilarating for Bella. It seemed as though it had been awaiting her arrival. As the horses led the luxurious carriage along the course of the Approach Road, Bella's eyes drank in the landscape.

She had always heard that a man, Frederick Law Olmsted, the one responsible for designing Central Park in New York City, had come to Biltmore and converted depleted farmland into vast forests by planting millions of trees. Bella could easily be impelled now.

"Wow," Bella inhaled the rich scent of honeysuckle, "this is beautiful."

Morton smiled, "Just wait until you see the house; it's remarkable." A kissing sound escaped his lips as he encouraged the horses to move along.

"I have heard that it is, although I can't fathom what could be found more amazing than this forest."

Morton only smiled and then noticed how Bella was continually ringing her hands. "Nervous?"

Bella drew her thumb and finger together, "Just a little."

"There's no need to be. Mrs. Vanderbilt will take a liking to you, I just know it."

Bella continued to ring her hands. "I hope you're right."

It was then, when the view of magnificence filled her vision. Bella's breath caught.   Never before had she seen anything like it. The massive structure was like nothing she could ever dream or imagine. Chimneys lined the rooftop, as domes spread upon domes harboring a significant amount of windows. Its size could not be assessed, for its vastness was inconceivable.

Bella's fingers fanned her heart as her mouth stood agape. Her eyes drank in the chateau as the carriage rolled past. Finally, coming to a stop, Morton stepped down, offering his hand for Bella.

"Welcome to Biltmore, Miss Bella Westbrook."

CHAPTER TWO

BELLA'S KNEES WOBBLED AS SHE stood before the lovely Biltmore House. Unwelcome fear gripped her heart as she soon realized that the position might not be for her after all. She felt she was too down to earth to ever measure up to the expectations that awaited her. Her simple, country-style raising would be of no profit to a place of such esteem.

For an instant, Bella thought about jumping back into the carriage and traveling the four and half miles back home, never giving a second glance. But as soon as visions of her Mama and Ashlynn flashed before her mind's eye, Bella could not gather the courage to turn back. Neither could she gather the courage to move forward. She just stood there, awestruck, not sure if she was ready to see what was behind the door.

Morton gripped her elbow gently and propelled her toward the door. She willed her feet to move in a timely manner, although she still seemed to lag behind a bit. Her face rose up toward the towering structure as she put one foot in front of the other.

"Servants normally enter through the back, but I wanted you to see the entire estate. It is much more magnificent entering through the front." Morton's casual tone did not match the uneasy feeling swarming inside Bella.

She instantly withdrew from Morton's grip, refusing to

advance to the forbidden entrance for her station. "I will not start off on the wrong foot, Uncle Morton." Bella grasped the suitcase but instead of loosening his grip, Morton held firm, refusing her stubbornness.

"I said we will enter through the front, and that is how it is going to be," Morton demanded.

Bella gripped the suitcase handle pulling it toward her again. "If I am to enter through the back, then I refuse to go through that DOOR!" To her surprise, Morton loosened the suitcase causing Bella to stumble backwards. Unable to regain her balance, Bella fumbled over her own two feet, and soon found herself sprawled before the open door.

A middle aged man stood perfectly still, his eyes wide and mouth agape. Bella wondered if he had heard her unladylike behavior, or did he simply label her as a rebellious little twit? Probably both.

Her eyes scanned the ground where she sat on her backside and discovered all her belongings were scattered abroad. At least her dress hid the unmentionables. Bella scooped it all up with one sweep of her hands, caring not the fashion it was laid, fastened the suitcase, and stood to her feet.

"I suppose I will enter through the front," Bella said, plastering a pretty smile onto her face, which was evidently fake, while her free hand dusted off her backside. Bella's eyes shifted from Morton then to the man who was obviously the butler. She righted her braid as she moved forward, politely ignoring her

Uncle Morton who was stepping close behind. Bella paused before the butler who had not moved his stance.

"Winston, I would like you to meet my niece, Bella." Morton spoke from behind bringing her pause to a complete stop. "Bella, meet Winston." The man's expression softened a little but his eyes still seemed to question her visitation.

Before Morton had a chance to share explicit details, a feminine voice echoed from the inside, "Morton? You are back already?"

Bella shifted her gaze to the tall, slender figure approaching them. The long white dress the woman wore flowed with elegance, and lace accents complimented the cuffs and modest neckline. In contrast to her creamy skin, the woman's hair was as dark as midnight, and fashioned elegantly atop her head. Her eyes lit up when she spotted Bella. She gasped, "You must be the beautiful niece Morton raves about."

Bella felt the heat consume her cheeks.

The woman's steps did not slow until she stood before Bella, gently taking her free hand. "Welcome to Biltmore, Bella. I am Mrs. Vanderbilt."

Bella stood there unmoving. She was at a loss for words. She had not expected the Mistress of the house to appear so human. Common. And especially so welcoming. Instead, Bella had pictured a lady adorned in pearls and fine silk, with a hat exploding with feathers, and a fan that never slowed down. But the woman that stood before her was not at all what she had expected.

Mrs. Vanderbilt turned to Morton and ordered him to care for the horses. With the motion of her hand, Mrs. Vanderbilt led the way through the foyer. "It is such a pleasure for you to join our family here at Biltmore," the woman glanced over her shoulder, "I have anticipated your arrival since I was enlightened of your decision."

The smile on Mrs. Vanderbilt's face encouraged Bella to keep marching. Maybe it wouldn't be so bad after all. And did she say *family*?

Bella had imagined that her duties here would rob her of what little freedom she ever possessed. She had never thought about growing close to anyone here except for her uncle. Maybe she had misjudged the circumstances entirely; perhaps something good could derive from her misfortune.

"I am privileged to acquire such a position," Bella said as she followed the Mistress. She had intended to say more, but her words fell flat as she stepped through the foyer and into the entrance hall. Though the room was dim, gentle rays of sunlight spilled through enormous archways, creating a natural glow of beauty, from the wooden vaulted ceiling to the polished marble floors.

Bella's feet turned her body in a complete circle as her eyes tried to drink in all of her surroundings. The stone archways were all about, in every direction, crowned by the vaulted ceiling.

Bella released the breath she hadn't realized she'd been holding. Her palms began to sweat as well as her brow. Good heavens, she thought, I will never learn my way around this massive structure!

Instead of leading Bella toward the luscious greenery that spilled over an iron fence, Mrs. Vanderbilt made hasty steps in the opposite direction. Just through the threshold, another immaculate sight stole away Bella's breath as she trailed behind the clicking heels. A grand marble staircase ascended toward the heavens in a spiral, as the enormous chandelier descended from the ceiling above.

Bella had never beheld something so awe-inspiring in all her life. And to think that this place would be called her second *home*. A place she would come to love and enjoy...

"Bella, I would like for you to meet Sophia." The mistress' words stole her attention away from the setting before her. A maid, probably about her age, settled back onto her heels, gently pushing back the strands of strawberry blonde that had escaped from her bun.

Bella could tell by the tight strain of her rosy cheeks that Sophia forced the smile onto her face. "Nice to meet you." The edge in her voice was quite noticeable, too.

"Likewise." Bella offered a faint but detectable grin and then noticed how red and chafed Sophia's hands were. She had obviously scrubbed from the top step all the way down to the bottom one. The bucket was half full of murky water with a small amount of suds. No doubt the poor girl was exhausted. Her droopy blue eyes told it all.

Bella sat her suitcase down and started pushing up her sleeves, "Here, allow me to help."

"Oh no, Bella. She is quite through. I was going to dismiss Sophia of her duties and allow her to show you to your room." Mrs. Vanderbilt cast a glance toward Sophia who had now risen to her feet and was drying her hands vigorously with her apron. "And then to Mrs. King."

Sophia raised her eyes to the mistress of the house. A look of defiance crossed her features, but she simply ducked her head and gave a half bow with an humble reply. "Yes, ma'am."

"Wonderful. Now you two hurry along, and don't keep the Matron waiting." Mrs. Vanderbilt turned on her heels and strode away in the direction from whence she came, vanishing into the far away corridor. The echoing of her heels were swallowed up by the hustle and bustle of everyday life at Biltmore House.

Bella clasped her suitcase once again and took a deep breath. She wasn't quite sure if she was going to be accepted by Sophia, not to mention who was awaiting her arrival. Mrs. King. Or should she say, the Matron.

Bella followed Sophia through a small doorway just to the right of the Grand Staircase. A twinge of regret swelled inside her chest. She almost wished to climb the remarkable stairway and trail her fingers along its iron rails, but there would be time for that later.

Bella had to merely run to keep up. The girl was traveling at breakneck speed down a stairway, her skirts rustling with every step taken. Bella bit back the urge to ask her to slow down; instead she trailed on Sophia's heels allowing little distance to grow between them. Sophia had taken so many turns that it was starting to cause a wave of dizziness to envelope Bella.

Finally, Sophia threw open a door, revealing a small room with a twin size bed, a small dresser and a rocking chair. Bella stepped inside and admired the accommodations that were beyond what she had anticipated. Although it was modestly situated, the pretty curtains and matching bed linens along with the illumination of the electric lights, seemed luxurious to Bella. And to think, it belonged to her. There would be no sharing the bed or the space offered by the tower of dresser drawers. She could turn the light on or leave it off if she desired to do so. She could stay awake until the wee hours of the morning reading by lamplight if she wished. Or she could sit and sew. Even though she hated to sew. Or she could-

"*That* will never do."

Bella's day dreaming was interrupted by Sophia's words. Bella spun around to face her.

Sophia already noted the look on Bella's face. Her eyes challenged Bella. "The braid. It will have to go, especially since you'll be in the kitchen."

Bella didn't appreciate the boldness of Sophia's demands. It wasn't like she had to answer to the maid's bidding anyhow. She glanced down to her shoulder where the honey-coated braid laid perfectly. It's thick and luscious shine was enough to make any girl envious.

She glanced back up at Sophia and noted how tightly she had

pulled her hair into a bun. Bella had never worn her hair in such a twist. To look at it was about to give her a splitting headache.

Bella folded her arms firmly across her chest and quirked her eyebrow, "I suppose I need to pull it into a bun like yours, so tightly that the corners of eyes touch my ears."

After Sophia thundered off in the opposite direction, Bella closed the door and thrust her back against it. A breath of frustrated air released from her lungs as her eyelids slid together. Her first day at Biltmore House could not get any worse. It had to get better. That is, if the Matron didn't give her an impossible list of duties to fill before nightfall.

Bella's heartbeat drummed mercilessly in her ear. That Sophia! What had Bella done to deserve such treatment? And what right did Sophia have to tell her whether to wear her hair in a bun or just as she always had?

Her chilled, petite hands patted her reddened cheeks, trying to cool them with the touch. She opened her eyes and scanned the room once again. Her eyes settled onto a black uniform with a crisp, white apron. Bella stepped closer. Her fingers reached out to touch such fine material. It even had white cuffs, shiny white buttons, and a big bow in the back.

Once Bella darned the uniform and secured the apron around her tiny waist, she glanced in the mirror. It was very different from the mirrors at home. There were no faded spots caused from age or mold; instead, the reflection was perfectly clear.

Her eyes roamed up and down the new *Bella*. Her uniform could not have fit any better. Its black material gave her a professional appearance along with the white accents and apron. She turned her body to the side, the skirts teasing the tops of her ankles. Again, she turned to view the plump bow in the back. It was tied perfectly, all full and fluff.

When she faced the mirror a second time, the long braid beckoned her attention. She would do something with her hair, if she could find the pins.

The screaking of the top dresser drawer testified of its many days being closed, not to mention the musty odor. She would definitely make time to stitch together a few sachets filled with cinnamon cloves.

After pulling out every drawer, Bella finally came to the conclusion that whoever had boarded the room before her hadn't left behind any hair pins.

Atop the bedside table, a tiny trinket box stole away her attention. She carefully lifted its lid. Inside it laid a numerous amount of tiny things. Bella tipped it over onto the bed in search for something to bind her hair. Her fingers scattered the contents. A button, a needle, a coin, a spool of thread, a ribbon, and finally, six hair pins. She silently hoped that six were enough as she scooped up the items and placed them back into the box where they belonged.

Standing before the mirror again, Bella spun her braid around its core and slid the pins in. She neatly tucked away a loose strand behind her ear and pressed the loose strands. The braided bun laid against the side of her head in a fashionable manner. It looked quite impressive.

KNOCK! KNOCK! KNOCK!

The unexpected knock on the door startled Bella. She spun around, pressing her hand to her heart. "Yes?" She asked with a weak voice as her feet directed her toward the door. Her sweaty palm twisted the knob to reveal who awaited her on the other side.

Sophia.

Her expression had changed little, if none at all. A cold glare was frozen onto her features. Her blue eyes had grown even icier than before. She scrutinized Bella from head to toe as if she were giving an inspection.

Bella bit her tongue, holding back the very idea of speaking her mind. A loose tongue could get her into deep trouble, she knew that, but it would almost be worth it.

Almost.

"Mrs. King is waiting," Sophia declared. "Let's not tarry."

Having spent most of the afternoon with the Matron, Bella soon discovered that Mrs. King was not intimidating at all. Besides the constant jingle of numerous keys, Bella found her company to be quite pleasant.

"All of the clocks are set exactly the same. They are synchronized. So there is never an excuse for tardiness, Bella," informed Mrs. King.

Bella just nodded her head as she stared into the face of the clock. The face that always told the truth. If she happened to be a bit late, it would never cover for her. Goodness! She would have to leave an hour before her appointed time until she learned the ins and outs of the place!

"Do not worry with chores today, Bella," Mrs. King said as she began walking down the corridor. "Just make yourself at home and get familiar with the Manor. As we have already discussed, your duties for now only consist of kitchen help. Bessie will be your superior. She is good at what she does." The Matron's steps slowed. "Just stand back and learn from observation. I like for you to know the next step without being told."

"Yes, ma'am," Bella replied.

"You will become acquainted with many employees here at Biltmore, both men and women alike." Mrs. King's dark eyes darted to Bella. She was very aware of the young lady's features. Any stable boy or footman would also be quick to notice.

"Fraternizing has never been tolerated and never will be. You do understand that servants here, except for the butler and chef, are expected to remain unmarried during their time of service, do you not?" Mrs. King inquired.

Bella's face jolted to her left where Mrs. King stood. Had she acted in such a way to receive such bold orders? The intensity in the woman's voice generated a rosy shade about Bella's cheeks. Would Mrs. King really think she would be susceptible to such conduct?

"There is nothing to fear, Mrs. King. For I am here to work

and to work only."

A gentle smile formed on the face of the aging woman. No doubt her many years at Biltmore had taken a great toll on her. "Good. That was what I expected to hear."

She placed her hand upon Bella's shoulder and looked directly into her eyes. "However, I do understand temptation. Just remember, if you think about someone else more than you think of Biltmore, you are putting your position here in great jeopardy."

CHAPTER THREE

DARBY FOUGHT AGAINST EVERY FORCE of opposition just to arrive where he stood.

Biltmore School of Forestry.

Ever since Pierson Enterprises had been established in 1890, his father, Charles Pierson, had anticipated Darby's interest in tree removal. But instead of carelessly wiping away the green forests of any age like he had been taught, Darby suggested logging with conservation, considering the tree's age and size.

However, when Darby decided to walk away from the muddy logging yard and seek a higher calling of caring for God's handiwork, Charles went into a rage.

"Ya mean yer gonna join up with them there scholars that knows nothin' bout puttin' a tree on the ground!" he railed trying to hold back the tobacco juice seeping through his lips.
Darby had heard this more than once and had tried clarifying his motives time and again, but there was no use. He ran his big hand through his thick, golden brown hair and let out a sigh. What was there to do? Go ahead anyway?

"Answer me, boy!" Charles demanded holding back no resistance when his fist met the top of the old kitchen table.

"Charles, leave the boy alone! If he wants to go, then so be it!" Odetta pleaded as she sat the steamy biscuits down between the two debaters.

"You stay outta this, Odetta! Somehow or 'nother he thinks it's his job to put back what's destroyed," Charles shook his head aggressively. "Dunno where he got that kinda idea from?"

Darby's appetite had faded, and he hated like everything to argue with his Pa in front of his Ma. There had to be a decision made, whether it hurt or not. Using his feet to push the chair away from the table, Darby stood, aware of the defeated expression on his Pa's face.

"I'm leaving," Darby declared. "I'm going to follow my heart."

"Hmph! Leaving! Just like that? Only b'cause you think God won't replant the trees we tear down? Why do ya think He put millions of 'em all over His green earth?!"

Darby turned from the table trying to ignore the tears welled up in his Ma's eyes and walked away.

"An' ya think them there scholars are gonna 'cept you with a limp like that?"

Darby slowed his uneven steps and almost stopped to remind his Pa that if safety around the log yard had been endorsed, then he wouldn't be left with a limp to contend with for the rest of his life. But what point was there in arguing with someone who always thought of the glass as half empty? Right now Darby was peering at the glass half full.

Darby felt a heavy hand settle onto his shoulder immediately pulling him back into the present hour. He briskly turned to find

Dr. Carl Schenck in the flesh. Darby had read many articles about the man when he first arrived at Biltmore in 1895. Having some 120,000 acres of mountain terrain, George Vanderbilt requested Carl Schenck to come to North America and manage the vast forests using scientific methods of forestry, making the German Forester the third trained forester in the United States.

Acting upon Vanderbilt's bidding, Schenck became the forester at Biltmore. He began his work there by creating tree nurseries and fish hatcheries, as well as log yards and saw mills, by which he applied all his knowledge of new scientific management. Then in September of 1898, George Vanderbilt granted him the opportunity to establish Biltmore Forest School.

Ever since Darby was a teenager, he had anticipated this very moment.

Feeling a sudden surge of enthusiasm, Darby felt his chest begin to swell. He did it. Going against all odds and the chance at losing his inheritance of Pierson Enterprises, he enrolled for a one year course of study at Biltmore Forest School, America's first forestry school.

"This is a paradise, is it not?" the overgrown mustache of his mentor danced with a jitter.

Darby tried to tear his eyes away from the common fashion of lengthened facial hair exceeding both sides of the cheek bones. Instinctively, Darby's hand went to his own face. A clean shave. That was how he had always liked it. He never understood why men chose to deal with the itchy stuff.

Finally, after a long moment of silence, Darby answered, "It is beautiful." His words seemed to blow in the wind that encircled him and soar above the highest peak of Mount Pisgah. As they stood there admiring the forever chain of the Blue Ridge Mountains, Darby wondered if he had made the right decision. If not, what price would he have to pay for an ambitious mistake?

He inhaled the rich scent of honeysuckle. It was soothing. Exhilarating maybe? It felt almost as if he were on the brink of success. A challenge. Perhaps even a life changing adventure. There was no telling what the next several months of his life could hold.

Darby's aching foot called for his attention. A thorn in the flesh. That's what it was. It deprived him of excessive hiking as he always loved to do, and it hindered him from being the person he wanted to be. He was handicapped now, and he would just have to deal with it. And if anybody was going to accept him, they would just have to ignore the uneven gait.

Darby was speechless when he was informed of his evening appointment with George Vanderbilt. He opened his mouth to speak, but instead, no words left his lips; his mouth stood agape.

"Mr. Vanderbilt is expecting the two of us to accompany him this evening at the Manor," Schenck repeated himself. "You are the son of Charles Pierson, are you not?"

What has Pa done now? Darby thought. He never doubted that his father would try to stop him from chasing his dream. Seasoned anger started working its ways through Darby's blood, bringing it to a boiling point in only seconds. He was unable to hide it; frustration marked his darkening eyes. They were no longer green but hazel. The edge in his voice was unmistakable.

"You know my Pa?" Darby asked as he folded his muscular arms across his broad chest.

The chuckle that vibrated from Schenck almost seemed sarcastic, yet Darby chose to ignore the remark.

"Isn't *he* the most profound southern lumber jack in the region? I am afraid that almost everyone could admit they have heard his name at least once in their lifetime," Schenck admitted.

Darby knew that his Pa was well known, but he didn't expect Carl Schenck to have reference of him, and especially not George Vanderbilt.

Schenck went on, "When Mr. Vanderbilt learned of your enrollment at Biltmore Forest School, he was impressed with your reasoning, knowing... well," Schenck paused as if to study his words carefully, "Pierson Enterprises would not operate under such regulations."

Oh! So Mr. Vanderbilt admired Darby's interest in learning such practices knowing that his father would never consent to abide by conservative principles. Impressive. A smile tugged at the corners of Darby's lips, but it didn't quite make it to his eyes. There was no reason to let his hopes rise higher than Mount Pisgah. At least not yet.

Now feeling more confident about himself, Darby allowed the tension in his body to relax, remembering that there was an appointment to be met, and he didn't want to keep George Vanderbilt waiting.

Exhaustion was swiftly taking over Bella as she scrubbed the last pot that was used to cook the potatoes. Somehow during her exploration of the house, she always ended up in the kitchen. After a few times of passing by and noticing that Bessie was pulling the heaviest end of the load, Bella offered help. The older lady was grateful and left the washing to Bella.

Only now did Bella wish that she had appeared only when the food was being served. It couldn't have been near as steamy as what she was doing now, and she certainly wouldn't be such a fright to look at.

Her bun was falling down. She could feel it. She used her shoulder to press it up again and again, but it was useless. The strands of hair were not as tamed as they were earlier. Each time Bella moved her face, she was constantly wiping them away with her forearm, not to mention the perspiration beading up across her forehead.

She couldn't wait to cave in on her bed and call it a day. It had certainly been a day.

But at least it had not gotten worse. The pins in her hair could have fallen into the dish water, but they did not. She could have broken priceless pieces of china, but she hadn't. She could have stained her white apron with grease, but fortunately it was still white and crisp. Sophia could have been assigned the kitchen too...

"Bella."

The unexpected sound of her name caused Bella's hands to free the pot she was scrubbing, allowing it land in the bubbly water, and drench her uniform. She cast her eyes down the front of herself. Steady drops of water fell from the hem of her skirt and onto her boots.

She averted her gaze to the one who was snickering. To even be caught thinking of the devil...

"Sophia," Bella's teeth ground.

The mischievous grin on the girl's face ignited like a match inside Bella. Why did she have to be the only one who got wet?

Without giving thought to her sudden reaction, Bella scooped up a handful of murky dish water and gave it a fling. Her aim was all too well. The sudsy water rolled past Sophia's forehead, and drizzled down her flaming cheeks.

Sophia gritted her teeth and growled as she leapt toward Bella. Her revenge was of no surprise.

Being the country girl she was, Bella grabbed for the girl's wrists and latched hold without mercy. The cry of pain didn't hinder the hold one bit. Instead, she gripped harder and challenged Sophia eye to eye.

"Let go of me! You drowned rat!" Sophia shouted.

Bella did. But before Sophia could get away, Bella grabbed for the pot that was still in the water and gave it all she had.

Lukewarm, discolored dish water covered Sophia. Her breath caught and thankfully, her mouth had been closed. She was speechless. Her hands wiped away the discolored dish water dripping from her eyelids.

"I didn't want to be the only drowned rat at Biltmore," Bella confidently folded her arms across her chest.

"I have a special place for drowned rats." The Matron's voice drew the attention of both young maids. Now they knew the meaning of *Matron*. The authority showed through the woman's eyes. Her hardened features proved she held herself in check, careful not to act upon instinct and strangle the little twits.

Both Bella and Sophia followed humbly behind Mrs. King. She led them through many corridors and had even taken a lift on the elevator. Under different circumstances, Bella would have found the tour delightful. But knowing that she was most likely fired and leaving as soon as she could pack her things, Bella found it hard to enjoy.

Finally, Mrs. King stopped before a closed door and rummaged through her keys. After opening the door and stepping inside, she allowed the girls their entrance.

The Matron settled behind a desk leaving both Bella and Sophia to stand at attention before her. She folded her hands firmly and directed her gaze toward Bella. "Do you mind explaining why you are wet, young lady?"

Bella glanced down at herself. Yes. She was still quite wet. "I… well, Sophia…"

"I did not!" Sophia's objected.

"Silence!" Mrs. King ordered. Both Bella and Sophia stiffened. Mrs. King released a breath, "Now, Bella, explain to me why you are wet."

"Sophia startled me while I was washing." Bella felt so dense. Such a hideous reaction that would cost her dearly. "I dropped the pot in the dish water, and it soaked me."

"Now explain why Sophia is also drenched." The Matron's eyes shot to Sophia and studied her. The poor girl's hair was matted to her head and her clothes held three times the amount of water than Bella's.

"She found my mishap humorous, ma'am," Bella admitted.

Mrs. King's eyes found Bella again. They seemed to say, well done, Bella.

"I used the pot to dash water onto her," Bella continued as she cast a glance toward Sophia. "Like I said, I didn't want to be the only drowned rat at Biltmore."

The Matron seemed to be restraining the urge to smile. She didn't ask to hear Sophia's tale of the matter. Instead, she said, "As much as I want to fire the both of you, I'm not going to." Her eyes shifted from one girl to the next. "Alternatively, you are going to be punished. The both of you will work side by side for the next three months or until you solve whatever conflict has transpired between the two of you."

Bella and Sophia both turned their faces one toward another. No doubt they both preferred to be fired other than ordered to work alongside one another for three long months. Together, they turned back to Mrs. King, both their eyes pleading for a different arrangement.

"You are to begin in the kitchen cleaning the mess both of you created," Mrs. King ordered. "You are dismissed."

Bella and Sophia walked the length of the corridor in silence. The quiet was speaking louder than audible words could ever express. As they neared the elevator, their steps drew up short when the door opened. Mr. Vanderbilt led two other men in the opposite direction.

Bella's mouth had gone bone dry. Why, of all times, did Mr. Vanderbilt have to see her in such a condition? She knew it was him because she had noticed him in portraits with his wife, Edith. Bella didn't know who the other men were; neither did she expect to. But the one who was younger, and much bigger, seemed oddly familiar, though she didn't know where she had seen him.

Neither Bella nor Sophia spoke a word as they made their way back to the kitchen to clean up the mess. It took several towels to absorb all the water that was lying in the floor.

The quiet seemed to grate on Bella's nerves more than conversing with her worst enemy. Bella had thought Rudy to be rude. She believed that Sophia had him beat by far. Maybe she was his sister?

Bella knew one thing. She would rather work at the Post Office any day than she had-

The Post Office!

That was where she had seen the tall, brown haired man who was nipping at Mr. Vanderbilt's heels!

Her hands paused on the towel she was using as she relived this morning's moments in town. He had been the one to buy the stamp! And he was definitely the most handsome man she had ever looked upon, not that she made a habit of doing so, but he was one who wouldn't go unnoticed.

And she had been the one to act so foolishly.

Bella shook her head trying to regain concentration of what she was supposed to be doing, and as soon as the last bit of water was dried, she was going outside for fresh air.

"And the idea? What do you think of a festival? Something to draw the attention of politics as well as lumber men like Charles Pierson." Schenck had proposed the idea in order to teach scientific methods to invited guests in a sequence of three days.

"And it marks the ten year anniversary of Biltmore Forest School." Vanderbilt had added. "Splendid. Simply splendid." George Vanderbilt directed his gaze toward Darby and studied him for a brief moment. "Mr. Pierson, I do say, I admire your attributes and independent motives to see a change come to our forests."

Darby nodded his head. "Thank you, Sir."

Mr. Vanderbilt arose from his desk where he had been seated and motioned with his hand. "Now, allow me to show you why I do what I do."

Darby obediently followed Mr. Vanderbilt up a spiraling staircase to the second story of the observatory and through a set of French doors leading to a balcony positioned above the main entrance tower.

Never had Darby imagined something so beautiful existed. The sun was setting just behind Mount Pisgah, creating an orange glow on the horizon. It simply stole his breath away. The landscape was even all the more amazing from this view point.

His eyes drank in his surroundings. He could see it all. The sunset, the mountains, the lush gardens, the-

Girl.

The maid that he had spotted when he stepped off the elevator.

She was just below the balcony undoing her hair. Darby stepped closer and gripped the railing firmly as he watched her fingers run through the honey-colored tresses. His throat constricted. His conscience told him he should look away, but he didn't. He watched as her head tilted back, and her eyes drifted closed. He drew in a shaky breath and inhaled the sweet smell of cinnamon wafting in the breeze.

"A beautiful sight, is it not?" Mr. Vanderbilt's voice echoed from behind him.

Darby's eyes still reined in on the lovely maid. "It most certainly is."

CHAPTER FOUR

NOW DARBY KNEW WHY HE was instructed to attend a private meeting with George Vanderbilt and Carl Schenck. He had been appointed president of his class of twenty five scholars. They emphasized how much they admired his common knowledge of forestry, the heritage which was given to him by his father.

Several times during their discussion, Mr. Vanderbilt asked for Darby's input concerning the festival. He had little to offer, but he did suggest a hike up Mount Pisgah, in which they thought the idea grand. He also mentioned mixing a little entertainment into the three day adventure. That too brought a smile to their faces.

Darby had really made some head way toward the road to success, and his classes hadn't even begun. However, all that had encouraged his self-esteem soon plummeted when he and Schenck returned to Schenck's home.

"When do you expect your foot to be well?" Schenck asked just before he turned toward his home.

"My foot?" Darby's voice faltered a bit. He had written the incident down onto the application; obviously, he left out the details about permanent functional damage.

Casting a glance to the ground where Darby had his foot positioned comfortably, Dr. Schenck inquired, "Yes, aren't you aware of the strenuous hikes and physical labor performed at Biltmore Forest School? Good physical condition is preferred."

Darby took in a deep breath. He didn't want to lie. Maybe right now a half-truth would suit because the last thing he wanted was to be turned away from his dream all because of a crippled foot. "I should be well in just a few weeks. I can see a difference already."

Only he didn't tell the difference was a downhill turn.

"Very well then. Good night." Schenck turned toward his home while Darby settled atop the horse. There would be no rest tonight. Instead of counting sheep, Darby would be asking the Shepherd for a miracle.

After a good warm bath, Bella finally called it a day. It had truly been a day. Certainly not the typical day she had expected it to be. Her head fell against the downy pillow; seemingly, it felt like a load lifted.

Although she and Sophia had not spoken another word to each other, the air had still been thick as if she could hear Sophia proclaiming that *this* wasn't over yet. Before they had retired to their rooms, Mrs. King sent a valet to deliver their chore of order for the following day.

Bella and Sophia were to begin their journey in the Library. The idea of being surrounded by hundreds of books sounded wonderful to Bella's ears, but the demands were quite unreasonable.

"Mrs. King desires to have each book removed, dusted, and returned to its proper place," the valet nodded his head and was ready to walk away when Bella asked, "How many books are there?"

"Over ten thousand books, ma'am," he answered and then turned on one heel and strode away.

Sophia released a grunt and rolled her eyes. Instead of arguing over the matter, she briskly went to her room and allowed the door to slam shut.

Bella was lying there staring at the ceiling above. Ten thousand books! It would take longer than three months to complete the job! What if Mrs. King demanded the job finished before they each filled their regular duties and went their separate ways?

Tears pricked the back of her eyes. Bella wished now that she had never come to Biltmore, no matter the amount of money she earned. Money couldn't buy her happiness. She would much rather be lying in the twin sized bed she shared with Ashlynn in the little shabby cottage than be lying where she was right now.

Ashlynn.

Bella said a silent prayer that Ashlynn was okay, still exercising like she had taught her. Her Mama promised she would see to it while Bella was away. A gray cloud filled her mind. What if Mama didn't take the time to work with Ashlynn? Many days without therapy would result in muscle loss. Muscle loss would result in weakness. Weakness would result in discouragement. Discouragement would result in a total loss.

"A total loss," Bella whispered into nothingness. "I won't settle for that."

Morning had come too soon. The hours of the night seemed like minutes, but here she was. After eating a scrumptious breakfast in the servants' hall, one like she never had before, Bella found herself at awe once again.

She was hoping that whoever had taken the time to count all of the books in the library had gotten the figures correct. If she were to make her own guess, Bella wouldn't dare say a number smaller than twenty grand.

Two stories made up the Library with a spiral staircase leading to the top. Books upon books were shelved from floor to ceiling. Oh, how she would love to hide out in a place like this for months on end, reading one book and then finding another and another. My, it would be heaven!

"I will take the top floor. You stay down here." Sophia's command revealed her presence.

Without protesting, Bella grabbed for the feather duster she had found in her room and went to work. Using a glimpse of common knowledge, Bella sought the ladder and climbed up a step. It only made sense to begin on the top shelf and work toward the bottom. Then she climbed another step. And then another. She shifted her gaze to the floor and swallowed the lump that had formed in her throat. This had been how her father died. Only he was much higher than she.

Upon making her last step toward the top, Bella grasped the first book and started counting.

Darby walked steadily as possible down the corridor toward the Library, thanking God that students attending Biltmore Forest School were welcome to the Library at any time. After lying awake most of the night, he finally decided upon searching for a medical book of some kind that might give step by step instructions for caring for an injured foot.

Had he only been paying better attention when Frank was wrapping the chain around the log that slipped, nearly dismembering Darby's foot, he would have noticed immediately that Frank was using improper methods just to finish faster.

But that was too long ago. Almost a year. And Darby could only pray there was still hope for improvement.

The heavy scent of hundreds, no thousands, of books welcomed Darby as he crossed the threshold. Wow! He hadn't expected the Library to contain such a vast amount of literature. Surely among all these books there had to be at least one with the answer to his problem.

The hard part would be finding it.

Darby's eyes roamed the room. It was spectacular. An enormous fireplace, fine furniture and tapestries, books lining from one wall to the next from floor to ceiling. It was definitely a sight to see. But not nearly as rousing when his focus reigned in on the pretty little maid he had observed yesterday evening.

It had to be her. Although her uniform was a different color, he would recognize her hair anywhere. There was never a color so unique. It wasn't quite blonde. Neither was it gold. And it wasn't brown. It was a gentle mix of all three.

Darby forced his steps to remain even as he drew near the ladder where she was. He longed to warn her against leaning too far over, but he refrained. Instead, he decided on plan in case she fell.

Bella was moving with great speed. From time to time, she glanced to see how far Sophia had progressed. Although no words were spoken, she knew she was in a race. She could feel it soaring through her veins. She wanted to be finished first. She needed to be finished first. So she stretched as far as she could, using her right hand to grab the next book and her left one to hold herself steady against the ladder.

I have to finish first, Bella encouraged herself.

Then a deep, masculine voice cleared his throat. "Excuse me?"

Bella had been in such deep thought that she hadn't even realized someone else was also in the Library. Seeing the figure of a man out of the corner of her eye nearly caused her to lose her wits. The hold she had on the ladder wasn't enough to steady her balance since one hand was reaching way too far for the next book.

Beads of sweat instantly formed along her forehead when Bella realized she could not regain her footing. Her body shifted. The book fell to the floor, and Bella was going next.

She squeezed her eyes shut. This would be the end of her; she just knew it. Bella felt her back bend, her arms swung nervously, but she couldn't swim in mid-air. One foot slipped and then the next.

She waited for the fall to end, but it was almost as if she never quit falling. The abrupt crash on the floor never came. Only the sound of a grunt ruptured from the form that enveloped her. Bella forced her eyes to open. She had to blink a few times to make sure she was awake instead of having a nightmare that led to a splendid happily ever after.

Yeah, she was awake.

This was no dream.

Green eyes stared into her deep pools of molasses. It was him. The man from the Post Office.

Bella's heart constricted as he eased her feet to the floor, and she tried to ignore the burning sensation his palm created on her shoulder. Once Bella steadied herself, she flattened her uniform with her palms and muttered, "Th-thank you. I'm glad you caught me-, I mean, I'm glad you kept me from falling-" Heat began to creep up her neck. "I mean, you know, falling to the floor." The lopsided smile on his face cause something to jolt inside Bella.

"I'm glad I was of assistance," he admitted, "but you really shouldn't have been leaning over so far. That's not safe."

Bella felt the heat rising from her collarbone. "I know," she whispered.

"Maybe you shouldn't risk yourself next time," he said as he folded his arms, "because I might not be here to catch you."

Bella flushed at the idea of being in his arms just moments ago.

The man cleared his throat, "Perhaps you can help me with something now that you aren't busy."

"Yes?" Bella shyly quizzed as she stepped back toward the shelf of books.

"I am searching for a book," he said, "one that gives instructions about caring for an injured foot."

Immediately, Bella shifted her gaze to the man's feet. Neither seemed to be in turmoil. She slowly lifted her eyes and studied a strong featured face. High cheekbones, a well-defined chin, and eyes as emeralds staring back at her. She had to remind herself to breathe.

Her mind flashed an image of her most treasured book in the entire world, *The Philosophy of Physiotherapy*. The book that her Papa had surprised her with on her sixteenth birthday. At this present moment, it was hidden safely away under her mattress, the exact place she kept it at home. But could she trust it in the hands of a stranger?

"Hello?" The man's big hand waved before Bella's face.

Bella blinked as a smile broke her refined lips. "Sorry," she said as she nervously tucked away an invisible strand of hair. "I-," she hesitated. Should she offer him her book or not? "I have a book that you might find interesting."

He released his folded arms, "Oh, really?"

"Yes, it explains how to treat all sorts of injuries and strengthen weakened muscles." Bella glanced back to the feet that seemed as normal as her own, neither did not seem to be lacking in muscle structure. When she met his eyes again, she found them far more intriguing than she should.

"The book you have, may I borrow it?" he asked.

Bella felt the walls about her heart start to crumble under his scrutiny and his beckoning tone of voice. Before she could drive an imaginary wedge into the broken crevice of her harbored heart, words of understanding began to spill from her lips. "Of course. I would go to the same limits to see someone I love find relief."

"Perfect," he sighed in relief. "When can we meet?"

CHAPTER FIVE

MRS. KING WALKED INTO THE Oak Sitting Room as she always did every morning to meet with Mrs. Vanderbilt and discuss the daily tasks at hand. Having spent most of the morning hours tying color coded ribbons around the fresh linens, she pondered who Mrs. Vanderbilt's next round of company might be.

Oft times Pauline, Mrs. Vanderbilt's sister, came to visit. Her stay was usually lengthy but she was very easy to please.

Then from time to time, Edith Stuyvesant Dresser Vanderbilt enjoyed a large number of visitors, ones that put the entire house of Biltmore in jeopardy. Maids would scurry from one room to the next, their duties never being fulfilled.

Among the many trunks of luggage toted throughout the entire manor, at least one of them were misplaced. Like the time Miss Parish could not locate the trunk that held her unmentionables. Every nook and cranny had been searched but still it hadn't turned up until late that evening. After Miss Parish had borrowed a chemise, among other things, it was brought to her attention that her luggage had been placed in the bachelor's quarters.

It did not take long to decipher who had found it. Mr.

Driftwood had been found nipping at her heels the remainder of her stay. Within the year, the two were joined in holy matrimony. Mrs. King always wondered what had inspired that union.

The steady echoing of heels stole Mrs. King's attention away from the marble fireplace. The mistress had arrived. She looked distressed, somewhat flustered.

"Ah, Mrs. King, I am terribly sorry for my delay. George and I had a bit of a heated discussion," Edith Vanderbilt spoke as she took her seat. "As you know, Cornelia will be turning seven on the twenty second day of this month." She sighed. "The child wants a dog. A dog! And George is willing to comply."

"Every child needs a dog. Besides, she doesn't have siblings to play with. Only the children from the village. Even that seems to be a bit less often than before."

"Ah, you are right," Mrs. Vanderbilt agreed. "Speaking of the village, I need to check up on Mrs. Baker. The doctor predicted she would recover from the pneumonia within a couple of weeks. Perhaps I can plan to visit her tomorrow and allow Cornelia to tag along."

"But she still needs a dog." Mrs. King added.

Cheerful bliss erupted from Mrs. Vanderbilt. "You will not allow me to forget. Besides, I would like to plan a surprise birthday party for Cornelia and invite some of the children from the village. That would be grand, would it not?"

"That would be wonderful," Mrs. King agreed. That's what Emily King admired about Edith Stuyvesant Dresser Vanderbilt.

She thought of more than just herself. Most women of her status would not care for anyone but themselves and especially not the unfortunate.

"Also, you are not going to believe this, Mrs. King. The founder of Biltmore Forest School, Dr. Carl Schenck, is conducting a festival in November. He is sending many invitations to renowned men across the United States. Our president is one of them."

"What?!" It came as a bit of a shock. The birthday party had been a small thing, but this event was a surprise. Why, it would take until then to prepare the house for such guests.

"Yes, this year marks the tenth anniversary of the school," Mrs. Vanderbilt added, "and he intends to demonstrate his idea of forestry all in the amount of three days."

"Oh, dear."

"That was my reaction, also, but to my relief, George asked that the men lodge at the Battery Park Hotel."

Relief melted over Mrs. King. "Good," she mumbled as she blew softly into her tea before sipping it.

"Oh, how is our Bella working out? I assume I will see her in the dining hall soon?" Mrs. Vanderbilt questioned as she slowly brought the teacup to her lips.

"Actually, she is in the Library as we speak. Dusting books."

"Dusting books?" Mrs. Vanderbilt eyed her suspiciously. "What has gone wrong?"

"Just ask me what has gone right. Nothing. She and Sophia had a bit of a water fight in the kitchen late yesterday. Cleaning the Library side by side is their punishment. As for Sophia, she has finally met her match."

The O that was formed by Mrs. Vanderbilt's mouth quickly turned to a smile. Everyone at Biltmore knew that sooner or later Sophia would meet the one to stop her in her steps and now Bella had to be that one.

"Well, we all realize that Sophia is very unhappy here." Mrs. Vanderbilt stirred the cup of tea and stared into its depths as if she were searching for something. "Maybe I should not have brought her here." Her words were audible, but had not intended to be.

"You have done your part. It is up to Sophia to make the best of it."

"Oh...I know. But wouldn't you rather live among loving, caring people in fine luxuries and not have to worry if dinner was to be served or not? Why, when I first saw the poor child, I soon realized she had gone without many meals; yet, I do believe she despises me for offering something better."

Emily King understood why Edith was second guessing herself. Had she opened the doors of her home to a homeless and helpless child, as was Sophia, and received cold treatment in return, she would probably send her packing. Mrs. Vanderbilt had a heaping load of mercy to go along with her hospitality.

"Maybe the scars of her childhood run too deeply. Perhaps time will heal what has been broken." Mrs. King added as she brought the cup of steaming tea to her lips again.

"I do hope you are right," Mrs. Vanderbilt said. "If not, maybe

Bella is the answer to her problem."

Bella's arms ached beyond belief. She had stretched and pulled all day. Now every fiber from her shoulders to her fingertips was protesting, begging for a rest. But she couldn't worry about that now. She only had a handful of minutes to find her way to the Library Terrace. She had foolishly agreed to meet the young man and hand her treasure over to him. Her book.

Her racing heart echoed in her ears. She had a right to be nervous. The man caused every nerve to unravel when in his presence.

At least before she left her room though, Bella had redone her hair and washed her face and hands so she wouldn't appear all grimy and dusty.

Bella hugged the book close to her bosom. It looked as though it were ancient. The binding had come loose, and some of the pages were hanging on by a thread due to the hours of study and research, but it still meant the world to her.

As her steps brought her to the terrace, Bella silently hoped she had not misjudged the man. After all, she didn't even know his name.

Crossing the threshold felt exhilarating. She hadn't given much thought about what to expect the terrace to offer. Bella hadn't dreamt of a canopy of Wisteria welcoming her to a peaceful calm, a perfect place to unwind after a noisy day of work. Neither had she expected hints of the evening sun to illuminate the man who stood waiting.

Bella wished for a cloud to dim the sun's beams and extinguish the gold flecks in the eyes of the man who was tearing down the walls about her heart one gaze at a time.

Darby waited patiently underneath the shelter of Mother Nature. The canopy of Wisteria shaded the entire terrace leaving little room for the setting sun to peek through. He was glad he had chosen such a secluded area so that no one would question their meeting. He would feel a bit embarrassed to admit that he was accepting help from a *girl.*

He had been resting his back against the massively, twisted vine and drinking in the view of the Blue Ridge Mountains when he heard faint, but detectible footsteps. His face turned slightly, catching a glimpse of the stilled figure. A rush of excitement whirled through Darby. It seemed like forever since he had spoken with her this morning, leaving a nagging anticipation to gnaw on him all day.

Finally, here he was. Here she was. He had to remind himself this appointment consisted of nothing more than just taking the book that she hesitantly agreed to let him borrow.

Darby's green irises instantly attached to her chocolate depths. He wasn't sure if it was the distinct contrast in color that drew them together, or something entirely different.

CHAPTER SIX

DARBY CAUGHT A WHIFF OF cinnamon in the gentle breeze. Instantly, he tagged the scent upon her. The closer she stepped, the more evident his suspicions became. The spice overpowered all the flourishing scents Mother Nature had to offer at the moment.

He moved away from the extraordinary vine that was braided and intertwined with many others and moved to meet her in the middle of the terrace.

"This is beautiful," he heard her say.

And just got lovelier, Darby thought but dared not to say it.

She boasted of the bountiful Wisteria although it was not showing off its lavender blooms in mid- August; its lush greenery was just as intriguing.

Her feet carried her to the far side where Darby had first stood. Her breath caught when she observed the Blue Ridge Mountains. The chain of forests seemed to trail on and on and on. "You should see the view from up there," Darby pointed toward the mountain.

She briskly turned her face to him. "You've been up there?"

Darby sidestepped her and rested his hip against the twisted vine once more. "Having had an undying interest in forestry, yeah, you could say I've hiked every mountain in this region."

Darby liked the way her eyes lit up.

"My Papa and I were supposed to hike Mount Pisgah this fall and see the changing of the leaves…" A saddened, distant look conquered the light that had just shown. "Anyway, here." She stretched out the book to Darby.

He took the worn book into his hands. It too smelled of cinnamon. It was still warm from where she had it clutched to her chest. He fingered the front cover as if he just realized how important the book was to her and then lifted his eyes. She had already been looking upon him, but inadvertently shifted her gaze to the book.

"You had better guard that with your life." A gentle grin tugged at the corners of her lips as she met his eyes again.

"Yes, ma'am."

"Thank you," she whispered and then cleared her throat. "Well, I guess this makes us even, huh?"

Darby's eyebrows drew together. Did she think she owed him for catching her when she fell? Maybe she was unaware of just how much he enjoyed it, and that it was no chore to be in her presence. "I'm afraid I'm not following you." His voice sounded warm and husky.

Bella cocked her head a little to the side, "You paid for the stamp."

Realization dawned on Darby. She had been the one at the Post Office. How could he not have noticed who she was before now?

Immediately, he held the book snug with one arm and

stretched out the other, offering his hand, "I'm Darby. Darby Pierson. And you are?"

She willingly stretched her hand to meet his. "I'm Bella." Their hands caught and held for a moment before she slowly released hers.

His gaze penetrated Bella's. He really liked what he saw in her eyes, but there was a shield there. One he hoped that would break down with time.

The sunset on the horizon declared it was time to depart, but neither moved. Instead, they shifted their gaze to study the orange glow behind the mountainous view.

"When should I return the book?" Darby asked.

Bella kept her focus on the mountainous view. "How long will you need it?"

"A week? Maybe two?"

Bella only nodded her head as if she was processing what he said. "Who has injured their foot?" she asked, her voice full of concern.

Darby could not believe she had not noticed his limp. Well, he had tried his best to conceal it. Obviously, he had succeeded. "Me," he answered dreadfully.

As quickly as the word met her ears, Bella met his gaze fully. "Really?" she asked in disbelief.

Darby sighed. "Unfortunately, yes. I got accepted into Biltmore Forest School, and my injury is a hindrance." He patted the hard cover of the book. "Hopefully, this has the answer."

Bella looked down at his booted foot. "Let me see it."

He took a brisk step backwards. "No!"

Darby's response startled Bella, causing her spine to stiffen.

Guilt flooded Darby's features. "Look, I'm sorry. I'm just sensitive, that's all."

Bella's mouth tilted. "I'll be easy."

Darby sighed. "No. You don't understand."

Bella took a brave step toward him. "Look, I've studied the ins and outs of Physiotherapy. I have a sister who is crippled. Trust me, I've seen it all."

"Listen, Bella," the use of her Christian name silenced her. "I meant that it is embarrassing to me. I'd rather you not see."

Bella smiled. "Do you think I've never seen a man's foot before?" The only male foot she had ever laid eyes on was her Papa's, but Darby didn't have to know that. She crossed her arms firmly across her chest and cocked her hip a notch.

Darby suppressed the urge to roll his eyes. "I have a- a limp."

"I can help you." Her voice pleaded.

Darby ran his hand through his hair. "No, Bella, I am *ashamed* of the limp. And you, of all people, would be the last I would ever want to see it."

"But-"

"No."

Bella's gaze searched his. "Don't you understand, Darby, we all have handicaps, or circumstances that create obstacles for us to overcome." She clasped her hands together and shrugged her shoulder. "While yours may be an injured foot, mine might be a broken heart."

"In which both require a healer," Darby added.

Bella stared deeply into his eyes, and for a moment he thought the earth shifted. Darby knew of certainty he wasn't the only one aware of the sudden variation of the wind. She felt it, too. Just as he was about to reach out and push back the tendril that had fallen about her brow, she stepped back.

"I-I must go," Bella muttered. "Just leave the book with Winston, the butler."

Darby followed her steps and called out, "Bella!"

She glanced over her shoulder and said, "Good night, Darby."

His steps slowed, and he watched as she walked away from the terrace. The sweet cinnamon scent lingered in her wake. Then he looked down at the book he was holding and lifted it to his nose. For a moment, he would have guessed she was still standing there offering help, but when his eyes lifted, she was nowhere to be seen. Again, his gaze rested on the book that was secured in his arm while his finger slid along the loose binding. He sighed, and then his feet led him down the steps and far away from the terrace. He needed to be far away because he didn't welcome the foreign emotion Bella caused anyway. Soon enough, he would reach his plateau of perfection, and his steps would be as before.

Smooth and flawless.

Sophia lingered in the shadows until the couple had dispersed from the terrace, and then she stepped to where Bella and the mysterious man had stood.

It had been easy to follow a safe distance behind Bella just to see what she was up to, but to Sophia's surprise, a man had been waiting for her on the terrace. Sophia had recognized him to be the same man who had visited the Library early this morning.

She had watched them exchange an object. A book maybe? Sophia wondered what kind of book it was and why he would be interested in it.

She stepped from beneath the security of the Wisteria and observed her surroundings before darting inside. She would be sure to find out what kind of connection Bella shared with the man. But more importantly, she wondered what kind of book they interchanged and why did it seem significant?

Darby had finally made it back to his quarters, the bunk that cost him six dollars a night to lodge.

His foot felt like it was on fire. After removing his boot, Darby propped it comfortably on a pillow. Immediately, the tension began to ease.

He took the book into his hands and stared at it. It was almost in shambles. Bella must have bought it in rugged condition because the spine of the book had been reassembled many times. When he opened the front cover, it didn't screak or pop like most books did. However, something was written on the inside. The script had faded, but it was still readable.

My Dearest Bella,

Darby absorbed the first three words. Something inside his chest tightened. Maybe a first love had gifted Bella with the book, and that was why it was so dear to her. Without reading the message, Darby skipped down to the signature. It was signed, *Papa.*

Why Darby felt an instant flush of relief, he could not fathom. So he took a deep breath and began to read.

My Dearest Bella,

I have had this book hidden away for some time now. I wanted to give it to you on your sixteenth birthday. Your growing love for your sister and the desire you have to see her walk again astonishes me.

You are far more than a Papa could ever ask for. Even during the storm, you've danced. You have even dragged me out in the worst of rains! But one thing you must remember, Bella, there will soon come a day when I won't be there to dance in the rain with you. But as sure as God kisses the early morning flowers with dew, He will send someone to dance in my place. That special person will shower you with love and hope and joy. But one thing you mustn't forget, no matter how much it hurts or how hard it pours, always remember to dance in the rain.

Love Always,

Papa

Darby swallowed the knot in his throat and reread it again. He had already sensed everything about Bella. Her Papa was correct. The young woman was astonishing, even though something deep inside told Darby not to admit it.

Having dismissed all thoughts of her, Darby turned to Chapter One, *Confirming Your Injury*. He read through the first chapter with a breeze and had gone on to the second one.

Still, only information that he had already known stared back at him. Having flipped through the book rather swiftly, he found a page marked where a diagram had been circled. It showed the effective movements for a stiffened foot.

The corner of the page appeared freshly bent, and the circle was all too new. He lifted the book to his nose. Just as Darby had predicted, the distinctive scent of cinnamon filled his nostrils. His heart flopped involuntarily. Had she taken the time to search out his need?

Darby retracted the book from his face and just stared.

This was going to be a long night.

CHAPTER SEVEN

IT WAS RAINING SO HARD Darby could barely see where his feet were leading him. Right now his only purpose in life was to protect what he was clutching under his coat, *The Philosophy of Physiotherapy*. His ankle and foot were protesting, begging for him to stop running, but he pressed on. Unable to see the branch that had fallen from the tree due to the violent storm, his foot caught and he was falling to the ground. Still refusing to loosen his grip on the book, Darby's shoulder plunged into the earth creating an agonizing pain.

He blinked his eyes trying to rid the excessive drops of rain when he saw a figure lurch forward and grab for the book. With harsh tugs of war, Darby fought. Once he thought he had lost it. Again he pulled, holding the book tightly.

He couldn't let them win. He refused to loosen his grip. Bella would be so heartbroken if he returned to her empty handed. Again, the figure pulled on the book, but much harder this time. Slowly, he felt it leaving his grasp. It was gliding through his fingertips.

"NO!"

Darby screamed, but as he raised up, he found himself in the middle of his bed panting for breath. He soon realized the book was clutched tightly to his chest. Relief melted over his sweaty body, cooling him down immediately.

It had only been a nightmare.

Darby heard the heavy drops of rain hitting against the window. Just as he was wondering the time, a flash of lightning lit up his room followed by a loud clap of thunder.

The book felt heavy in his arms. He needed to put it somewhere safe. Somewhere only he knew. After pondering the thought, his feet settled onto the cold, wooden floor. Hiding places weren't easily found in the dark.

Again the lightning illuminated the room. His gaze dropped to the rumpled bed.

The mattress! That by far would be the safest place to keep it. He lifted its edge and slid the book under it.

Once settled onto the bed again, he placed his hands behind his head and stared at the ceiling. Sleep seemed to have been driven far from him, and one particular face was impossible to remove from his mind.

The awakening dawn followed the thunderstorm that thrived last night. Birds were chirping, singing their good morn praise. It looked as though God dumped all of the tears of the heavens upon the earth beneath. Vibrant green leaves looked glassy, as did the blades of grass. Sluggish drops of rain made their way down the window pane where Darby stood.

He had an agonizing morning. Darby had worked his foot according to the book, but found no relief at all. It was still as stiff as ever.

His uneven steps led him outdoors. The smell of summer rain greeted him. He loved that smell. Even as a child, he remembered going outside after the rain. Nothing about it had changed. Even the birds tended to chirp louder, probably giving more thanks because God let the rain draw the worms to surface, making it much easier to find food for the day. Darby was reminded that God even cares if the sparrow is fed. To be caught thinking about food, his gut let him know he was fifteen minutes late for breakfast.

Darby's plate was loaded with biscuits, smothered with steamy gravy. Scrambled eggs were mounted up beside the crispy bacon. Just what he needed to begin a good day.

He took cautious steps to his seat. "Mornin', boys."

"Mornin', Pierson." Hunter Morris eyed Darby's plate, "Not very hungry, are ya?"

Darby just smiled. He wasn't hungry. He was famished. Without giving thought of his manners, Darby devoured the country breakfast, leaving no trace of a single crumb.

"Where were you last night?" Hunter queried.

Darby almost choked on his milk. He brought his eyes up to his peers. Every single one of the scholars were interrogating him with their curious gazes.

"Maybe he was fasting," one of the young men jested.

"Does it look like he knows the meaning of that term?" another scholar added.

"I think he ate supper with Mr. Schenck."

"Actually," Darby could not wipe the smile away with his napkin, "I went to *nun ya*," he said as he pushed the chair away from the table and stood.

"Huh?" the crowd began to buzz.

"*Nun ya* business." Darby dipped his head and hobbled away.

He would let them believe he ate supper at the king's table yesterday, as long as they didn't know he had spent the evening on the terrace without a single meal.

Later that day, Darby fought for steadiness as he descended the steps of Biltmore Forest School, following behind his mentor, Dr. Carl Schenck.

The group of young men marched accordingly giving their full attention to what Schenck was instructing. "To produce lively plants, we must make certain they are settled in healthy soil. It is like the parable of the sower." Schenck turned to the group of eager students.

"If seeds fall carelessly to the ground, the fowl will devour them. Yet if they fall unto stony places and cannot take root, the sun will scorch them. However, if we care not about the seed and plant it in the midst of thorns, surely we will harvest thorns. But if we use the wisdom God granted us already, and sow the seed in good ground, meaning fertile soil, then our trees flourish and we will harvest fruit in abundance.

"We must first understand soil composition. It is made up of four parts; air, water, organic matter, and mineral matter."

Schenck went on to state the soil composition varied from different parts of the climate, due to temperature and location.

He also explained the need for minerals and living organisms in order to produce vibrant plant life.

Having assigned every student to gather his own soil and study the composition, Schenck moved along observing the methods the young men were practicing, not that it mattered what fashion was used to scoop up the dirt to fill their buckets.

Dr. Schenck's gaze settled upon Darby. He watched how Darby observed the dirt in his hands and let the grains of soil slip through his fingers. He had known Darby was a natural; he could see in the young man's eyes the unwavering devotion to protect the earth, but only one thing worried him.

Darby's limp.

It was plainly stated in the application that strong physical health was a requirement, but as he watched now, Darby struggled. Since Darby was the son and heir of renowned business owner, Charles Pierson, that had been his admission ticket. As Schenck observed Darby's complicated foot, he decided it was best to dismiss the scholar from strenuous activity.

"Does the earth in these parts contain water?" Schenck asked as he approached Darby.

Darby unsteadily raised to his feet and dusted his hands, "Plenty of it. Probably from the storm last night."

"Most likely," Schenck agreed. "I see you are still not well." He gestured toward Darby's foot.

Darby paled. "Today has been worse," he explained, "probably due to the weather."

Schenck tapped his chin. "Beginning next month, we will be taking daily hikes up to Mount Pisgah marking diverse trails to prepare for November. I have plans to invite many prestigious men, and I do not wish to bore them." Schenck studied a moment in silence. "As for you, I am afraid you are not in the condition for such activity."

"What are you saying?" Darby asked, his brows almost connecting.

Schenck thought for a moment. He didn't intend to dismiss Darby entirely because there were some things he could do, but he wasn't capable of hiking or tree removal. So what could *he* do? Plant small things and nourish them and watch them grow?

Carl Schenck understood the dream of a man. He also understood the drive of a man. When a man wanted something badly enough, he would do everything in his power to conquer his goal. In Darby's case, if he would seek proper medical attention, most likely his problem would diminish a great deal.

"Other than dismissing entirely," Schenck said, "I will give you exactly one month to improve. I do not expect you to be healed in that length of time, but I do expect to see a large fraction of that limp put behind you." Schenck bent over to grasp the pail of dirt. "I'll carry the bucket. You get the shovel."

Darby slowed his uneven steps and allowed a gap to form between him and his mentor. Dismissed entirely? Had Dr. Schenck considered denying him the title as class president? Darby's chest tightened at the thought of being forced to walk away from his dream. His life felt just like the grains of dirt that had passed through his fingers earlier. His ambitions were swiftly slipping from his grasp. And it was all because of a limp!

Darby stopped and drove the shovel into the sodden dirt. His palm pressed against the dome of the handle while he allowed his aching foot to find relief. His other hand ran through his hair. One month! Well, at least Dr. Schenck didn't say one week.

Darby sighed and shook his head because there was just one solution to this complicated situation. He just silently hoped that *she* would give him a second chance.

Bella had finally worked her way down to the bottom book shelf. It had been a peaceful day. Few people had visited the Library which was good. Less distraction. More conquered. And Sophia had been relatively quiet.

She enjoyed the quiet since it offered plenty of time for her to think. Images of Ashlynn and Mama flitted through her mind. She had written and rewritten letters in her thoughts, but still she had not conquered penning them down.

As much as she tried, Bella could not erase the face that haunted her sleep last night. She chided herself for whispering his name when she thought no one was listening. How foolish.

She didn't even know when she would encounter him again, and when she did, would she have the nerve to apologize for not responding to his bidding when she fled the terrace?

There was something about him she could not lay a finger on. Never before had a man's eyes had an effect on her like Darby's. And when in his presence, her heart refused to slow its pace. And why did her palms become sweaty? And why did she enjoy the sound of her name flowing from his lips?

"Good afternoon, Bella."

Bella yelped as she turned, only to find an amused Darby standing much closer than she had expected. She stepped back against the large shelf of books. "Do you make a habit of scaring people?"

He smiled the same tormenting smile that caused her heart to jolt. "Why do you ask that?" he quizzed.

Bella opened her mouth to speak, but no words came. Instead, she held her breath when he closed the distance between them and reached his fingers to her hair.

"You had a feather in your hair." He held it up. "See?"

Heat filled her cheeks. She could feel it. Her eyes darted to the feather he held. It must've fallen from the duster.

"I hope you weren't planning to fly away," he said as he trailed the feather down her cheek before sliding it into the pocket of his shirt.

Her gaze followed the feather. Finally, she looked up into his eyes. "No, why?"

"I was hoping the offer was still good." He pleaded with his eyes, "I need your help, Bella."

She questioned his motives and what had caused the sudden change. Just yesterday, he refused her help. What made him decide that he *needed* her?

"Why?" she questioned.

Darby released a sigh. "I have exactly one month to improve." He pointed to his foot. "If not," he choked, "if not, then I will be permanently dismissed from Biltmore Forest School."

Bella felt the pain she saw flash through his eyes. Her chest ached for him.

But was one month enough time? She was only granted one evening off a week, which thankfully was tomorrow, and then half a day every other Sunday. There would only be eight evenings she could give him. He, of course, would have to be faithful to everything she taught him and that included exercising his foot daily.

Bella cleared her throat. "I think it's possible."

Hope filled Darby's eyes. "Is that a yes?" he asked.

The corners of her mouth lifted. "I suppose it is."

CHAPTER EIGHT

BELLA HAD SPENT THE ENTIRE morning writing to Ashlynn and told her of all the remarkable things about Biltmore and how she had fallen into step. She left out the bit of details about Sophia, but she did mention the many books her hands had held the past few days. Feeling the urge to write a little something about Darby, Bella decided otherwise.

She promised to return home for a visit as soon as she received her wages and bid them her love and God's blessings.

Bella examined herself in the mirror once again before leaving for the terrace. She was wearing the gingham dress she had brought from home. It was pressed and starched, of course. Her hair lay loose across her shoulder in its usual braid. She ran her hands over her flat tummy making sure that the wonderful meals here at Biltmore weren't catching up with her.

Her fingers trailed her perfectly arched eyebrows, smoothing them like it mattered. It didn't. Bella didn't even understand why she was actually giving thought about her appearance.

She took a deep breath. She was ready.

Bella had to search for her next breath when she stepped onto the terrace. Darby was already there, waiting, which was no surprise. He was seated on a bench just off to the left. Beside him was her book.

As she stepped closer, Bella tried not to acknowledge how taut his white, button down shirt fit his broad figure and how damp his hair was. She tried extinguishing the rich scent of spice wafting in the breeze, but there was no use. It kept making its way back to her, bringing alive the foreign fibers inside her person.

Seeing Bella at work was something, but seeing her now was much more glorious. She looked much like the day she was at the Post Office except maybe the dress was different. But her hair, goodness her hair was beautiful! It wasn't concealed in a tight bun on the side like he was used to seeing it, but instead it laid loose across her shoulder in a twist of some kind.

"I hope your day went well," Bella finally spoke.

And just got better, Darby thought. "Ah," he shrugged. "Any typical day. Digging dirt, planting trees and getting filthy."

He noticed how she paused her step and performed a quick assessment of his appearance. He knew what she was thinking. At least he hoped he knew what she was thinking.

"It doesn't look like you've been playing in dirt all day," she said.

He knew. A smile formed on his face, "I didn't want my feet to stink."

Bella's lips parted with a smile, revealing her perfect, white teeth. Her eyes darted to his feet. "Well," she stepped closer, "let's get started."

"Right." Darby took his seat again and began removing his shoe.

"Both."

"Huh?" His hands froze when he looked up and watched her kneel down onto her knees in front of him.

"I need to see both of your feet."

Darby paled under her command.

"But you can leave your socks on," she said playfully.

Relief washed over Darby. "Good."

Bella knelt before him and took his injured foot into her hand. She was gentle. After comparing the flexibility of both feet, she barely pressed his toes back toward him. "Tell me if it hurts too much." She peeped up at him through her lashes. "Are you okay?"

"Yeah." He barely made the word audible.

She repeated the exercise ten counts. Then she placed her left hand under his foot for support, laying her right hand on top. She gently pressed his toes downward. Again, she repeated the movement ten counts.

Darby observed how her hands worked his weakened limb. He had thought Bella astonishing like her Papa, too, had thought, but his opinion of her just became greater. There was a gift in her touch. Already his foot was beginning to relax. It had been aching terribly before she arrived, but now it felt like cool water was flowing through it.

How did she do it? It puzzled him.

She rested his foot beside the other and cleared her throat. She tucked a strand of hair behind her ear as she always did when she was nervous. "Your foot seems a bit more flexible, doesn't it?"

He only nodded.

"Now, I'm going to press my hand onto the bottom of your foot, applying little resistance at first, but then it will intensify. I need you to press your toes toward me."

Darby bit the inside of his cheek as his foot worked. Sharp pain shot up his foot and through his ankle, but the more he worked it, the easier it became. He felt the resistance, but it didn't seem so hard.

His eyes were locked onto his foot. He was doing it!

Bella felt bubbly inside. It was working! Simply a miracle!

She stole glances up at him, but his determined features were focused on his foot and its movements.

Darby continued to press, and she could feel the force from his foot become stronger with each count. She couldn't help but smile. Her eyes started to fill with water. Bella felt so good for him.

"Ready to walk?" she asked.

"Definitely," he answered full of confidence.

Before he could protest, Bella had already slipped his shoe on one foot and was ready to slip on the other. When she stood, she offered him her hand.

At first she thought he would refuse her help. Instead he slid his warm hand in hers. She tried ignoring the pulsating current that generated from their touch. Bella found his determined gaze, "Rely on my assistance as much as you need, but it's time to press your foot all the way down, okay?"

"All right." Darby's voice had gone from excited to hoarse.

Did he feel the same electrical charges shooting up his arm?

Darby flattened his foot. Bella wondered how long it had been since he stood firm on both feet.

He took a deep breath and stepped forward, his weaker limb following behind. To Bella's surprise, it willingly complied. The step was beautiful.

Together in silence, they walked the length of the terrace and back. Again, they walked its length.

Bella had to fight the tears that were begging to be loosed. His gait was forming into perfection. She watched him as he watched his feet. He was strong. His well-set jaw bone declared that.

She couldn't help but notice how nice he looked, even though his shirt looked a size too small. She wondered if he rolled his sleeves up to his elbows because they were too short to begin with. Her gaze fell upon his tanned forearm. He, no doubt, had spent many days in the log woods. His big hand was anchored in hers. Together, they made a good team. Too bad they hadn't met under different circumstances. Bella couldn't help but wonder which road they would have traveled together.

"I'm walking, Bella!" The edge of excitement in his voice couldn't be denied.

He began to work his hand loose from hers. She let go. Instantly, her hand felt ice cold. She pressed it against her stomach as she observed each step Darby made. He was becoming weaker as a slight limp was starting to form.

She stepped up to his side and took his hand without permission.

Darby felt defeated. It had been so perfect until he tried it on his own. He jerked his hand away from Bella and limped toward the bench where he had been sitting. He didn't sit down, but he just stood there and peered out into open air. He could smell the rain coming. He needed to be going. There was no sense in wasting any more of Bella's time.

He retrieved the book from the bench and asked as he turned, "Do you mind if I take this?"

"You can't expect to be healed in one day, Darby. It takes patience and perseverance," Bella said as she barely laid her fingers on his arm.

"But you don't understand, Bella," Darby explained as he withdrew his arm from her touch. "This is my life!" His big hand fanned his chest. "My dreams and all I ever hoped for depends on this."

Bella retracted her hand as though she had been burnt. "And

you think I don't have dreams?" her accusing glare chilled Darby. "Do you think I *choose* to work here?"

"I thought all ladies wished to be employed by the Vanderbilts, just like all men desire to be a forester."

"You're wrong, Darby." Her eyes blackened. "You're dead wrong."

He propped his hands on his hips to relieve the growing tension in his foot. "Tell me, Bella, what on earth are you going to find more satisfying than living in fine luxuries as this?" his hand fanned the vastness of the estate.

Her jaw slacked. Her eyes held an immense measure of grief. Immediately, Darby regretted his choice of words.

"I see," she said, "the world revolves around *you*." A sympathetic smile formed on Bella's face. "Obviously, you have never had to sacrifice your will for anyone." Her eyes darted to his foot as if she just realized pain resided there. "I thought you were different," she said as she lifted her eyes to meet his again. "But you're just like everyone else." Bella turned and fled the terrace paying no heed to the pouring rain.

"Bella!" Darby called out, but the loud crack of thunder prevented his beckoning to be heard.

CHAPTER NINE

Darby had called Bella's name but as he expected, she didn't stop. Yet he couldn't let her go. Not alone. So he hobbled after her. He could barely see her through the sheets of rain that were coming so quickly.

He called her name again and again, but she chose not to stop. Due to the sound of the rain, she probably couldn't even hear him. He paid little attention to his aching foot. He had to reach Bella. He was sorry. He was so sorry for being selfish.

Darby followed her steps. She had gone under the Wisteria Pergola, probably to escape the beating force of the raindrops. Once he struggled down the steps, he could see her again but she was still running.

"Bella!"

He called out, but she refused to acknowledge his bidding.

Finally, he made it safely underneath the arbor. After wiping away the droplets of rain from his eyelids, he saw her plummet to the ground.

"Bella!"

Ignoring all sign of pain and torture, Darby dashed toward Bella. When he finally made it to her side, he held no restraints. He took her cold, shaky form into his arms and rocked her while she wept. "I'm sorry, Bella," Darby spoke against her wet hair. "I'm so sorry for being selfish."

Darby would have held Bella like this until the end of time if she needed him to.

Forget the dreams. Forget the school. Forget the therapy.

He soon realized that *this* was what mattered most. Healing a broken heart. Providing refuge from the storm. Becoming a sanctuary for Bella.

Bella pulled away from Darby's embrace. The distance between them did not silence the echo of his heart drumming, while the sudden chill reminded her of how safe she felt in his arms, although she denied that it felt right.

Darby neared her face, but she wouldn't look at him. He drew close to her ear and whispered, "I'm sorry, Bella. I didn't mean for those thoughtless words to escape my lips."

Her spine stiffened. What the reaction meant, she didn't rightly know.

His finger settled on the side of her chin, and he willed her face to turn. His green orbs penetrated her dark cocoa depths. She began to squirm under his scrutiny. His finger slowly slid from her chin, his hand going to rest on his knee.

"You're beautiful," he whispered.

Darby's words caused Bella's heart to take on a different beat. No man, other than her Papa, had ever spoken such flattery to her before. She remained frozen by his compliment while she watched his finger make its way back to her face and push back a damp strand of hair from her forehead.

"Do you believe me?" Darby sincerely asked as he placed his hand back to his knee where it belonged.

"Do I believe that you think I'm beautiful, or are you asking if I agree with you?" Bella couldn't help but return his contagious smile.

"Actually, I was relating the question to what I said before that." He was blushing. Darby had embarrassed himself. "Do you believe I meant that I was sorry, and those greedy words will never slip from my lips again?"

"Oh." At the mention of his lips, she dropped her gaze to their form. Goodness, they were full and perfectly bow shaped, but now they were lifting at the corners. She brought her eyes back to his. "Forgiven."

"Good."

Bella watched his Adam's apple bob up and down. For a second, she thought she heard him swallow.

"Well," Bella really didn't know what to say. She needed to go since she was freezing, but did she really want to? To her own surprise, she was really enjoying getting to know *this* side of Darby.

"Do you mind sharing what's weighing heavily on your mind?" Darby asked.

His question took her by surprise. Her gaze settled on the dancing rain drops falling from the clouds. For an instant, Bella thought she imagined a little girl and her Papa laughing and dancing in the rain.

Immediately, Bella rebuked the mirage.

"My Papa passed away last month." Her words fell in a whisper. "I promised him I would see that my Mama and sister were well taken care of."

"Isn't that what you're doing?" he asked.

Her head only nodded, "I just wish I could see them more often. My sister needs me."

"How so?"

Bella found Darby's eyes once again. Compassion, mixed with an unknown emotion, radiated from his green irises. She turned her attention back to the rain.

"She's handicapped." Immediately, her gaze shifted to Darby's foot. "Ashlynn suffered from Polio disease when she was five, leaving her left side paralyzed." She swallowed the bitter taste in her mouth. "Together, we have come so far, but if she discontinues everything I taught her," Bella shrugged, "we will lose all that was fought for."

She watched Darby's foot work from side to side. He, too, understood the importance of the continuation of the strength building exercises.

Darby took Bella's hand in his and examined its structure. She tried hard not to notice the warmth of his grip. She watched as he memorized her fingers. Her palm. Her wrist.

"There is a gift in your touch, Bella." His voice spoke just as warmly as his hand felt. "After all, I am very thankful that you and I crossed paths." He gave her hand a gentle squeeze. "If not, then you would have paid one dime for a stamp."

Together they laughed.

"I would not have given Rudy Moyers the satisfaction of being duped."

"Yes, you would've," Darby argued.

"I don't think so." She shook her head as she pulled her hand away from his.

Bella stood to her feet and inhaled deeply, "Ah, the sweet smell of rain."

Darby struggled to his feet. "Yeah, it reminds me of when I was a boy."

"Hmmm." Bella wondered what the rain meant to him. Did he dance? Or was it just a simple childhood memory?

"We probably need to be going." His voice dissolved the thoughts she was imagining at the moment.

"Right." She agreed, but neither moved. They stood still and watched the rising fog.

"Bella!"

The sudden sound of Bella's name from the opposite end of the arbor jolted them both. Within the moment, they were both facing their intruder.

Sophia.

She was holding Bella's book.

"Does this belong to you?!" Sophia called out.

"I'm sorry, Bella. I must have left it on the bench." Darby apologized.

"Don't worry about it," Bella mumbled. "I have a feeling her motives were driven by something entirely different."

Sophia had found great satisfaction intruding on Bella and her beau. The man departed as soon as Bella gave him her book. She had spied them again and witnessed the both of them fleeing the terrace. When they hadn't returned, she wandered about carefully, not drawing much attention to herself. Finally, she spotted them underneath the Wisteria Pergola. She remembered the book and knew exactly how to break up the little tryst.

It worked, and it would work again and again.

As long as they didn't realize she was lurking in the shadows.

Bella had not seen or heard from Darby in several days. Finally, she and Sophia finished the work in the Library, but that still didn't solve her problem. Now they had both been assigned the kitchen. Today would be a bit more exciting than usual. Cornelia Vanderbilt turned seven today, and the Mistress of the house had planned a surprise birthday party that would be taking place this afternoon in the Banquet Hall.

Bessie had told Bella that many children from the village had been invited. "That's just how our Mrs. Vanderbilt is, Bella." Bessie had said. "She reaches out to the poor and showers them with gifts and with love."

Bessie had been right. The children that were starting to enter the Banquet Hall were not wealthy like one would think. They were adorned in clothes like Bella was used to wearing. And to think, they would be served as luxurious guests for one day. The thought made Bella smile.

She and Sophia had been given the opportunity to prepare the table. Fine foods were to be served, as well as a scrumptious birthday cake. Games were played and the prizes were quite extraordinary. One gift was a bird cage with a chirping canary inside it. Bella silently hoped she could play that game and win the prize.

She stood back to watch the children and observe the glow on their faces as they took in their surroundings. A little fella, named Johnny, asked Mrs. Vanderbilt what each flag stood for. She patiently explained each and every one to him. His eyes lit up when she pointed out the American flag and explained what each symbol meant.

It was time for another game. All the children formed a circle, Cornelia the object of attention of course. Then they started passing a potato. "One potato, two potato, three potato, four!" The children exclaimed. "Five potato, six potato, seven potato, OR!"

The children jumped up and down with glee. All except for the unlucky one, of course. Finally, the game was over. A little girl, Francis, won. She received one dollar for her prize.

It was now time for cake. Together, Bella and Sophia brought in the cake. It was beautiful. Three layers ascended toward the high ceiling above them. White fluffy icing was spiraling along the cake's edge holding tight to edible pink pearls.

"Now, inside the cake are metal charms. They are safely wrapped in wax paper," Mrs. Vanderbilt explained.

"There is a sewing machine and if you find it, then it means you will be a seamstress when you grow up." Mrs. Vanderbilt went on. "Also, there is a cow, meaning you will be a dairy farmer. And there is a fish, meaning you will be a fisherman."

Mrs. Vanderbilt clasped her hands together. "And lastly, there is a dime. If you find it, it means that you will be rich." The children's eyes grew large.

The cake was being cut and served when Mrs. Vanderbilt spoke again. "Oh, I almost forgot. There is a heart, also." She blushed when her gaze settled on her husband. "It means you will find true love."

The children snickered.

"Be sure you do not swallow your token!" the Mistress exclaimed.

Bella stood back and observed the children once more. Boys and girls, alike, were devouring their pieces of cake. A little girl, one much like herself, found the cow in her piece. She didn't seem too disappointed to find out she would make her living by milking cows.

A little boy found the fish. He said that was what he was hoping for.

A chunky little girl at the far end of the table found the sewing machine. Now, it only left the dime and the heart.

Bessie was making hasty steps toward her and Sophia. She had two pieces of cake. "Here, girls. Enjoy!"

They each silently took their piece. Bella had never tasted a cake so good in all her life. The icing was just right. It wasn't gritty nor was it too creamy, and the cake was just as perfect. Neither was it too dry nor too moist. It was just-

Crunch!

Pain shot through Bella's jaw. Goodness! It scared her. Oh, but she must've found one of the charms! The form was thick. It was not the dime. That she was sure of. And why did all of a sudden everyone in the room turn their eyes toward her? Did they hear the crunch, too?

She tried smiling the best she could. She politely laid her fork onto her dish and quickly removed the charm from her mouth. The children were cheering, begging her to unwrap it.

She stepped closer to the forty foot long table and began to unravel the wax paper. Her heart stopped when she realized what was lying in the palm of her hand.

The heart.

It was gorgeous. It was gold plated and speckled with diamonds.

"True love!" the children started shouting. Heat crept up Bella's neck. Her gaze shot to Mrs. Vanderbilt, who was also smiling.

Then all of the sudden, the children hushed. The room took on a different atmosphere.

Mrs. Vanderbilt turned her attention to the one who had just entered the Banquet Hall.

Bella followed her gaze.

Darby.

CHAPTER TEN

BELLA ENCLOSED HER FINGERS TIGHTLY around the charm and stuffed it into her apron pocket. Darby, of all people, would be the last she would want to learn of her fortunate finding. It was just a silly game for kids. Bella knew that, but why did her heart flutter when the wax paper fell from its form to reveal its beauty?

Mr. Vanderbilt made his way over to where Darby stood. He held a box with a beautiful red bow tied around it. Mr. Vanderbilt directed Darby to where the presents were stacked and gestured toward the cake table.

Immediately, his gaze collided with Bella. He had caught her staring at him. Well, she wasn't exactly staring at him. The gift he was carrying held her captivated.

"Bella?" Mrs. Vanderbilt spoke her name, gaining her undivided attention. "Would you mind serving our guest, Mr. Pierson, a piece of cake?"

Bella's features froze, as well as her heart. She took a deep breath and answered, "Yes ma'am." The thawing of her heart came quickly, as well as the innumerable beats.

Bella could feel her cheeks become ignited. She tried taking deep breaths to calm herself.

Bella didn't need anyone to notice that she and Darby were already acquainted. And how was she going to tell him to act nonchalant?

Bella decided she would deal with that in a moment. Right now, she needed to concentrate on keeping her hand still so she could slice the cake.

Darby was relieved when Mr. Vanderbilt chose to stay and babysit the gift he had delivered. The wobbling critter just wouldn't be still, and Darby knew at any time it would start barking because the pest had whined the entire distance from the school to the house.

Darby was glad to find Bella alone at the cake table. At least he would have the chance to say *hello*. By all means, he knew to act casual, showing no sign of familiarity. He watched her as she nervously sliced a rather large chunk of cake and dumped it onto a dish. Obviously, she had not gotten used to serving yet.

"Bella?"

She swung around with the cake. Her grip almost loosened enough to send it flying. Darby reached for the plate to ensure that he did not wear it all the way back to his bunk. His hands clasped onto hers, and the touch ignited a flame that spread like wild fire up their arms.

Both Darby and Bella retracted their hands as if they had been burnt, leaving the fine piece of china to shatter in a hundred pieces and the blob of cake to stick to Darby's boot.

The room fell silent. Bella wouldn't even look at him. He observed her as she took in the disaster. All color drained from her cheeks. She probably just realized the broken dish cost more than her earned wages.

And the cake? Good heavens! It was mounted atop his foot!

Bella fell to her knees and held out her apron. She began piling the broken shards of glass onto it. Darby knelt down beside her and scooped up pieces of glass, carefully placing them in her apron.

"Here, Bella, use the broom." Bessie stood there offering it to her. Before Bella could stand to grasp it, Darby had already taken it into his large hands.

Mrs. Vanderbilt approached them quietly. Before she could utter a word, Darby said, "I'm very sorry, Mrs. Vanderbilt. It was entirely my fault, and I will pay handsomely to see that the dish is replaced."

Mrs. Vanderbilt fanned the open air with her hand. "Think nothing of it, Mr. Pierson. There are at least one hundred more dishes of the same design." She smiled warmly at the both of them. "Do not worry with it," she said as her gaze shifted to the floor. "Oh! Look!" Mrs. Vanderbilt shouted.

Everyone did look. Darby felt their gaze.

"We no longer have to worry if one of the children swallowed the dime! It is stuck to your boot, Mr. Pierson!" Mrs. Vanderbilt lost her control and laughed as did the entire room full of people. She strode away and motioned for the children. "It is time for gifts!" she cheered.

Bella remained on her knees, so Darby offered his hand, but still she arose with little grace. She held the shards of glass in the safety of her apron, and she refused to meet his stare.

"Come here," Darby beckoned. "You've got a blob of icing right there." Bella stiffened as Darby's finger slid easily up her chin and to the corner of her mouth. "You're even cute when you're mad," he said as he withdrew his finger and consumed the icing. He watched her gasp, and then ever so slowly her cheeks heated. He liked causing this kind of reaction.

Darby cleared his throat. "Tell me, *Bella*, what does finding the dime have to do with a birthday party?"

"The person who finds the dime is supposed to be rich when he grows up." She looked him over boldly, her gaze lingering on his boot, "Looks like you're a little late for that one."

Darby knew she had no idea who she was talking to. He would inherit much wealth, but at the ripe age of twenty four, he had his mind on other things. And the southern belle in front of him was one of them.

"So, *Bella*," Darby stressed her name again, and smiled when he saw her stiffen, "what did *you* find?"

Bella paled. "Not everyone found a token." She shrugged her shoulder. "Lucky you." She turned to walk away, but he caught her by the arm and stalled the action.

"What did *you* find?" he asked again.

Bella swallowed. "I told you. Not everyone found a token." Her voice wavered.

"I do not believe you for a minute," Darby declared as he

cocked his head to the side. "Why is that, *Bella*?" He stressed her name again. He knew it flustered her.

"Please let go. People are looking," she said through gritted teeth.

"I will. But first tell me what token you found," he bargained.

Bella tried tearing her eyes away from his, but his gaze held her captive. Finally, she whispered, "I found a heart."

"Oh?" Darby pressed on. "What is the *heart* supposed to mean?"

Bella surrendered unto his gaze. "I am supposed to find true love."

Darby looked Bella over boldly and said, "I guess you're a little late for that one."

He loosened the grip on her arm and strode toward his exit.

Bella placed a hand over the spot Darby had held, and followed him with her gaze. When he was about to cross the threshold, his face turned back to steal a glance.

And to Bella's downright destruction, he winked.

The party had ended soon after Darby made his exit. When Cornelia opened the last gift, which was the one Darby had delivered, she squealed with excitement. "A puppy!" She pulled it out of the box, but the little thing squirmed its way right out of her arms. The group of children parted like the Red Sea, leaving a path for the puppy to escape.

Then like Pharaoh's army, the children chased after it. The yelping critter took one lap around the extravagant table, then it took off through the entryway, and down the corridor. Mrs. Vanderbilt was nipping at their heels, demanding the dog to stop. But of course it didn't.

Such an easy way to make rid of all the guests, Bella playfully thought.

Finally, after cleaning the entire Banquet Hall, Bella retired to her room. Her feet and legs were aching beyond relief. She pulled the charm from her apron pocket and dove onto her bed. The sparkles shone brightly as she stared at it in the palm of her hand. She fingered the bumpy texture where the diamonds were engraved.

Bella had never owned such a beautiful item before. She supposed it would be the only piece of gold she would ever possess.

Bella pondered her own heart. The one that God allowed to beat with time. The one God allowed to be broken. The one that seemed so hard. The one that she purposely built a wall around so it couldn't be hurt again.

The one that Darby Pierson could see through her eyes. The one that fluttered every time he was near.

How could one heart possibly take on so many phases?

Perhaps her heart was much like the one she held in her hand. The many phases were the numerous diamonds. Behind the diamonds was a gold plated form of a heart.

Did she really have a heart of gold?

Bella pondered the thought of finding true love. How could she find it if she wasn't looking for it? Maybe Mrs. Vanderbilt meant that true love would find her. But if there was always a wall about her heart, then how could love find its ways there?

What if love was strong enough to tear down the wall?

Bella rehearsed the stolen moments with Darby. Although she should have found it annoying, she didn't. Even when they broke the very precious piece of china.

She could still feel the tingly sensation in her hands when she thought about his hands cupping over hers. And Darby ate the icing he scooped from her chin! Did he mean for the gesture to seem so intimate?

The emotional roller coaster was a bit more than Bella had bargained for. She didn't understand the meaning of all these feelings that were swarming inside like butterflies in spring.

She fell into a deep sleep while she was trying to sort out all her feelings. While she dreamt, she gripped the heart in the palm of her hand, refusing to let it go unless it fell unto the person she loved.

The next morning when Bella awoke, she found herself still in her bed wearing her uniform from the day before. Her attention was drawn to the lump in her hand.

The charm.

She smiled as she remembered the events from yesterday, and her heart skipped a beat when she was reminded she would see Darby today. Although she had to work half of her Sunday, the evening meeting seemed to melt away all dreads of physical labor.

Bella scanned her tiny room for a safe haven to hide the charm. Her gaze landed upon the trinket box. Yes, that would definitely be the safest place to tuck it away. So when she lay down at night, it would be within arm's-reach and she could cherish it as long as she liked.

So Bella opened its lid and lay the heart directly on top of the other trinkets. It glistened and shined greater than any of the others. Bella closed the lid and fled the room unaware of the person patiently waiting to intrude.

A smirk formed on the prowler's face. If the beautiful charm was *not* in Bella's pocket, then it should be in her possession within a whole five minutes.

When Bella was out of sight, Sophia stepped inside the tiny room and scanned it carefully. If Bella were to hide something, where would she hide it? Under a pillow maybe? It was not there. A pang of disappointment smote Sophia's heart. Maybe this wasn't going to be as easy as she had first thought.

Sophia opened and closed every drawer. Still nothing. Then her gaze settled onto the tiny trinket box. Could it possibly be hidden away there?

Her steps were light, careful not to create much commotion. She lifted its lid. The shine was nearly blinding. The tiny diamonds sparkled brighter than anything Sophia had ever seen.

She picked up the precious stone and studied it. This really belonged to her. She was going to make a grab for that piece of cake, but Bella rudely intercepted it. True love was meant for *her*. She had searched for it far too long.

Sophia kissed the lucky charm and slid it into her pocket.

With a surge of victory, she vacated the room, not even giving a second glance.

CHAPTER ELEVEN

BELLA FELT A SPRING IN her step all day. Everything had gone perfectly and time had been flying. Even Sophia had been kind. Hopefully, the barrier between them was about to be broken and fate would have its way.

After Bella dried the last pot, she glanced at the clock. She had exactly half an hour before she was to meet Darby on the Library Terrace. That was a good thing. At least she would have time to redo her hair.

Just as Bella rounded the corner to make her way to her room, an arm intercepted her.

"Uncle Morton!" Bella threw her arms around him. "I thought I would see you more often! Where have you been?"

Morton was smiling. "I see Biltmore is treating you well. It's good to see that you're happy."

"I couldn't be happier!" Bella exclaimed.

He offered his arm. "How about a walk outside and you tell me just how wonderful this place is?"

Bella knew she really needed to go to her room and at least look into the mirror. Her hand felt for her bun. Before she could protest, Morton took her arm, "Come on, you look fine."

Soon Bella found herself outside, being escorted by her Uncle Morton. She felt like she owed him this time. After all, he had been the reason she had a job here at Biltmore.

"Why do I never see you?" Bella asked.

"I thought you were going to fill me in on your first two weeks?" Morton countered.

"Oh...okay," Bella began. "First of all, I met this girl named Sophia..."

Sophia peered from a distance and spied the man who had just stepped onto the terrace. It was the same man who delivered the gift to Cornelia's birthday celebration. Also, he had been the one to visit the Library. Sophia hungered to know the connection between him and Bella, and to know what they were up to when they met.

When she examined his masculine form, Sophia entertained the idea of winning his attentions. That would be one way to get even with Bella for all the turmoil she had added to her life.

A smirk formed on her face when she gripped the charm. Fate had never been so good to her.

Darby had arrived a bit early, hoping he could steal a few extra moments with Bella. The canopy of Wisteria offered plenty of shade from the scorching sun.

His foot had been doing very well. He owed her. He owed her a lot for dedicating her spare time to help him. The sacrifices Bella made for him only made his growing attraction toward her stronger.

He had found sleep hard to come by last night. He couldn't erase her image from his mind. And the icing he scooped from her chin had been the sweetest he had ever tasted. Darby had then realized he had forgotten to eat a piece of cake since his had taken a dive to the floor. Oh, well. The taste of the icing was of the utmost satisfaction, and the time spent with Bella was worth it.

And to think she found the heart. Darby smiled. He wouldn't mind playing a role to make *that* come true. He felt like he could easily love her, but he wasn't sure if she would return the same emotion. Hopefully, he could wiggle his way into her heart before she realized it.

Darby heard the sound of faint, but detectable, footfalls echo from behind him. He turned his face to discover that he was no longer alone. It was the same maid who had rudely interrupted their last meeting. He watched her as she stepped onto the terrace and confidently walked in the opposite direction as he.

She slid her finger along the banister as if she were checking for dust. He noticed that tendrils of her red hair had escaped her bun and danced around her face as the gentle breeze blew.

Darby pondered her intentions and decided that the terrace was probably her sanctuary, a place where she came to get away from the hustle and bustle going on inside the house.

Darby turned his gaze from her and peered from the banister where his elbows were propped for support. His eyes took in the beautiful scenery. The mountains outlined the horizon. Lush gardens were thriving with color and floral scent.

Just perfect. Until...

Bella clung to her uncle's arm as they ascended the steps leading back toward the terrace. "I've met someone else, Uncle Morton."

"A man?" Morton questioned, his tone at a medium.

"Well," Bella licked her lips, "he needed my help. He is a student at Biltmore Forest School, and his position there is in jeopardy..."

"If you let Mrs. King or Mrs. Vanderbilt, and heaven forbid, if Mr. Vanderbilt were to hear of it, then your position will be in jeopardy as well," Morton declared.

Bella knew that already. She chose to ignore the comment, as well as her uncle's cold glare. "Listen, I'm just helping him. Nothing more."

There wasn't anything else to it, was there? Of course not.

"Good," Morton released a breath, "because there is no man good enough for my wonderful niece."

"What you really mean is I'm not good enough for any man," Bella said as she playfully punched him on the arm and went on to jabber about Darby and the priceless piece of shattered china.

Darby couldn't hear what Bella was saying to the man, but he did see her drive a fist playfully into the man's arm. He felt it all the way to his gut. Although the man looked a bit older than Bella, in his thirties maybe, he was still a man. He could hear her cackling from where he stood. She never laughed like that with him, and she certainly never walked with her arm locked in his like she was with this man.

Darby noticed the maid drawing closer to where he stood. She kept her back and neck straight, her hands clasped together against her middle. As if she sensed his gaze, she turned and smiled. Her smile was pretty, but nothing like Bella's. He barely nodded his head and looked away.

"It's a beautiful evening, is it not?" Darby was surprised when she spoke. A bold little maid.

"It is." His answer was flat.

"Do you visit the terrace often?" she asked as she scooted closer to where he stood.

"Often enough." Darby answered as he scooted further toward the massive twist of vine.

"Are you next?" she asked.

The question won Darby's undivided attention. "What do you mean?" he asked as his eyes grew fierce.

She cleared her throat and answered, "Well, with Bella, of course."

Darby turned to face the little maid fully. He noticed how she took a tiny step back. "What do you mean *with* Bella?" he asked.

The maid shrugged her shoulder gently and sighed, "If you think you're the only one she meets here, then guess again."

"There's others?" his voice spilled the words bitterly.

She gracefully walked past him and said, "A few. I just thought you needed to know."

Darby followed her with his gaze. "I hardly see how she has time for anyone else."

The maid quirked her brow. "She's with someone else now, isn't she?"

Darby turned his face to sound of Bella's voice. The maid was right. Bella was with someone else. He swallowed the lump in his throat and turned back to thank the maid for informing him, but she was gone. She had vanished. He even stepped away from the banister and turned a complete circle.

But she was gone.

Bella loosed her arm from Morton's and bid him farewell. He had promised to take her to visit Mama and Ashlynn on her next day off. That just topped it all. And to think that the next hour of her life would be spent with Darby! She bounced up the steps and was surprised to find him already waiting. She couldn't help but smile. He looked absolutely wonderful as the sunlight outlined his figure. However, her smile froze when she realized he was not returning one.

The bounce in Bella's step was no longer there, and her smile slowly melted away. She watched him as he stood up from where he was leaning and made his way to the bench. He hadn't even greeted her.

Bella had to will her feet to move. All the hopes and dreams she had fed on all day soon plummeted to the ground beneath her feet.

"How are you doing?" Bella asked Darby, aware of the thick air surrounding them.

"Good. We'll get this over. I have an exam to study for." He still refused to look into her eyes.

Bella took her usual position at his feet and worked them accordingly. The compressions declared the muscle strength building in Darby's foot. "I see you've been exercising your foot regularly." Bella dared to look up to his face. She caught his eyes for a moment, before they darted back to his foot.

"I have." His answer was short.

Her hands froze while her eyes sought him, hoping to see a glimpse of what was there before. "Darby?"

He lifted his eyes but they were shaded. "Huh?"

For a moment Bella thought she detected the smile in his eyes when he looked at her, but as quickly as it came, it left. He bent down to remove her hands from his foot, and then started to put on his shoes.

"But we aren't finished, Darby."

"I am."

As his words swirled through her mind, Bella concluded that he directed that statement somewhere other than just toward the therapy for his injured foot.

When he started to stand, Bella stood also.

"We could walk the length of the terrace," Bella pleaded.

Darby awarded her with a glance. "Actually it's probably time for me to go."

"But we just got here."

"No," Darby's icy glare met Bella's eyes, "you just got here."

Bella couldn't argue with him because he was right. He had

been there waiting, but she couldn't help that he had arrived before the appointed time.

She watched him as his tall, masculine form limped away from the terrace. Away from her.

And why it hurt she didn't know.

Bella wandered about aimlessly in her own world trying to sort out her thoughts and the confused feelings. Not that it really mattered because it didn't. She would have to work here at Biltmore for years just to support her Mama and Ashlynn.

At the age of twenty, Bella had never before felt what she felt when Darby was near. She sensed his presence. Her heart raced. Her tummy flopped. Her cheeks heated. Her palms grew clammy. And now....now she was more confused than ever.

Her feet guided her back to the terrace. Her fingers slid up the twisted vine that created the canopy of greenery. That's how she felt inside. Twisted. Perplexed. But knowing this, Bella purposed to ensure a wall about her heart, and promised herself not to give Darby Pierson a second glance.

Once Bella was in the privacy of her own room, she allowed her heart to ache a little. Just a little. She couldn't erase the way Darby looked in her eyes yesterday and how flustered she had become when he winked at her. The butterflies that were swarming inside her had all flown away leaving her to feel deserted. But what had changed? Nothing.

Bella remembered the heart and smiled. Still, if the fable was true, she would find true love. A love she could give, and she wouldn't always feel empty and void. But sooner or later, she would embrace love, true and undeniable love. When she found it, Bella would cherish the unconditional gift that returns the same measure of reward.

She stepped over to her bedside table and lifted the lid of the trinket box. Her heart faltered. She lifted the box from the table and dumped its contents onto her bed searching frantically for the charm.

But it was gone.

The room began to grow smaller and suddenly Bella felt as though she was being watched. Slowly her feet turned her body. Everything else seemed as it should be.

Again, Bella's gaze settled onto her bed where the heart should have been lying and shining like the stars in the heavens, but it wasn't there.

Bella swallowed nervously as she tried to think of who would do such a thing. Hardly no one even knew of the charm, just the handful of those who were in attendance at Cornelia's birthday celebration. But who could it be?

She was far too exhausted to even think clearly. After giving her pillow a nice fluff, Bella fell onto the bed. Even the electric lamp didn't seem to fascinate her. The bed didn't seem as comfortable as it did last night, and the quilt wasn't nearly as warm.

Dare she even think it, but her heart wasn't beating like it was yesterday.

Darby laid there staring into the ceiling. He felt like a halfwit for walking away from Bella. His aching foot declared the same thing, but he had no desire to be played as a pawn in a woman's game. Darby recalled the many times he had stared into her eyes. He had thought the emotion genuine, but he also knew that women were good at that sort of thing. They could wiggle their way into a man's heart, rob what was inside, and leave it to rot.

He couldn't let a woman have that sort of effect on him. Even if her smile caused his heart to constrict, or if her touch ignited a consuming fire, he would have to forget about her.

He would definitely sere the memory of scooping the icing from her chin. He would mute the sound of her voice that echoed in his ears. He would omit the vivid memory of her hair falling freely down her back. And what of her scent? How could he extinguish the desire for cinnamon?

Ah! Darby shook his head. He had to quit thinking about her. *Bella.*

And whatever it took, he would keep her at arms'-length.

CHAPTER TWELVE

BELLA FELT TEMPTED TO LOOSEN her braid and let her hair ripple in the breeze as she sat perched beside her uncle in the carriage. Morton had stood true to his word, and Bella couldn't wait to see her Mama and Ashlynn. She had missed them so, and she had thought about them plenty at night while she was lying in bed. She wondered what they had done during the day while she worked. Had Ashlynn continued exercising her weak limbs? Had Mama kept her word?

Guilt gnawed at Bella because she failed to forget about the appointment on the terrace this evening. As much as she tried to pay no heed to the thought, the more frequently she found herself thinking of him. Darby.

Bella worried her lip while she imagined his silhouette outlined by the glinting sunlight and waiting for her as usual. How long would he wait there until he realized she had cancelled? Maybe she should've left a message for him? Then again, maybe not.

Bella sighed and tried to dismiss his image from her mind.

Morton cleared his throat. "Are you okay, Bella?"

She smoothed the tendrils of hair that had escaped her braid. "I'm fine, Uncle Morton. Why do you ask?"

"I-well, you just seemed distracted," his voice full of concern.

I am. Bella crossed her fingers. "I'm fine, really."

Morton eyed her curiously as his hands flicked the reins. He redirected his gaze to the road before them and said, "I was privileged to meet the forestry scholars this morning."

Bella gasped, "Really?!"

Morton turned his face slightly.

"I mean," Bella cleared her throat, "Really?"

"Yes," Morton confirmed his statement, "they were preparing to hike Mount Pisgah."

Bella turned to face Morton fully. "What?!" She ran her hands along her cheeks as her eyes began to roam aimlessly. "He can't go hiking," she mumbled.

"Who can't go hiking?" Morton asked suspiciously.

Bella folded her hands and swallowed the lump in her throat. "No one," she mumbled. Instead of looking to the left or to the right, Bella fastened her eyes ahead and focused on the road before them. What if Darby goes hiking? He hadn't reached the goal, and his foot was certainly not strong enough for strenuous activity. What if he loses all that was fought for?

The rest of the distance was travelled in silence, and it wasn't long before Bella found herself staring at the little cottage. It seemed different. The door was closed and so were all the windows and curtains. On a normal day, the windows would be open and the tail of the curtain would be waving.

But not today.

"I'll return for you in a couple hours," Morton said as they approached the cottage. "I need to take care of some business in town."

"I'll be ready," Bella said as the horses slowed to a mere trot and then came to a stop. Once she stepped down from the carriage, Bella curiously observed the house she called home. Each step screaked as she ascended the old wooden steps leading to the front door. Soon her hand gripped the old rusty door knob and gave it a strong twist. The door whined as it opened, the dust particles danced in all directions.

"Mama?" Bella called out, but there was no answer. Her steps led her through the kitchen.

"Ashlynn?" Still no answer.

After Bella peered into every room, she concluded they weren't home. She continued to look around taking note that the house was a little more cluttered than before. The beds had not been made and the dishes had not been washed. Her eyes sized up the pile of dirty laundry in the corner. Perhaps they are in the back preparing the ringer washer.

Bella opened the back door leading to the outside. The yard appeared empty, all except the clothesline that needed another brace in the middle to keep it from sagging.

Where could they be? Bella thought.

Just as she was about to enter into the house, Bella heard her Mama's voice echoing from the kitchen.

"Ashlynn! Go!"

Bella's spine stiffened. Never in all her days of living at home did Bella hear Mama's tone grow so fierce. Especially with Ashlynn.

"I'm goin', Mama." Ashlynn solemnly replied.

Bella knew she should make an appearance, but instead she stood behind the back door that was still slightly ajar and listened for anything else out of the ordinary.

Nothing else was said. Bella strained her ear to hear, but all she heard was silence.

She easily widened the door but saw nothing. Ever so slowly, she allowed the door to open further. After quietly stepping inside, she tiptoed through the kitchen and peered into the living room. Bella was surprised to find her Mama sprawled out on the old, worn out couch.

Odd.

When Bella stepped into the living room, the wooden plank squeaked. Bella froze, but her Mama's slumber was not disturbed.

"Mama?" Bella followed the sound of Ashlynn's voice and was taken aback when she opened the bedroom door.

"Bella!" Ashlynn cheered.

Immediately, Bella shushed her sister's excitement. "Shhh, don't wake Mama," she whispered as she stepped into the room.

"Why, Bella? She would be real happy to see you." Ashlynn's eyes shined much like the sunshine.

Refusing to answer Ashlynn's question, Bella stepped to the window and pulled back the curtain. With a forceful thrust, she opened the window and was relieved to inhale some fresh air.

"Why are you in bed in the middle of the day?" Bella asked.

Ashlynn shrugged. "Mama's not been feelin' well since you left."

"What's wrong with her?" Bella asked as she planted her knees into the well-seasoned floor boards, peeling back the thin sheet and began working Ashlynn's weakened leg.

Ashlynn's innocent features were not perplexed like Bella's insides. "I don't know," Ashlynn solemnly replied, "she just sleeps a lot."

Bella's hands continued to massage the stiffened muscle.

"Her friend comes by every day," Ashlynn said, "and he brings her medicine."

Bella's hands froze. A friend? And medicine? Bella tried to remain calm. "What kind of medicine does her friend bring?"

Ashlynn just shrugged her shoulder. "I don't know. Her friend brings it to her every day." A sour expression filled her child like features, "He always brings it in a flask, and it smells bad, too." Ashlynn laid her small hand on Bella's arm, "But Mama must be very sick because she drinks a lot of it."

Bella felt queasy. *He*? As in a man? And what was *he* bringing her to drink? This couldn't be happening. It wasn't possible. "Does Mama's friend have a name?"

"Oh yes!" Ashlynn's eyes lit up. "Mr. Farmer! And he brings me a sucker every time he comes."

Bella's gut twisted into knots. The Farmers had a reputation. Needless to say, not one of the best. And furthermore, Mama's friend had to be a man. Not that Bella had a right to judge when her thoughts were suddenly plagued by visions of Darby, but it hadn't even been two months.

Two months since her Papa's death!

Bella tried not to show her distress. She knew Ashlynn didn't understand, and she probably enjoyed his company. Especially since he brought her a sucker every time he came around. Just what would he give Bella if she were here? A hard time?

"How long has he been coming here?" Bella asked.

"Bella?" Mama's voice silenced the room.

Bella slowly turned her face, and she nearly gasped at the sight of her Mama. Dark circles marked her droopy eyes, and her skin was no longer creamy but pale.

So different from two weeks ago.

Is this why Mama urged her to take the job at Biltmore?

"Mama." Bella could not mask her disappointment as her eyes connected with her mother's.

There was no shame to be found on her Mama's face. Instead, she smiled wearily. "So nice of you to just show up. I would'a at least tried to pick up a bit."

Show up? Was this not Bella's home? The one she was born and raised in, and now she has to ask for permission to visit?

Bella cleared her throat. She didn't exactly know what to say. Bile crept up the back of her throat, and the room she was in was starting to spin like a bottomless vortex.

Darby politely declined the offer to hike Mount Pisgah. Although hiking was among his most favorite tasks, he decided to stay behind and plant trees.

Darby had gone to the shed to retrieve a shovel and spade, and discovered he was accompanied by a fellow scholar. "I thought you were hiking with the rest of the boys," Darby stated as he limped toward the planting sight.

"I wasn't about to leave you behind," Hunter Morris scanned the forest's edge. "You never know what's lurking around here."

Darby stopped and assessed the tall, lanky young man and wondered just how Hunter planned to ward off a predator if there was one. Darby just shook his head and continued to limp along.

"I seen that," Hunter admitted.

"Seen what?" Darby asked as he drove the spade into the ground.

Hunter joined him and took the spade from Darby's hand. "Let me do the digging, and you can do the planting."

Darby opened his mouth to protest, but Hunter started whistling. "I can see that your foot is much better," Hunter explained. "There's no reason to put it in a strain, is there?"

Darby sighed and agreed, "I guess not."

"So, Pierson, tell me the secret," Hunter said as he drove the spade into the dirt.

Darby propped his wrists on the shovel's handle. "The secret?"

"Yeah, how's your foot getting better?" he asked.

Darby cleared his throat. "I'm just exercising it."

"Really? That's good. Then maybe you'll feel like joining the guys this evening," said Hunter.

"Oh?" Darby questioned.

"We're goin' horseback riding."

Darby pondered his options. Either he could meet Bella on the terrace as planned, or he could join the guys.

Still, when he turned the pages of her precious book, he smelled her scent. When he closed his eyes at night, he saw her smile, so a distraction might do him some good. Darby kicked the toe of his boot into the dirt. Finally, he said, "Sure, I'll go."

That evening the entire host of forestry scholars set out on their adventure. Darby lagged behind a bit as he found himself bombarded with thoughts of Bella. Oddly, his gut twisted with guilt when he haphazardly found himself thinking of her. He had tried all day to refrain from thinking. Especially about her. But for the life of him, Darby couldn't escape that nagging feeling that Bella was hurting.

Now he had an unexplainable notion to heal that pain. But how could it be possible when he was running from her presence and refusing to attend their meetings?

As Darby's muscular form gave way while the four legged beast trotted along the forest's edge, he contemplated turning back. But what would the guys say? That would be something he would have to live with the rest of his term at Biltmore Forest School.

"Let's stop and rest the horses here! There is a stream just over there!" Hunter Morris' voice rang out as he pointed to their right.

Yes, there was a stream, and Darby had been too caught up in his thoughts to hear the trickling water.

He followed last and dismounted last. When his foot connected with the ground, pain shot up his leg and into his hip. His breath caught tight in his chest. He had to force himself to breathe.

"Y'all right, Pierson?" Gregory Yeary patted him hard on the shoulder as he passed him.

"Yeah. Just a little pain in the foot." Darby spoke weakly.

Perhaps he should ride back toward the estate and search for the one who had the touch to make the pain go away.

Bella finally worked her legs enough to stand. She had hoped that neither Mama nor Ashlynn noticed how distraught she had become. She was well aware of the change in her Mama's disposition, and she wondered if Mr. Farmer was expected to arrive at any given time. The glare on her Mama's face told her that her speculation was probably correct.

"I will help you get everything in order, Mama." Bella offered politely.

Mama waved her hand in the air as she turned to walk away. "Don't bother. Won't do any good."

Bella turned toward Ashlynn who still seemed unaffected by their Mama's behavior.

"I got yer letter!" Ashlynn clapped her hands. "It sounds like a wonderful place!"

Bella suddenly realized how peaceful Biltmore was, even in all of the hustle and bustle of its everyday life. Even though Sophia existed there. Even though there was a man there tearing her heart into shreds.

Yes, compared to the heartache she was feeling right now, Biltmore was a wonderful place. And for some strange reason, Bella could not wait to return.

Morton returned a little later than he had intended, but that was okay. At least Bella had gotten all of the dishes washed, rinsed and put away.

"Goodbye, Mama." Bella smoothed the gray strand of hair away from her Mama's brow.

"Uh..." Mama barely opened her eyes. Before she muttered goodbye, they were closed again.

Bella slowly stood to her feet thinking surely she would find her heart lying there because it had truly been ripped away. She turned. Ashlynn stood against the splintery door-jam with open arms. Bella embraced her.

"Please come back, Bella. It gets lonely without you," Ashlynn begged.

Bella pulled back and looked into her sister's eyes. A sad smile formed on her lips. "I will, but I can't promise how soon."

Ashlynn's shoulders sagged. "But you will?"

"Yes, and until then keep exercising like I taught you. *Please*?" Bella pleaded.

Ashlynn's bright smile warmed Bella's heart. "I will and thank you. Thank you for helping me today."

Bella tweaked her nose. "No need to thank me, sis. I love you. I must go, Uncle Morton is waiting."

Bella couldn't help but hold her tears in check when she settled into the comfortably cushioned carriage. She would miss Ashlynn. Ashlynn needed her. She needed Ashlynn. Together they had no choice but to be strong.

Morton eyed Bella from where he sat. Her gaze was somewhere afar off, and she hadn't spoken a single word to him since they departed. "How was your visit?" he finally asked as the horses led the carriage along the Approach Road.

Bella squirmed a bit. "It was okay."

"Just okay?"

Bella inhaled. "Well... it was different."

"What do you mean?" he asked.

"Mama. She looked terrible."

"She's just grieving, Bella. That's normal. I remember when my Pap went on to be with The Lord. Mam did the same thing."

"That's not it, Uncle Morton," Bella snapped. "There is a man, already." Tears suddenly brimmed her eyes, then steadily rolled down her cheeks, and dropped onto her lap.

"Oh." It was quiet for a moment, all except the beating of the horse's hooves. "Bella, she may need someone."

"A Farmer?" she asked sarcastically.

"So he's a farmer, huh?" Morton grinned. "Well, at least you won't have to worry if they need any milk or bacon."

Bella just shook her head. "He's not a farmer. He is a Farmer."

Morton raised his brow. "Okay, Bella. That made no sense to me whatsoever."

A tiny grin formed on her lips. "I meant that his name is *Mr. Farmer.*"

Morton's smile slid away. He even paled and his eyes were screaming, NO!

"How do you know?" he asked.

"Ashlynn told me."

As the words slid off her tongue, the silhouette of a man on the back of a horse filled her vision. He had slowed the beast down to a mere trot. As he came closer, the evening sun outlined his form. He stood tall, his broad shoulders refused to jolt from the steady pouncing of the horse's hooves. He looked strong. Masculine. His hair was glistening in the light. His eyes were green as grass, yet cold as ice.

Darby.

CHAPTER THIRTEEN

DARBY SLOWED CHESTNUT AND MOVED over toward the edge of the Approach Road as the carriage drew closer. He managed to escape the guys by casting the blame on his inflamed foot.

Which was true.

But he needed to see Bella.

His foot desperately needed her attention now, but he was fifteen minutes late and she was nowhere near the terrace. He assumed she had given up on him.

Chestnut's trot came to a pause when Darby's strong hands pulled tight on the reins. His forearms contracted, as well as his heart. His skin prickled along every nerve ending. Suddenly, Darby became numb.

His eyes connected with the young lady riding in front, which was entirely against the customs. The shock of the passenger being Bella had been a bit much. It only grew more intense when Darby recognized the driver. It was the same man he had seen with Bella just a few days ago walking arm in arm underneath the Wisteria Pergola.

Darby wasn't quite sure if he kept his composure in check as they passed, but he felt certain that he did not return the smile that Bella offered because his insides were severed into pieces that could never be mended.

Bella felt a pang of disappointment when Darby barely nodded his head as he rode past. Guilt began to swell in the deeper part of her chest. He had come back. Darby had been waiting for her, but she let a trickle of pride prevent her from keeping her word. Her throat suddenly became dry. She tried swallowing, but it only became dryer. Morton's words finally drew her back into the present.

"That was one of the students from Biltmore Forest School."

Bella swiftly turned her face to her uncle. "How did you know?"

Morton detected the familiarity in her voice. "You know him?"

Bella's cheeks heated uncontrollably. "I recognized him, yes. It just puzzled me that you would know him." She nervously tucked a strand of hair behind her ear.

"He's a Pierson. Everybody should know him."

Including Bella? Because she had only become acquainted with him when she began working at Biltmore, and that was because she had the book he needed.

And the knowledge of physiotherapy.

"I'm confused, Uncle Morton. I only learned of his existence just a couple of weeks ago," Bella admitted.

"He is the son of Charles Pierson, owner and operator of Pierson Enterprises."

Bella's throat began to close. She had been assisting Darby Pierson as in *Pierson Enterprises*, the most well-known lumber company in all of North Carolina? The company who supplied her Papa with building materials? The one who had been generous enough to cover the funeral costs? That was who *Darby Pierson* was?

Her heartbeat echoed in her ears when she realized how naive she had been. He was by far one of the wealthiest of people in all of Asheville. Well, except the Vanderbilts, of course.

And she was among one of the poorest.

The carriage came to a stop, and Morton extended his hand to assist Bella as she descended. "All of the employees will receive Saturday evening off to attend the barn gathering. Are you going?"

"I don't know," Bella shook her head, "I'm not much of a dancer."

"I'd like to think you're one of the best," Morton complimented.

Bella just shook her head again.

"Come on, Bella." Morton took her hand gently. "You need to mingle with the other employees. It's just good clean fun. You need to go. It will help free your mind of things."

Wasn't that the truth! It sounded nice. Maybe she could momentarily forget about her troubles with Darby, and Mama, and just enjoy life. Even if it was just for one evening.

She thought about it for a moment. "Sure. I will see you there, Uncle Morton." Bella wrapped her arms around his neck. "Thank you so much for being there for me."

Morton returned the hug and watched her walk away. The massive house swallowed up her figure as she entered. He released his breath and said a silent prayer in hopes that she would forget about her troubles and just dance.

That night, Darby dove onto his bed and opened the Book.

Not the Philosophy of Physiotherapy.

But the Book. The One his Ma always turned to for answers. Maybe he could find some answers of his own.

He was so confused. He kept hearing the words that the little red haired maid had spoken to him on the terrace just days ago. His heart was telling him to disregard what he had been told and just go on.

Instead, Darby started flipping through his Ma's Bible, very aware of the scent of paper and ink wafting in the air. She had been sure to send it with him when he left home. She obviously knew he would need it.

Taking note of the many marked scriptures, he skimmed page by page until he found himself in the book of Ecclesiastes. He never even knew that the book existed. Instantly, he was hooked,

The Words of the Preacher…

He read and read until his eyes drifted to the underlined words on the next page.

To everything there is a season…..

He related to that. He had heard Dr. Carl Schenck speak plenty about the seasons.

A time to plant, and a time to pluck up that which is planted.

Darby smiled and wondered just where Schenck may have gotten his lectures from.

He read on.

A time to weep... Darby's throat constricted. Maybe he should just cry.

A time to laugh... Again, Darby smiled, although his eyes were glassy.

A time to mourn... Hmmm, Darby thought.

A time to dance... Darby glanced down at his foot and wiggled it a bit. Maybe if he'd just dance then everything would fall into place. But he hadn't danced in ages. Could he even remember how it's done?

A time to embrace... Then he thought of Bella.

What would it be like to dance with her in his arms? Perhaps dancing could be the next step to physical therapy.

Darby contemplated the idea and decided against it. For now. First, he'd do what he could. The barn gathering tomorrow evening would be just the place to try some buck dancing, and if that went well, he might join in on the square dance.

"We will be serving in the Banquet Hall soon." Sophia said to Bella as she handed her the dripping pot. Bella enclosed the towel around the heavy utensil and began drying.

"Really? Is there a party arriving that I haven't heard about?" Bella questioned.

"The festival will draw many people here." Sophia's voice dipped to a whisper. "Even the President of the United States has been invited."

Bella almost dropped the pot. "What? How do you know this?"

Sophia just gingerly shrugged her shoulder. "Word gets around. Anyhow, you'd best be learning how to serve. How would you like to present a platter to Theodore Roosevelt?" Sophia arched her eyebrow.

"I don't think so." Bella shook her head. "To change the subject, are you going to the barn gathering tonight?" Bella asked as she dried her hands.

Sophia smiled. "Of course. I've never missed one."

"Good. At least I'll know someone besides my Uncle Morton."

"You'll know Bessie."

"Bessie goes?"

"Of course I go, Bella! Ain't never missed a one." The graying middle aged woman said. "And you're going too." Bessie demanded.

"I'm afraid there is no choice in the matter, huh?" Bella smiled. She enjoyed Bessie's company and she certainly didn't want to miss seeing her carry on like a young woman.

Bessie twisted her hips. "You have no choice, Bella! You'll have the time of your life."

I hope so, she thought.

Bella understood now why the festivity had been called a barn gathering. Because it took place inside a real barn. She pulled her arm away from Morton's. "Go on," she said as she gestured him toward the open door of the barn, "I will be inside in a bit."

"Are you sure?" he asked.

"I'm sure, Uncle Morton," she replied. "Sophia and Bessie are here somewhere. Now, go!"

Morton bowed elegantly and strode toward the entrance.

Bella watched as the sound of banjo strings and fiddle playing swallowed up his form. Her heart had already faltered countless times, but it seemed much weaker right now. The music echoing through the door stalled her steps. Her trembling hands wiped away the beads of sweat from her forehead. Bella forced herself to breathe, but fresh air seemed to have hidden itself.

She was suddenly reminded that her Papa would not be inside awaiting her arrival. He was the *only* person she had ever danced with; therefore she would be dancing alone or perhaps not dancing at all.

Bella willed her feet to move toward the door although her insides were knotted. She allowed her eyes to drift closed for a moment as she tried to calm herself. The pounding of her heartbeat jolted through her veins as she drew herself up.

Finally, her feet began to carry her across the threshold. She was welcomed with a heavy scent of fresh cut hay. Groups of people of all ages were scattered abroad. Music filled the air, as well as an abundance of chatter. Bella scanned the crowd in hopes of finding Bessie, but the abundance of dancing dust particles prevented that. She did not see Sophia either, which was perfectly fine.

Hunter Morris let out a low whistle. "Boys, if you'll excuse me, I believe I may have just found myself a dance partner." He patted Darby on the shoulder and then made long strides toward the open door.

Darby's heart leapt to his throat. Bella's form was radiated by the setting sun. Her hair hung across her shoulder in a loose braid just as it had before, but she was wearing a different dress. It was pale yellow, which made her hair shine more radiantly.

Darby stepped deeper into the shadows, but he kept his eyes fastened on her. And Hunter.

Darby broke out into a cold sweat when he observed the smile Bella awarded Hunter. A lump formed in his throat when he witnessed their handshake. Even worse than that, she placed her hand in the crook of Hunter's arm.

Darby's heart pounded mercilessly when he thought of Bella's hand in Hunter's. Why his gut knotted he didn't know. He was supposed to be immune to her presence, not affected by it, but it wasn't working. The more he was aware of her, the more vulnerable he became.

Darby shifted his foot to relieve the growing tension while his gaze followed the pair as they made their way to a vacant table. For a moment, Darby thought of joining them, but he decided against it. Instead, he would stand in the shadows and pretend that the dull throbbing in his chest wasn't there.

The only ache he felt was in his foot.

CHAPTER FOURTEEN

SOPHIA WAS DRAWN TOWARD THE barn by the abundant sound of banjo strings. Her hand felt for her hair. She had worn it differently this time, in a more attractive notion. Instead of the tight bun that pulled at her scalp, she had twisted it delicately and pinned it on the side much like Bella's.

Before she entered the barn, she withdrew the charm from her pocket and kissed it for a measure of good luck. Then she made her entrance. The people were already dancing a hoedown. Men, women, boys, and girls alike, were spinning from one person to the next.

Sophia successfully scanned the crowd. Immediately, her gaze attached onto the *one* she was hoping would be present, but her teeth ground until they hurt when he looked away. Instead of walking in the opposite direction like she wanted to, Sophia made bold steps toward the tall man of masculinity.

The stout smell of spice drew her steps up short. She nearly choked. "Good evening," she muttered trying to hold her breath.

"Good evening." The edge in his voice proved that he wasn't flattered by her appearance.

She offered her hand, "I believe we have met before. I'm Sophia."

Surprised that he willingly complied, their hands met. "I'm Darby."

"Do you attend the barn gatherings often?" Sophia asked although she already knew that he did not.

"First time." When Darby answered, he returned his focus to something or someone on the other side of the barn.

Sophia followed his gaze and was surprised to find Bella engaged in a cheerful conversation with another man.

"She doesn't know I'm here." Darby declared.

Sophia turned to the man who was now facing her. Darby.

Again, she realized just how big this man was. He was at least a foot taller than she and twice as broad. Suddenly she felt the need to shrink away and appear unnoticed.

After searching for an ounce of boldness, Sophia asked, "Then why are you standing in the shadows? If I wanted Bella to know I was here, I would be in the middle of the dance floor."

Before Sophia gave him a moment to reject, she slipped her arm into his and propelled Darby toward his doom.

Bella hadn't laughed so hard in ages. Her sides hurt as she tried catching her breath.

"Then Dr. Schenck asked if I was *chewing gum*. I said, No! I am Hunter Morris!"

Bella burst into another spill of laughter. "Please stop," she wheezed. "I can't laugh anymore." She lifted the cup of cool water to her lips and drank. She nearly choked when her eyes caught a glimpse of Darby.

He was dancing.

With Sophia.

An odd pain jolted through her body.

Why is he here with Sophia? Bella thought.

She became very aware of the nauseous feeling growing in the pit of her stomach. Suddenly she felt isolated. Hunter cracked another joke and everyone sitting at the table cackled uncontrollably, except for her. Then she became flushed. She needed fresh air. She had to escape.

"Are you all right, Bella?" Hunter's voice echoed from a faraway distance.

"Huh?" Bella asked.

"You don't look so good. Do you feel all right?" he asked.

Bella turned to Hunter and politely excused herself. She thought she had managed to escape without being noticed until a firm hand took her arm, forcing her body to turn in mid-stride.

"Rudy!" Bella shouted. "What are you doing here?!"

The scoundrel's smile nearly caused her to wretch.

"I see you have missed me, my *belle*."

Bella's glare challenged him, but he only laughed. "I am not your *belle*, nor will I ever be!"

Rudy laughed even harder and pulled her to him. She fought his grip, but it was too strong. "Let go of me!"

"Not without a dance," he demanded as he pulled Bella by the arm toward the dance floor.

Finally, Bella stopped trying to pull her arm away. His grip was too firm. His fingers felt like they were digging into her skin.

Tears pricked the back of her eyes. She did not want to dance. Especially not with Rudy.

"You know, Rudy, there is a lot of strength in those skinny arms of yours!"

The look of defiance in his eyes declared her victory. Just as he was about to wrap his lanky arm around her, the music changed. Everyone shouted with glee and began to exchange partners.

Bessie came skipping along and took Rudy into her arms. Bella waved him off as she noted the look of fright on his face. She would thank her friend later for intervening during her moment of distress.

She was about to bolt toward her exit when Morton scooped his arm into hers, throwing her right in the middle of the dance.

"Uncle Morton!"

"Just dance, Bella!"

She had spotted Darby as soon as her uncle cast her off to the next gentleman. Eventually, he would come around to being her partner. She couldn't wait to latch onto his arm and pull him out. His foot would be inflamed if he didn't stop.

She knew he was watching her. She could feel it. She momentarily cast a glimpse his way and noted that her arm would be in his within the minute.

Just as she was about to latch onto him, the music changed.

"Darby!" she cast him an accusing glare as she clung to his arm. But soon she found herself speechless. He swung his big arm around her waist and took her hand.

Away they went.

"What are you doing?! You shouldn't be dancing!" Bella protested, but to her surprise, he ignored her complaint. Instead, he fastened his eyes onto hers. Suddenly she felt the need to squirm her way out of his grip. His gaze was far too powerful, and she knew Darby had the gift of seeing inside her heart.

Did he know she enjoyed his partnership far more than any other dancer she had danced with tonight?

Darby felt his surroundings slowly melt away. Right now, it was just him and Bella. It seemed all too right. He had not felt *this*, whatever *this* is, whenever someone else was latched onto his arm.

He tried to ignore just how well Bella's hand fit into his and how perfect her steps were. She never missed a beat. She was a dancer for sure. A very skilled dancer. And to think, she was dancing with him.

Then he remembered, *A time to dance*.

It was almost as if an audible voice whispered the words into Darby's ears. Before he knew it, he was smiling, and the dancers had stepped back giving him and Bella the floor.

"Stop." Bella muttered the word through her clinched teeth.

"Why?" Darby managed to ask.

Bella hesitated before she unleashed her frustration. "I need to stop dancing! I'm not even supposed to be on the floor!"

"Why?" Darby asked before he sent her spinning again.

"The dancers shouldn't be clapping, Darby! The music shouldn't be playing." Her voice weakened.

When he didn't render unto her plea, she shouted, "Stop!" Bella was none too careful about the tone of voice she used, but he still refused to quit. Instead, he performed a flawless Dosey Doe and then latched onto her again.

She tried tearing her eyes from his, but his gaze held her captive.

"Darby, your foot!"

"It's fine!" Darby could hardly hear himself speak over the music and the consistent clapping of hands.

"It won't be!" Bella's words bit back breathlessly.

"Just dance, Bella!"

Darby tried his best to concentrate on every step his feet made, but the lovely young woman in his arms weakened his focus. The distant look in her eyes told him all he needed to know. She wasn't enjoying this nearly as much as he was. To be such a dancer, she truly didn't want to be on the floor.

The music had begun to slow and so had their steps. He took note of her raspy breaths. Perhaps she was just tired. "You're a great dancer," he said.

Bella just shook her head and cast her gaze to the floor.

"Look at me."

Bella barely raised her eyes to his. Although their steps had slowed a great deal, her breathing was still flustered. "Why don't you like to dance?" he asked.

"I..." Bella just shook her head. "I shouldn't even be on the floor."

His thumb caressed her wrist. "Why?"

Her mouth opened but no words spilled out. Instead her eyes took on the distant phase again. She tugged at her hand. "If you'll excuse me."

Darby tightened his hold. "Where are you going?"

"I just need some fresh air," she said as she pulled her hand away from his.

"Bella, wait!" Darby called out, but she barely glanced over her shoulder while her feet led her toward the exit.

Darby's feet froze in place. He watched her as she stepped past the door, not giving him a second glance. He rebuked the tightness that constricted inside his chest, and he wondered if her reaction would have been the same if Hunter had asked her to wait. Or the mysterious man he had seen her with. Would she have clave to their hand?

"You look stranded."

Darby turned his gaze toward the voice. Sophia.

She gingerly shrugged her shoulder. "She's known for that sort of thing."

Frustration started to mount inside Darby. "You show up at all the wrong times, Sophia. Did you know that?"

She just smiled. "I would like to think I show up at all the right times."

"It's according to how you look at it," he said.

Sophia arched her brow. "And just how are you looking at it, Darby? It looks to me like you are in desperate need of a dance partner."

CHAPTER FIFTEEN

BELLA HAD TO GET SOME fresh air. If she didn't, she would surely suffocate. She inhaled the evening air deeply, but nearly gasped when she heard her name being called by a very familiar voice.

Had Darby come looking for her?

She opened her eyes that had drifted closed. Darby's figure filled her vision. At the sight of him, her heart fluttered. She tried to keep it from happening, but it just didn't work like that. It was a spontaneous reaction. It just happened before she knew it.

"Darby!" Bella read the expression of relief on his face when he turned and saw her. He started stepping toward her, but something wasn't right. His features were hardened. His steps were uneven.

Bella's heart sank. "Oh no," she whispered as she grabbed a handful of her skirts and dashed toward him.

Darby's pale stricken face revealed that he felt faint. The excruciating pain was etched about his brow. He almost collapsed onto the ground, but Bella prevented the fall. Her arm wrapped around his waist and she braced herself against his side, pulling his arm over her shoulder. She gently guided him toward a nearby stump.

"Easy now. Just keep your weight off of it." Bella told Darby as they inched along.

"Thanks." Darby barely mumbled the word.

"We're almost there. Hang on just another step or two, Darby. Try not to put any pressure on that foot," Bella warned as she helped him settle back onto the stump.

She heard him grunt. She knew he was in pain and she almost felt like it was her fault. Now *he's* paying for it.

Instinctively, Bella dove to her knees and removed his shoe with care. Then she removed his sock to see if his foot was red and swollen. It was. Which was no surprise. She looked up only to find his eyes squeezed shut.

He was biting back the pain. She knew it.

"Tell me if it hurts, Darby." He only nodded his head.

Bella's left hand held his foot while her right hand gently pressed the top of it. He showed no reaction to pain, so she pressed on. Her fingers slid to his ankle. Which was swollen, too.

Slowly and ever so easily, Bella encouraged Darby's foot to work with her assistance. It was very stiff. She dreaded to tell him that he needed to stay off it for a while. Days probably. Maybe weeks. He would continue to grow worse if he didn't allow what was already hurt to mend.

Bella made slow circles with her fingertips. The motion traveled up his foot and made way to his ankle and then back down to his foot again. She repeated the movement several times until she felt Darby's foot begin to relax. Relief flooded her. There was still a ray of hope.

Bella raised her eyes. To her surprise, Darby had leaned

forward without her noticing. His eyes were open now. His features had also relaxed. Her fingers froze. Bella couldn't function when he looked at her that way.

"There is healing in your touch." Darby declared. "Why is that, Bella?"

His eyes searched hers. He wanted answers. He expected answers. But Bella knew he would be disappointed because she didn't have any.

Right now, she was more confused than Eve on Mother's Day.

"I don't understand." She shook her head trying to tear her eyes away, but found it quite hard as he leaned closer. Their faces were only inches apart.

"The pain is gone. Explain that to me, Bella."

He had said her name again. He was so close that she could feel his hot breath fanning her face. She didn't know why his pain fled when she touched his aching foot.

"You need rest, Darby. Dancing was not wise." Bella had hoped that would satisfy, but the gleam in his eyes revealed to her that it did not.

"I would do it a thousand times over." His rich voice flowed like sweet milk and wild honey. Bella felt it hard to keep her composure because she surely thought his flattering words would cause her heart to melt away. Instead, her heart drummed mercilessly in her chest.

"Would you?" he asked as his eyes penetrated hers.

"Would I what?" Bella found it hard to speak. Her voice was barely audible.

Darby's finger caught her chin smoothly. "Would you dance with me a thousand times over, Bella?"

Bella tried to tear her eyes away, but the hold was much stronger than she.

Was he asking her to dance? Or was that his way of knowing whether or not she enjoyed it? Or was he insinuating that if there were a thousand times to come, they would be found dancing together?

Bella licked her dry lips. She didn't know what to say. Yes, she would love to dance with him again. And yes, she very much enjoyed it. And yes.....if there were a thousand more dances, she would want to be in his arms.

Before she could part her lips to speak, Darby's free hand felt for hers. Slowly his fingertips fanned her palm, then his fingers slid between hers. Still his eyes were reined in on her, searching the hidden parts of her heart. He was unwilling to let go so easily. His gaze held her captive. His fingers interlaced with hers. Everything about him imprisoned her heart, but to Darby she didn't mind being bound. Slowly, Bella felt herself surrender unto the unknown emotion.

Darby felt himself drowning in Bella's eyes. He tried to ignore the pulsating charges traveling through his hand and up his arm, then exploding inside his chest. He inched closer. Now they were only a hair breadth apart.

"Bella." Her name fell from his lips in a whisper. He watched her eyes drift closed. Before his slid together, he thought surely he saw her lips part.

"Uh-hum!"

Darby dropped Bella's hand as if it were a ball of fire and withdrew himself from her face, creating a safe distance although something inside him was already saying that it was too late. When he lifted his eyes, Darby could hardly believe who was standing there.

Bella sprang to her feet as quickly as Darby dropped her hand. She could feel her cheeks burning. They had almost been caught. Well, maybe not almost. They *had* been caught. When her eyes connected with a very angry uncle, Bella paled.

"Morton." She had meant to say *Uncle Morton*, but right now Bella was doing well to remember his name.

"Bella? Is everything all right?" Morton folded his arms firmly across his chest as he cast Darby an ugly glare.

Bella cleared her throat. She was unsure where to start explaining. First of all, there should be an introduction made. She turned to her uncle.

"Uncle Morton, this is Darby." And then she turned to Darby. "Darby, this is my Uncle Morton."

"He's your uncle?" Darby's curious gaze held a glint of humor as he started to rise to his feet.

"Yes, I am her uncle," Morton answered instead of Bella. Then he turned to her and said, "It's time to go."

Her eyes darted to Morton. "It's not even dark yet."

"Exactly." His anger kindled behind his grinding teeth.

"I can see that she gets back to the house safely." Darby took an unsteady step toward Bella.

Morton scrutinized Darby with an unforgiving glare, "I don't think so. She's going with me."

Bella just hung her head. She knew she had crossed the line when she invited the foreign emotion to slip inside her heart. Her uncle had warned her about it, yet she allowed it to happen anyway. She lifted her eyes and shifted her gaze from one man to the other. One man was angry, *very* angry, while the other man could see through the broken crevices of her heart with compassion.

"Actually, I will find my way back alone," she said.

"No!" they shouted in unison.

Finally, the men agreed upon one thing.

"Go with your uncle, Bella."

She didn't understand why Darby surrendered to Morton so easily. Maybe she wasn't worth fighting for. "But we weren't finished yet," she argued.

Darby ran his fingers through his hair. "Just go on with your uncle, Bella."

She felt her temperature rise several degrees. "Don't expect to meet me on the terrace and pick up where we left off."

Darby just shook his head. "Go on. Now." He barely whispered.

"I am going to prepare the carriage, Bella." Morton said, winning her attention. "Five minutes."

His firm tone sent shivers down her spine. She would be sure to be there within four minutes. She watched as her uncle's silhouette faded in the distance, and then she turned to Darby.

"You have the gift of choosing the wrong words, did you know that, Bella?"

Bella's mouth dropped. "Thank you, I appreciate the compliment." She stepped closer to Darby. "But I don't understand why you just solemnly agreed that I do as my uncle said."

"He's your *uncle*."

"Why did you seem relieved to have learned that tiny piece of information?" she quizzed.

"It doesn't matter." Darby answered after he ran his hand through his hair a second time, allowing it to settle on the back of his neck that was now full of tension.

"Tell me, Darby." Bella's hands rang with sarcastic enthusiasm. "I'm just dying to know!"

Bella watched Darby's eyes take on a distant look. Whatever strain was relieved by knowing that Morton was her uncle *did* matter. Finally he returned to the present moment. "You better be going," he retrieved his pocket watch that was attached to a shiny gold chain, "time's up."

"Just like that." Bella snapped her fingers. Her chocolate coated eyes blackened. "I believe my uncle was right," she started to back away, "poor girls need to stay away from the rich boys."

Darby matched each step she took. His hand grasped her arm gently. "You are by no means poor."

Bella laughed. "I'm glad you keep lying to yourself, Darby. If you knew just how poor I was, you wouldn't be caught in my presence." She glanced to where his hand held her firmly. "And you surely wouldn't be caught touching me. Which brings me to the conclusion that my absence will not sting too bad."

His finger silenced her lips. "Being rich has nothing to do with money in my books." His finger slid to her chin while his eyes penetrated hers without boundaries. "Being rich is having a smile on a beautiful face when you don't have two coins to rub together. Being rich is to know love when all that surrounds you is oppression. Being rich is to dance even when you don't feel like dancing." Darby dropped his hand and backed up a step. "When can I see you again?"

"I don't know."

Darby just nodded his head as though he was trying to digest her answer. "Good night, Bella. Your uncle is waiting."

Bella swallowed the lump in her throat. Despite her gift of choosing the wrong words, Darby was gifted to say the right words. She had never looked at life from that perspective. From the rich man's point of view. She only assessed life from where she stood.

Bella watched as Darby turned away and walked back toward the barn.

"Good night, Darby," she whispered, not sure if he heard her or not.

CHAPTER SIXTEEN

THE FULL MOON SHONE DOWN from above. Bella tried to concentrate on the countless stars instead of all the fun she was missing out on. Morton had been quiet and hadn't spoken to her since they left the gathering. His silence was beginning to make Bella uncomfortable. She knew when he was quiet that he was thinking, and she had a good idea what was on his mind right now.

"Did he kiss you?"

Yes, she knew exactly what he was thinking. The very same thing she had been trying to keep far from her mind. Hard as it was, Bella couldn't help but wonder just how it would have felt. Would it have been soft? Warm? Sweet? She squeezed her eyes shut. She had to stop thinking about it.

"No." Bella finally answered.

"Good, because it would have cost your job. It wouldn't have been worth it."

Bella wished that she felt that way about it. Since her departure, Bella felt a rapid growth of emptiness take control. Maybe a part of her did belong to Darby, but did anything about Darby belong to her?

Obviously not. He walked away too easily.

"So, you meet him often?" Morton asked flatly, leaving only the echoing of the horse's hooves to sound in the night.

Bella turned her gaze upward trying to soak in the beauty of the sparkling sky, only to discover that the sky above was falling upon her world. "Yes," she whispered.

"How often?" Morton inquired.

"Twice a week."

"On your days off?"

"Yes."

Morton let out a sigh, "I am not going to ask why."

"It's not what you think, Uncle Morton. He is desperate to find relief for his foot." Bella argued.

"So, you *did* recognize him when we passed on the Approach Road?" Morton didn't acknowledge her argument, or the statement she made about Darby's foot.

Bella chose to remain silent. Debating the topic would profit little, if none at all.

"Avoid him at all cost," Morton instructed, "or you'll be caught in a trap you've made yourself. Trust me, those are the hardest ones to escape, and their consequences are fierce."

"How do you know?" she asked.

Morton kept his eyes locked onto the road stretched before him. "I've been there and done that." His voice choked. "He's not worth it; trust me."

Bella wondered just what her uncle may have been talking about, but she decided not to pry. If he wanted her to know then he would say so. Bella let out a sigh, "I suppose you're right."

"You speak as though the words taste terrible."

"You have no idea," Bella admitted with disgust. She now realized that the emotion running deep inside was not going to be easy to make rid of. Considering that she needed the job she had, there had to be a choice made. She couldn't travel two separate paths leading to opposite destinations.

Either she could chose the path of self-sacrifice in which its destination led to a place of promise, or she could continue tiptoeing along the road leading her heart to destruction. The thought caused a gnawing pain to envelope Bella. She didn't know how many times a heart could be broken and put back together. She just knew the process was agonizing and she didn't intend to allow it to be broken more than necessary.

Sophia was surprised when Darby strutted back into the barn alone. For that she was glad.

No Bella.

Right now was a perfect time to intercept him. Slowly she ventured to the opposite end of the barn where he now stood. He looked fine dressed in black and white. Her nervous hands flattened her skirt as she silently hoped that he found her appearance all the same.

Sophia smiled sheepishly as she approached him. She knew he had to see her although he acted like he didn't. How hard was she to overlook?

"You disappear fast," she said.

Finally he looked, turning to face her fully. "You do too."

Sophia stepped back, creating a breathable distance. "What do you mean?" she asked curiously.

The music hummed without restraint making it hard to hear one another's words, so he matched the step she had taken back. "After you said your piece on the terrace, you were nowhere to be found."

"Oh," she said flatly.

"Which makes me curious. Bella doesn't meet anyone else on the terrace, does she?"

His irritable tone caused a chill to venture down Sophia's arm. Or maybe it was the look in his eyes. She started to cower under his scrutiny.

"You wouldn't *lie*, would you, Sophia?" Darby asked.

She felt the urge to turn away from the man, but she couldn't quite do it justly. He had somehow figured her out. Instead of running from the truth, she smiled and said, "Lie? Me?" Sophia laughed, "I call it a gift."

"A gift to lead others astray?"

"No, a gift to shine a light on the truth."

Darby excused himself from the pest. He needed some fresh air. Again. Once he was outside, Darby sought the stump he had sat on earlier. He couldn't erase Bella's image from his mind. No matter how hard he tried, her chocolate eyes were staring back at him.

Darby had to form a plan. A plan that would diminish her resolve. Something to change Bella's mind and cause her to follow her heart instead of the words of her uncle. And, too, she must realize that wealth has absolutely nothing to do with love.

He needed to return her book. He would make the visitation brief without showing his feelings or revealing his intentions. He would allow some time to elapse and then he would seek her out again. If he detected the same glint in her eyes that was once there, then Darby would know without a doubt that she still cared for him.

But what if she didn't? Darby swallowed.

He would cross that bridge when he came to it.

Darby arose from the stump, unaware of his visitor.

Her shadowy figure stepped forward. "I wondered where you had gone to," she said as she stepped nearer.

Darby gritted his teeth. "I just needed some fresh air."

"Oh, well, I need a favor."

Darby couldn't see Sophia's face to read her expression. How could he possibly help her?

When Darby didn't respond she moved closer. "Unfortunately, my ride has left me." She shrugged her shoulders, "Could you take me back to the manor?"

What? She was asking him to return her to Biltmore House? "I'm sorry, I don't have a carriage."

"I can ride horseback!" Sophia twirled on the tips of her toes and faced him again. "I love horseback riding!"

Bella ventured toward the door in which she was to enter, but instead she stalled her steps and waited for her uncle to leave. She knew she should probably go in and lie down, but sleep was far from her mind.

Her feet carried her away from the house and toward the terrace. Bella's steps were slow. Her fingers traced her long braid. Her thoughts were on no one but the forbidden. Bella wondered why she desired to have the forbidden the most. Why could she not be content with her job? Why could she not find satisfaction in seeing Mama and Ashlynn less often than she saw the full moon?

Her heart pondered these words, although the answers never revealed themselves. She doubted to ever see Darby on the terrace again. Although she would be there at their appointed time, Bella didn't expect to see him there. She wondered if he would continue to exercise his foot. If he did, then he would be preparing Biltmore Forest Fair. It was creeping upon them. He would be too busy to worry about her anyway. His dreams were being fulfilled. For him she was glad. She would like to be there to watch him hike Mount Pisgah.

She desired to see Darby conquer his mountain. The thought made her smile.

Although darkness evaded all light except that of the moon, Bella fingered the flower in her hand. The one she picked before stepping onto the terrace. As childish as it seemed, she started chanting, "He loves me.....He loves me not."

A trail of petals followed behind her footsteps as she picked one and then the other. Her feet were nearing the edge of the terrace. "He loves me.....He loves me not.....He loves me."

The echoing sound of hoof beats dominated the chirping crickets. Bella ducked behind the massive twist of vine.

Who would be arriving at this hour? She thought.

The silhouette of two people atop a horse filled her vision. Because of the streaks of silver light seeping through the Wisteria, Bella could plainly see it was a man and a woman. Her heart quickened. It was probably an employee of the Vanderbilts and if she was seen…

If there was time to run, Bella would have run.

The horse ceased its gallop and the man dismounted. He assisted the lady. The voices sounded quite familiar as Bella tried to ignore the words exchanged. It was none of her business who violated the Vanderbilts' wishes.

Bella thought surely her heart had stopped beating when she heard the mention of Darby's name. Now, it became her business. She strained her eyes to see and her ears to hear. Realization poured over her body like a cloud of doom. The remains of the flower in her hand fell to earth. She didn't need a flower to reveal a fantasy.

The man was Darby.

Good heavens, the woman was…Sophia.

CHAPTER SEVENTEEN

ALMOST A WEEK HAD PASSED since Bella attended the barn gathering. She found herself in a distant world, her thoughts far from what she was doing. The day had been quite a challenge. First thing this morning she was pulled out of bed an hour earlier than usual because Greta, a chambermaid, had been ill and needed temporary relief from her chores.

Bella cared not how she had left her room. She just twisted her hair in an unfashionable bun and slid a few pins through its core. She must have grabbed two different socks because one felt higher than the other. Her apron was tied much too tight or else her waistline was expanding. To say the least, it had been a very uncomfortable day.

Having worked alongside of Fran, Bella wished the woman could be a part of her everyday schedule here at Biltmore House. "Oh, honey, I would slide down the laundry chute if I could ever catch the Vanderbilts gone and the Matron busy."

Bella laughed. She could see it now. The lady was nearly three times her size and carried a wide range set of hips. Bella couldn't fathom how Fran's wild idea could possibly come to pass. Literally.

"When you decide to take the chance, please inform me. I will be waiting at the bottom." Bella said as she gathered an arm load of bed linens.

"You can count on it. And while I'm at it, I'm going to dive into the pool."

Bella tried to suppress her grin. If she had to choose which scenario to witness, the deciding moment would be quite difficult.

"Speaking of the pool, I just might be your partner in crime," Bella added.

"You swim?" Fran asked as her forearm pushed back a strand of her dark hair.

"Oh yes! My Papa often took me to Lake Toxaway to fish." Bella's shoulder lifted, "I never found much interest in fishing. I always ended up in the lake."

Fran paused her actions. Instead of pressing the fresh linen onto the bed, she stood there studying Bella. "It seems we have a lot in common, except I never had a Papa."

Bella detected the sad note that rang in Fran's voice. The longing in her pale blue eyes was evident.

"Tell me more about him, Bella," said Fran.

A nagging feeling gnawed at Bella. She didn't wish to talk about her Papa. Instead, she wanted the memories of him to be at rest. But when she looked into the curious gaze of a middle-aged woman who never knew about a Papa, Bella couldn't retain the countless moments of years gone by.

"Okay, I will share with you one of my most favorite times spent with Papa." Bella allowed the ball of bed linens to fall to the floor. "I remember it like it was yesterday…"

"Bella!" Papa had shouted her name from the porch. "Please hurry! We're late!"

The loud footfalls echoed from inside as ten year old Bella came running through the kitchen. His eyes grew wide when she stumbled out the door. "Where do you think you're going dressed like that?" his big arms fixed firmly across his chest.

Bella's head dipped to examine herself more carefully. Had she picked out the wrong color? The red plaid shirt of her Papa's was stuffed down into her skirt. The sleeves had been much too long, so Bella had rolled them up past her wrists. Peeking out from underneath the hem of her skirt was Papa's boots he had discarded some time ago. Bella had them in safe keeping under her bed. She lifted her face and was relieved to find him smiling down on her.

He offered his hand, "Come on, Bella. Let's get outta here."

Bella felt big as the world as she walked hand in hand with her Papa. She noticed many compliments were given to her father as they walked down the busy street. Finally, the town church came into view.

Pastor Jackson stood beside the door to greet the folks as usual. A group of children were gathered around playing Ring Around the Rosie. The excitement broke out when Rudy Moyers called her name.

"Hey, everybody! Look at Bella! She musta forgot to wash her Sunday dress!"

Bella's cheeks were aflame. She heard the group of children

snickering. She really wanted to give the little freckle faced boy a piece of her mind, but a gentle tug from Papa encouraged her to move forward.

Bella didn't hear one word during Pastor Jimmy Jackson's sermon. All she could feel were the eyes of her peers staring at her. What had been wrong with how she dressed today? She wanted to be just like her Papa, her hero. Dressing like him seemed to be a good start. Or so she thought. She allowed her face to turn slightly. Only enough to capture a glimpse of her Papa. His hair was combed nicely and was the exact shade of her own. Golden honey. His beard, thank God, had been shaven. Bella didn't want to imagine herself with a beard. His features were strong, almost seemed to be unmovable. Her hand felt for her own cheekbone. Yes, hers was just as defined as his. She studied his nose for a second. Was hers the same length as his? She laid her pointer finger on top of her nose. When he glanced down at her, she withdrew her hand from her face and placed it in her lap. She was relieved when he smiled down on her.

On their way home, Bella was quiet. She kept her hand folded inside her Papa's. She tried not to think of the remarks she had received at church, but it was hard.

"Have you ever wondered if it was possible to make everybody happy?" Papa asked as they took slow, steady steps.

"Me? No. Why?" Bella questioned.

"Something I learned when I was young was to pay no mind of what others think as long as I am happy and God is happy,"

Papa explained.

Bella turned her face to Papa. "Oh, you mean like today?"

Papa chuckled, "Yes, like today. I knew when you stepped onto the porch that you'd be in for it."

Bella withdrew her hand and folded her arms. She refused to take another step. "Why did you let me?"

"You'll not learn any younger."

"Huh?" Bella wondered what the phrase meant.

Papa looked ahead of him. They were almost home. "Bet ya can't catch me!"

A smile spread on her face. She'd catch him. Then her gaze fell to her feet. At least she'd try.

Gray clouds had settled over the Carolina sky. Bella could almost reach out and touch her Papa's arm, but the sudden down pour of heavy rain prevented it. Instead, Papa turned and took Bella's hands in his and twirled her around until she became dizzy. The large boots fell from her feet revealing her ten perfect toes. When her feet settled onto the ground, together, hand in hand, Bella and Papa danced until they could dance no more.

"Papa," Bella said breathlessly, "I wanna be jus' like you."

That night after Bella had gotten dressed and ready for bed, she decided to speak to her Papa once more. She tiptoed from her room and stopped short when she heard him talking to someone. She didn't know they had company, so she peeked around the corner only to find Papa by himself. Even Mama was nowhere around. Strange.

Bella heard him say, "Father, she wants to be just like me." He buried his face in his hands. "Please help me to be just like You."

"Papa?"

Startled, he lifted his face. "Bella, I thought you were in bed asleep."

Bella stepped cautiously not sure if she was welcome or not. He patted the spot beside him. "Come here, sit." Bella took her seat and waited for him to speak. "You know how today at church when those children poked fun at you?" Bella nodded. "It bothered you, I could tell. But did you pay attention that once you started dancing in the rain with me, you forgot about everything that was causing you pain?"

Bella hadn't realized it until now, but yes, she hadn't give the incident a second thought. "That's how life is, darlin'." He stroked her cheek with his thumb. "Life and its twists are not fair, but that's how you learn to deal with it. You just dance in the rain that your storm brings."

Fran removed her handkerchief from the cuff of her dress and wiped her eyes. "That's the most beautiful story I've ever been told, Bella." She started blowing her nose. "There is a life lesson in it whether you realize it or not."

Bella just nodded. She could see the value in it, of course. But how could she apply it to her current storm? She hadn't slept in what seemed like an eternity, and as much as she tried pushing her problems far from her, they always made their way back to the forefront thoughts of her mind. Was it possible to face them and dance in the rain at the same time?

"I wish I had a wise Papa like you've got," Fran said.

"Like I had, you mean." The sorrow in Bella's voice was none to be hid. "He passed earlier this year."

"Oh, Bella. I'm so sorry." Fran was sympathetic, but Bella didn't need sympathy nor pity. She just needed to be set free from the hold of one certain person.

A knock on the open door startled them as they both looked upon their intruder. It was Check, the valet. "Miss Bella, you have a visitor."

"Me?" Bella gasped.

"Are you Bella?" the young man cast her a wistful smile.

Feeling somewhat of a dimwit, Bella stood. "Oh, Fran, I must help you finish the chores."

"No, Bella, you go on," Fran said. "I'll only be a handful of minutes anyway."

Bella followed Check down the corridor. Her hand felt nervously for her hair. She was a mess that much she could tell. Her heart sped up as she neared the entrance, the place where she assumed her visitor had been left waiting. She pondered who it might be, but no one came to mind. She took a deep breath before she rounded the corner.

Bella's throat constricted when her eyes took in the familiar figure leaning against the iron railing that encircled the Winter Garden. She had to force her feet to move. She could do this and remain unaffected, right?

"Thank you, Check." Bella dismissed the valet while gaining Darby's attention all in the same moment. She watched him as he stood and made even steps toward her.

So he has been exercising his foot regularly, she thought. Bella cast her focus to what was in his hand. Her book. Relief washed over her like a mid- summer rain. He had kept his word.

"Darby." At the mention of his name Bella's chest tightened just like it had the many times she had said his name before. "You sent for me?" She questioned why he had not just left the book to be delivered unto her. Did he have something he wanted to say? Was he hoping to catch a glimpse of Sophia?

"Yes, I was returning your book." He held it out to her. She reached for it, and her fingers barely grazed his during the exchange. Again, like every time they touched, she felt it clear to her toes. She dared a glance at his eyes. Still that same reasoning rested in his piercing gaze.

"Thank you." Bella fingered its cover like it was a foreign object she had never possessed.

"Thank you, Bella." He won her attention at the mention of her name. "All because of you, I will continue my stay at Biltmore Forest School."

All because of her? Exactly how did he mean for that message to be interpreted? He was only staying there because of her, or because he is well enough to maintain his position?

"Bella, if you'll excuse me, I have an appointment within the hour." With a nod, he excused himself and walked away.

Bella never found the words to say goodbye. Instead, her hand ascended into the air, leaving her fingers to grasp at nothing. She turned away also, not sure where her feet would guide her. With her book clutched tightly to her chest, Bella wondered whom Darby was supposed to meet. On a normal day, he would have been waiting on the terrace, but not now. His motives were different and only because Bella directed him in another direction. This was what she had wanted. This was all for the best according to her uncle's wisdom. But why did her Papa's words flow smoothly when all else seemed to be upside down.

Just remember, Bella, life and its twists are not fair. You just have to learn to dance in the rain that the storm brings.

CHAPTER EIGHTEEN

"SOPHIA, I EXPECT YOU TO teach Bella exactly how serving is done in a traditional manner." Mrs. King's keen eye settled onto the maid who was now beginning to squirm. "You will be serving the guests of Mr. Vanderbilt this evening in the Banquet Hall, and the only women present will be Mrs. Vanderbilt and Mrs. Schenck." Mrs. King folded her hands firmly upon her desk. "Instruct Bella to meet the ladies assistance first. Then fall into routine serving Mr. Vanderbilt, Mr. Schenck, and then the scholars from Biltmore Forest School." The Matron arose from her desk, "You are dismissed."

Sophia released the breath she had not realized she had been holding. When Mrs. King had requested her presence, her mind had begun to whirl. What had she done this time?

Now an edge of excitement surged through her veins. The scholars of Biltmore Forest School were going to be present in the Banquet Hall this evening. There was one student in particular whom she desired to see.

The man had not shown the attention toward her that she had hoped for, although he was gullible enough to believe that she had gotten left behind at the barn gathering. The ride back to Biltmore had been perfect bliss. For Sophia at least. He seemed reserved, careful not to show much emotion.

So, Darby would be there tonight. In the Banquet Hall. So would Bella. That kind of put Sophia in a pickle. There would definitely be some competition, but there was always a chance at winning.

Sophia pondered her next move. Besides putting on her best uniform and plenty of perfumes, she knew just the thing to be the one to leave the Banquet Hall victorious. A smirk formed on her face. At first Sophia hated the thought of teaching Bella how to serve, but now with her brilliant plan intact, she looked forward to seeing Bella make all the wrong moves.

"You always serve the gentlemen first." Sophia stated as she placed the serving tray on Bella's arm.

"Really? I would have imagined the women receiving first." Bella shrugged her shoulder and performed as Sophia had instructed.

"We do everything differently here at Biltmore. I would have guessed you had figured that out already." Sophia smiled triumphantly. *Strike One.*

Sophia sat herself at a small table. "Now, when you are serving the guest a dish, always serve it from the right side. Now practice," Sophia ordered. *Strike Two.*

Bella moved to Sophia's right and placed the dish in front of her. "Perfect," Sophia said. "Now, always remove it from the left so further dishes can move in on the right." Bella did as she was told. *Strike Three.* "Perfect, are you sure you've not done this before? You are catching on too quickly."

Bella smiled and shrugged her shoulder, "Maybe I'm a

natural."

Sophia bit back a grin. "That you are, Bella, a natural indeed."

Bella had found it easier to tolerate Sophia today. She had been very helpful and patient concerning her serving skills. She had even offered to practice again before entering the Banquet Hall, but Bella politely declined. She felt confident she could perform without a fault or a spill.

Bella had taken the time to return to her room, darn on a fresh uniform, and redo her hair. She didn't know who the special guests were, but she would put forth her best effort in order to please her employers, especially since this was her first opportunity to serve.

Sophia was already standing at attention when Bella arrived at her post. She ordered Bella to start with the right side of the table, and she would take the left so that Bella could use her as reference in case she had forgotten the next step.

The immaculate room was being filled with guests as quickly as Bella could blink. She noted the guests were mostly men. At the opposite end of the table sat Mrs. Vanderbilt and another lady whom Bella didn't recognize.

Just as soon as the guests were seated, a stampede of servants swarmed like they were fighting fire. Sophia had forgotten to mention this little detail. Immediately, Bella was thrown into action. The sudden act of serving caught her off guard. She had intended to move carefully and gracefully. At this rate, Bella doubted she was doing so. She broke into a cold sweat. This task had been underestimated. Serving wine had not been on her studies. Trying to balance the tray with half-filled wine glasses was an obstacle course in itself. Bella supposed that the guests should receive their drinks from the right as well. One man almost knocked the glass from her hand, but thank goodness, her grip was tight.

Bella tried catching a glimpse of Sophia, but she was long gone. However, she did acknowledge the stare from the two women who were still sitting there with nothing but utensils in front of them. Bella bit her lip. Her gut told her to bypass the gentlemen and serve the women, but Sophia had instructed her differently.

Bella slid the next guest his dish from the right and removed the dome lid. She did the same for the next and the next. Obviously, she was serving in the wrong direction. Other servants were nearly trampling over her. Despite the wonderful smell of luxurious food, Oysters Rockefeller, Bella had heard one of the men say, the sight nearly caused her to gag. She kept her focus trained on what she was doing instead of glancing at their dish.

There was no time to pause or even blink. Each time Bella thought there would be a break, she would spot an empty glass and retrieve it from the left just as she had been taught. When she was returning a new glass of wine, Bella bumped into Check, the valet, who had been walking in her direction with a stack of dirty dishes. Bella braced her empty hand to prevent them from falling, but the tray on her other hand wobbled. Not sure which one to guard the most, Bella lost the balance of her tray. It toppled from one side and then the other. It was impossible to regain control when all of the sudden, *CRASH!*

The shattering of the priceless crystal silenced the room. Bella felt the intense gazing from the onlookers. She had not been given specific instructions on what to do if an accident occurred, so she simply knelt down and started picking up the shards of glass and laying them in her apron. All of the sudden, Bella noticed that she was not alone.

Mr. Vanderbilt had joined her. "I am so sorry," Bella apologized. "It is my fault, I should have been..."

Her employer cut her words off with his own protest. "Allow me; it is nothing."

Together, Bella and Mr. Vanderbilt picked up the visible pieces of the shattered goblets. Minute by minute, the conversations began again, leaving the incident forgotten about.

A towel fell from above causing Bella to look up only to discover Sophia hovering over her. Was that a gleaming look in her eyes, or was Bella just imagining it?

"Thank you." Bella whispered as she took the towel into her hands and dried up the precious wine that had been wasted.

After disposing the evidence of the mishap and making rid of the towel, Bella returned to the Banquet Hall to clean. Her steps drew short when she heard Mr. Vanderbilt give Dr. Carl Schenck the liberty to reveal the schedule for the Forest Festival. She recognized the name to be the founder of Biltmore Forest

School, Darby's mentor.

Had these men been part of the school? The scholars perhaps? Bella swallowed the lump that had suddenly formed in her throat. Instinctively, she felt Darby's gaze. He had been there all along. He had witnessed her poor serving skills and the accident. Heat slowly crept up her neck and flushed her cheeks. Still, she refused to render unto his beckoning; instead, she listened to what Dr. Schenck had to say.

"The festival will last three consecutive days. During that time, I will make known unto many the ways to conserve our forests." He moved away from his chair, and Bella followed him with her eyes. "Also, we will present effective ways to reforest already corroded and depleted land. With the help of my students, we will demonstrate proper tree planting and seed extraction. I will give each attendee the option to plant his own tree on the property of George Vanderbilt." The statement earned an applause, one to which Bella found herself participating.

He continued to venture down the length of the forty foot long table explaining that he believed this event would not only be beneficial for the surrounding forests, but also for the entire country. Bella found herself nodding in agreement.

Schenck stopped directly behind one of the men seated at the table. Bella allowed her eyes to roam as the man kept talking. Like magnetic attraction, she found herself staring into a familiar set of eyes. Her heart flopped. Then it flopped again. She tried to look away, but his gaze had her pinned down. Darby was trying not to smile, that much she could tell. Finally, she pulled her eyes away. Hard as it was, she tried not to look back.

Bella kept giving quick glances in Darby's direction. He had not been looking. Instead, she watched him withdraw a small piece of paper and a pen from his pocket. He wrote something on the paper as Bella watched him. His lips lifted a notch when he looked up and found her already ogling him.

While he had her undivided attention, he took the note, slid it underneath his napkin and then patted it gently. Bella had to remind herself to breathe. He had written something. To her. She tried to remain calm and neutral, but something inside said that she was flustered and not too well at hiding it.

Bella was glad when Dr. Schenck's presentation had ended. She was ready to make an escape, but not before she retrieved the piece of paper. Her gaze shifted around the room. When her eyes rested upon Sophia, she felt a silent challenge. Then Sophia's eyes darted to the place where Darby was sitting and then back to Bella. She knew. She had witnessed every detail. Sophia had seen the written message.

Finally, the group stood to leave. Bella ignored Darby and refused to look upon him again. She would not surrender to him. Did he think she had forgotten what had transpired between them? Probably not. But one thing was certain. She couldn't wait to get her hands on that piece of paper.

Once the group had dispersed, Bella made hasty steps to the place where Darby had been seated. She spotted the napkin that hid the message. She pulled it away from the table. Nothing.

There was no sign of a paper note. She looked under each napkin just in case she missed it, but it wasn't there.

Bella stopped and glanced about the room. Sophia was making her exit, but before she crossed the threshold, she stopped and waved the piece of paper in the air.

With an evil smirk, Sophia darted out of the Banquet Hall without giving a second glance.

CHAPTER NINETEEN

D
ARBY HAD BEEN WAITING ON the terrace much longer than he had expected. He was beginning to wonder if Bella was going to decline his invitation. He had watched her all evening at his free will because she hadn't noticed his presence. Even he, being a country boy, had known that she was going about everything the wrong way. Darby couldn't fathom why she hadn't been successfully trained before she was thrown into serving a host of guests as large as the group of forestry scholars. Something wasn't adding up, but he couldn't seem to lay a finger on it.

Bless her heart, he wanted to get down on his hands and knees to help her clean up the many pieces of shattered crystal, but he decided against it. Then to his surprise, Mr. Vanderbilt had assisted her. Darby worried for Bella. He feared that tomorrow would bear disappointment unto her. What if her position was now in jeopardy because of her poor serving skills?

He let out a sigh as he looked up into the darkening sky. Only by the light of the moon and twinkling stars was Darby aware of his surroundings. He would wait five more minutes for Bella and if she didn't arrive then, he would take his leave.

Darby gave her the benefit of the doubt and waited five minutes longer, but Bella didn't show. He turned to leave when he spotted a shadowy figure stepping toward him. Excitement surged through his veins. Relief melted over him. Bella had accepted the invitation he had written on the paper note.

He watched her with a steady gaze as she approached him. Although she was moving quite slowly, Darby could still determine the outline of her figure. Her hair was still in a tidy bun, and she was facing him boldly. Her head held high and her shoulders stood tall. Had she grown an inch or two since he left the Banquet Hall? Maybe she had changed her shoes.

Darby warned his heart to slow its pace when he stepped away from the banister. Flecks of moonlight filtered through the canopy of Wisteria revealing her face unto him. His feet froze. He didn't find the smooth chocolate eyes staring back at him. Instead, they were bluish. The form of the maid did not belong to Bella. Anger and disappointment mixed like a destructive tornado inside Darby's person. He knew who this was. Sophia.

"What are you doing here?" the edge in his voice revealed his frustration.

"Bella sent me," she said as she stepped closer.

"Why did she send you?" he asked skeptically.

Sophia gingerly shrugged her shoulder. "She doesn't wish to see you. I tried to pull her along with me, but she refused and retired to her chamber."

Darby folded his arms across his chest. He didn't believe the little twit, yet how had she known to meet him here? "Can you give Bella a message for me?"

Delight shown on Sophia's face by a force. She had not wished to talk about Bella. That much was evident. "Of course, anything."

"Tell her I wanted to see her, not you." Darby watched Sophia's countenance climb several degrees. Good. "Tell her it disappointed me that she sent you." Her temperature warmed a great deal. Even better.

"Is that all?" Sophia's foot tapped non-stop.

"No, there's one more thing."

"Out with it." She demanded.

"Tell her that I said she did a wonderful job serving tonight."

Sophia's mouth dropped. "Tell her yourself, you big ogre!" her words spat out like a venom. She turned and marched away leaving only the sound of something metallic to fall to the ground.

Thankfully, there was a full moon or Darby would have never found it. He stared at the charm lying in the palm of his hand. It belonged to Bella, but why had Sophia had it? He shoved it into his pocket.

At least he possessed Bella's heart.

Bella paced the length of the dim hallway just outside of Sophia's room. She knew Sophia would return. Eventually. A raging storm swirled inside Bella. Her heartbeat echoed like thunder. Her chilled hands felt for her face. She was aflame. Bella had tried following Sophia, but she had already gotten out of sight. Bella should have rightfully received the message Darby had written her. When she replayed the scene in her mind's eye, Bella failed to remember just how Sophia could have retrieved it before her.

    Sophia's sudden change in behavior had caught Bella off guard. She had actually believed that they were finally breaking down the barrier that stood between them. Not now. A bitter gnawing agitated the pits of Bella's stomach. It was hard to forgive someone so deceitful. Learning of Sophia's slyness, Bella wondered if Sophia had even been truthful in teaching her serving skills. Everything had gone drastically wrong. Something wasn't adding up, but Bella felt confident she would discover the missing factors.

    Bella had paused her pacing when she heard faint footfalls. Could it be Sophia?

    The surprise of Bella's presence ceased Sophia's steps which did nothing to slow Bella. Instantaneously, she moved toward the conniving foe with great confidence. There was nothing that felt more victorious than witnessing one's adversary cower under the scrutiny of her opponent.

    The weak side of Sophia revealed itself on her pale stricken cheeks. For a moment, Bella thought the witch might break and make a run for it. It probably would have been in her best interest to do so. Instead, Sophia drew herself up and squarely looked Bella in the eye.

    "Sophia-," Bella forced the word from her lips. "You know," Bella studied the blank look staring back at her, "you completely contradict the meaning of your name. You are from what I would call *holy wisdom*!"

    Sophia's mouth stood agape as if she couldn't believe that

Bella had said such a thing.

"Ever since the moment I stepped foot in this house, you have detested me! Deceived me! You've tried with every ounce of your strength to destroy me!" Sophia flinched at Bella's words. "Now tell me. What! Is! Your! Problem?!"

"You want to know my problem?!" Sophia bit back. "You! You had him all to yourself! Just you and him! While I had no one! Absolutely no one!"

Bella stepped back from Sophia and lifted her palms. "Listen, Darby does not belong to me. He is not mine, and I'm sure he would agree."

"I'm not talking about Darby!" Sophia lashed out. "Does the name Walter Westbrook sound familiar to you?!"

Bella blinked rapidly. "Yes, that's my Papa, but what does that mean to you?"

Tears were now dripping from Sophia's chin, and her chest heaved. The anger mounting up in her blue eyes was unmistakable. "Oh, that's *your* Papa! Quite possessive, don't you think?" She matched each step forward that Bella had taken backwards. "Just what makes you think that he was all yours, huh? Just Papa and Bella!" Sophia mocked.

Bella backed further away. "I'm confused."

"Your Papa is-," Sophia stuttered and buried her face in the palms of her hands. "Your Papa is my .....Papa." She finally lifted her face. "Bella, you are my sister." Her gaze collided with the floor.

Bella felt the pull of gravity become greater than she had ever felt. She surely thought she was falling to the floor beneath her feet. Her Papa had another child? It was impossible. Well, maybe it was possible, but why did Bella never hear of it? Besides, Sophia looked nothing like him. Her hair was a unique shade of red; her eyes blue. She had a steeper nose. Her eyebrows didn't arch in a defined shape like her own. Her heart was cold and bitter. Papa's was warm and sweet. Everything visible seemed to protest Sophia's statement.

If Bella had ever been lied to, she prayed it was now. "Why?" the word fell in a whisper. Bella had too many questions. There would never be enough time to ask them all. The moment fell silent. She wasn't sure what to say, but she could read the sincerity in Sophia's eyes for the first time.

"It wasn't fair, Bella."

"What do you mean?" Bella asked.

Sophia slowly knelt down where she stood. "Can't you see that I wanted him to be my Papa just like he was to you? But no, I got the bad end of the deal." Bella joined Sophia where she now sat. "Morton knows," Sophia clarified.

"He does?" Bella asked.

Sophia nodded her head. Her downcast eyes were in a faraway land. "My Mam wouldn't let him see me. That's when he moved away and married your Ma."

The words were hard for Bella to swallow. What if he had not met her Mama? What if Sophia had been his baby girl? What if he had taught Sophia how to dance in the rain? Then she probably wouldn't be sitting in the floor wondering what could have been. Instead, she would be counting her blessings.

Bella didn't know what to say. She just knew she needed rest. Lots of it. Maybe she would wake up and find out this was all just a bad dream. As she looked upon Sophia, Bella wondered if she could ever care for Sophia just as she did for Ashlynn. Could she find it in her heart to forgive? Would there ever come a day in which she could honestly call her *sister*? Bella just shook her head and rose to her feet.

"I need rest." She said as she turned to walk away.

"Wait!" Sophia shouted as she too stood to her feet. After reaching into her pocket, Sophia pulled out the paper note. "Here."

Bella took it into her hands. She wanted to open it, but she decided against it. She looked up and found Sophia staring at her. The bitter taste in her mouth prevented spoken words. Instead, she walked away as she first intended.

Once Bella was inside the safety of her room, she opened the small piece of paper. *Meet me on the terrace.* She could have guessed that. An ache settled in her chest. "Oh, Darby," she whispered as her tears broke free. She needed him now. His safety and shelter in the midst of this betraying storm. She probably would have gone to meet him, but instead Sophia made a mess of it.

Sophia.

Or should she say, *sister*?

CHAPTER TWENTY

BELLA TRIED IGNORING SOPHIA'S PRESENCE while the continual banging of pots and pans echoed in her ears. Though the night had felt quite long without rest, Bella found herself very alert. Perhaps she was too emotionally distraught to let a sleepless night affect her ability to function properly. Every time Sophia cast a glance in her direction, Bella felt it. She refused to bridge the gap between them. Instead, Bella kept her focus on the soapy suds that buried her hands.

"Bella."

The sudden mention of her name jolted Bella as she turned to find Bessie staring at her curiously. "Are you okay, dear?" Bessie's hand collided with Bella's forehead. "You're not feverish."

"I'm fine, Bessie, thank you."

"Bella, you haven't washed a single pot in the last thirty minutes." Bessie's all-knowing eyes searched Bella for answers for this unusual behavior.

Bella looked down at her hands. A rag gripped in one and shriveled fingers on the other. "My apologies." Bella's hands swam in the water searching for a pot to wash.

"Is it because of what happened yesterday?" Bessie asked as she moved to Bella's side.

Oh yes, yesterday had been nothing short of a nightmare.

"I'm fine, Bessie."

"You and I are going to work on those serving skills…"

Bessie's words faded into the air as her first serving experience came to mind. It had been horrible but nothing in comparison to the feeling she was left with last night. Bella felt herself nodding in agreement with Bessie, but her thoughts were still far from the present.

"Bella?"

"Huh?" Bella jerked her gaze back toward Bessie.

"You didn't hear a word I said, did you?"

No, Bella hadn't.

"I said, Mrs. King has requested your presence."

Bella's heart drummed in her ears as her fist knocked gently on the door before her. She knew it wasn't a good thing to be called upon by the Matron, and she probably wouldn't have to guess why she was being summoned.

"Enter!"

The Matron's voice sent chills down her spine. This was it. She was probably being fired for the blundering mistakes she made yesterday evening. Bella's tongue slid between her lips, her eyes drifting closed for only a moment before twisting the knob. The door opened without protest leaving Bella no choice but to enter. Mrs. King was seated behind her desk as usual, but to her surprise, Mr. Vanderbilt stood patiently beside the chair.

Oh boy. Panic surged through her veins. She was definitely

going to be sent packing, which was fine. She needed to be home. Ashlynn needed her. Mama needed her. She needed them.

"Please be seated, Bella." It had been Mr. Vanderbilt who gave the order. Bella didn't have a voice to reply. Obediently, she moved toward the chair and took her seat.

"How are you today, Bella?" Mrs. King asked.

"Fine, thank you." Bella replied evenly.

"Very well." Mrs. King smiled slightly. "I assume you ate a good breakfast this morning."

"Yes, thank you." Bella replied, knowing that it was probably the last breakfast she would consume at Biltmore.

"Mr. Vanderbilt." Mrs. King nodded her head in his direction. Bella forced herself to give him her full attention.

He smiled. "Thank you, Mrs. King." He directed his gaze toward Bella. "The Matron and I have come to a crossroad concerning your position." His long fingers smoothed his moustache. "However, I do wish to consider your opinion, Bella. I concluded that serving is too great a challenge at this point. My instincts tell me to promote you to chambermaid."

Bella felt her stiffened spine relax. Chambermaid? The idea sounded grand. She wouldn't have to dwell in the presence of Sophia. In the matter of fact, she would probably never see her. She felt her lips lift a notch. The gesture indicated her approval toward the idea.

"You will work alongside of Fran. Unfortunately, Greta is too ill to return to her normal duties." He turned to Mrs. King, "I will leave the remains to you. Good day, ladies." With a curt nod, Mr.

Vanderbilt left the room only leaving the heavy scent of spicy cologne to linger in his absence. Bella held back the sneeze that tickled her nose and prayed for a breath of fresh air.

"Bella, I have just a few questions to ask, and then we will go about discussing your new position." There was no humor in Mrs. King's dark eyes, "In your own words, tell me how to serve a guest."

Relief washed over Bella when she had been given direct orders not to return to the basement and finish scrubbing the pots and pans. Although she would miss Bessie's presence, something inside Bella leapt with joy knowing that Sophia would only be an afterthought.

The Matron had asked many questions concerning the prior evening and Bella's serving techniques. Mrs. King confirmed Bella's assumptions. Sophia had taught her backwards. Instead of serving on the left and removing from the right, Sophia had instructed her just the opposite. That explained why Bella fumbled the entire evening.

Bella smiled a victorious smile when her gaze landed upon Fran. Everything was working out for the good. Well, maybe not everything, but it sure seemed like it.

The next morning Bella pondered skipping breakfast instead of joining the other servants. She intended to just grab an apple and escape when a firm grip took her by the arm. She almost gasped. When Bella turned, she was glad to see that it was only her uncle. "Good morning, Uncle Morton."

He dipped his head, "Good morning to you, and congratulations on your promotion. I can't wait to hear how it all happened." He continued to hold on to her arm and escorted her to a nearby chair at the table. Bella's eyes roamed cautiously, but they never found Sophia. Soon she was indulging in her most favorite breakfast platter of biscuits, eggs, and grits. She quickly forgot about her adversary.

"Promoted after shattering priceless pieces of crystal?" the head chambermaid asked with a smile, "how did you manage that?"

Morton spoke up. "Grace, we all know that you drowned the mistress of the house in her own wine." Morton smiled upon the blushing maid, "Now tell me, which is worse?" Grace didn't answer; instead, she studied her plate. "That's what I thought." Morton spoke triumphantly.

Before Bella escaped the servants' dining hall, Morton proposed to take Bella on a horseback ride that evening in honor of her promotion. She tried to decline, but he insisted. "Come on, you've not seen the half of the estate and I already worked it out with Humphrey. He has reserved the gentlest horse just for you."

"I don't know," her gaze roamed around the empty room. Everyone else had already taken their post. "I need to go. I have work to do."

"Meet me at the barn, I'll be waiting." Morton didn't give her a chance to protest.

Bella released her breath. The ride sounded nice. At least she would get to enjoy the autumn air and the changing of leaves. Then her mind went to Sophia. She hadn't made an appearance this morning. Bella couldn't help but wonder where she might have been. Had she wished to dodge Bella as well? Or had she been fired and forced to leave Biltmore? Bella wanted to smile about Sophia's misfortune, but what was this tiny ache she felt inside?

The evening had crept upon Bella. Working with someone as interesting as Fran sure made a difference in one's day, but still she couldn't escape the nagging feeling concerning Sophia. Bella felt compelled to peek inside the kitchen to see if she was there. She wasn't. Could she possibly be sick and tucked away in bed? Bella quietly made her way toward the servant's rooms. The door to Sophia's room was closed. Bella gently laid her ear upon the door. Silence. Her fingers enclosed about the knob. A little twist indicated that it wasn't locked. The door opened with a screeking sound, but Bella found the room empty. Where had Sophia gone?

Bella questioned what she should do. Should she ask where Sophia had been sent?

The chiming of the clock reminded Bella that she had an appointment with her uncle, but as soon as she returned, she would find out what had happened to her...sister.

Morton had been right. Humphrey did reserve the gentlest beast for Bella. She had fed him a handful of oats before they had ridden out. Her hand felt for her pocket. She even took some along with her just in case the golden colored horse decided to be stubborn.

She hadn't ridden a horse in ages, but she hadn't forgotten how it was done. Her back was ram rod straight. Her fingers held onto the reins tightly. She could do this; she just knew it.

"Come on, Bella. We need to pick up the pace if you want to return before dark!" Morton called over his shoulder.

"Where are we going?" she asked curiously.

"I want you to see the highest point of Mount Pisgah and since we will be so close, I'll take you to a knoll where you can see the backside of the entire estate."

"Really?!"

"Yes, but like I said, we have to pick up the pace." With that being said, Morton dug his heels into the sides of the beast and away he went. Bella took a deep breath and did the same.

Bella tried to absorb every ounce of peach and red and pink and yellow. The beauty of the autumn leaves dangled above her head as Morton led the way. Thankfully, she had thought to grab her cloak. The evening air held a crisp chill, even more so at the rate of speed they were traveling.

They must have ventured at least a mile when Morton slowed his horse, allowing the beast to stop. Bella did the same. She followed suit when he led his horse toward the waters of the French Broad River.

Soon they were back onto their path. The sun had already begun to set, but thankfully, they were close to their destination.

The broadened trail forked, and the path became very narrow. The abundance of trees prevented very little light from spilling through. The terrain grew steeper, but still Bella hung in there.

When the curve ahead revealed an entire group of riders, they stopped. Bella felt the steadiness of her horse melt away. Was it becoming nervous? Bella didn't rightly know. But before she could ask, Morton had already become engaged in a heavy conversation with the leader. She felt tempted to pull out some of the oats from her pocket, but before she loosened her grip on the reins, the horse reared up onto its two back hooves and plunged its front hooves into the dirt. Bella screamed. At the sound of her fright, the beast lurched forward at a breakneck speed. Bella closed her eyes and held onto the reins with all of her might. She expected a crash. She expected to be thrown into midair. But instead, the horse had found its way around the crowd. It weaved in and out of the surrounding trees and found the path ahead of them. It ran like the wind leaving only the dust to dance in their absence.

Darby dug his heels deeper into Chestnut. He had to get to Bella. He had been in the back of the group, yet he was closest to Bella's rescue. The dust stung his eyes as he neared the wild beast. Darby tried blinking it away, but it was impossible. He willed his eyes to remain fastened onto Bella. Finally he managed to ride parallel of her and the wild beast.

"Bella!" he called out.

When she turned to him, she screamed. "Darby! Help! Please help me!"

He freed his right hand and held onto the reins with his left. He stretched out his arm. "The reins!" Bella looked even more frightened. Her nervous hands lifted them toward him. With a powerful tug, the beast slowed and then come to a stop.

Bella collapsed onto the neck of the beast that almost killed her. She was panting for breath. Darby feared she was going into shock. He jumped down from Chestnut's back and took Bella's weak body into his arms and carried her to a grassy spot atop the knoll. Then he brought the canteen to her lips.

"Here, drink." Darby coaxed her, and she willingly complied.

When she lifted her eyes, she smiled. She hadn't expected her first view from the knoll to be so breathtaking. Orange and pink strokes highlighted the evening sky just beyond the house, but the most beautiful sight was the smile on Darby's lips.

"Thank you." Bella's voice stammered.

"No need to thank me. Just thank God that you're alive." His finger pushed back a tendril of hair from her brow. "What happened anyway?"

Bella shrugged. "I have no idea."

Darby tried suppressing the smile that formed on his face, "Maybe I should give you some riding lessons."

"In your dreams, Darby."

CHAPTER TWENTY ONE

THE NEXT MORNING DARBY FOUND himself unable to focus on the task at hand. It was difficult to erase Bella's image from his mind, the way her braid had come undone during the escapade on the wild horse, revealing an abundance of honey dipped waves strong enough to paralyze any man's heart. Although the encounter was not an ordinary one, he was glad he had been nearby to rescue her. Had he not been there planting the countless trees...

Just after Darby had given Bella a sip of water, the thundering hoof beats had revealed nothing other than a group of forestry scholars led by that fuming uncle of hers. Regret had surged through his veins when she had abruptly stood and dusted off her skirt. Darby knew Morton didn't like her being near him. The cold stare he received from the man testified as much. Darby had barely heard her mumble *goodbye* when she departed on her uncle's horse. He had felt a pang of disappointment when she left and never once looked back.

Darby leaned back against a sycamore tree and withdrew the charm from his pocket. He hadn't thought to give it back yesterday. Still, he would guard it with his life. He slipped it back into his pocket and inhaled the autumn air bristling through the trees. Bright hues of pink, peach, and red synchronized with the October breeze. It had been a perfect morning to admire the handiwork of God, but instead, he had spent his time mooning over Bella and creating sign boards to mark each Tip.

The Tips were designed to identify each portion of ground from plantation to plantation in the order of that which all guests of the Forest Fair would receive in their brochure. There were sixty three of them altogether, although Darby would have guessed many more according to the ache in his arm. Finally, Darby pushed himself away from the tall tree and hammered the last of the nails into sign board sixty three. The heavy tool fell to the ground. Now it was time to start staking them.

That evening Darby joined Schenck and several other students just beyond the school where the ground marking began. Tip One was placed where depleted and corroded land had once been. Now a white pine plantation dominated the hillside. The trees had grown so close together that Darby would have had to crawl underneath the numerous branches just to make an entrance.

"This plantation is about ten years old, one of my first projects on the estate." Schenck declared.

"Yeah, I can tell." Hunter Morris added. The mouths of the other students stood agape. No one ever made such remarks toward their mentor. Ever.

Schenck abruptly brought his feet to halt, challenging his student with sternness. The extensive release of frustration echoed from every student present, except Hunter of course. He stood there smiling. For some reason, he always found it amusing to ruffle the doctor's feathers once in a while.

"Perhaps I have forgotten to share a bit of valuable information, Mr. Morris." Carl Schenck eyed the student. "Not only is this type of plantation capable of self-pruning, but it is also a resultant of superb lumber. Now, let me remind you that is the reason you are here. That is the reason I stand where I stand. Our purpose lies much deeper than the soil. We take it to the root."

"Mr. Pierson, would you please?" the forester motioned with his hand and directed Darby to the exact place where he wished for the sign board to be driven into the ground.

Pang! Pang! Pang! The sign was in place.

Tip Two was driven into the ground while Schenck explained the purpose of the thriving white and yellow pine. "You see, first I planted the field in Chestnut, Shagbark, and Bitternut Hickory." He shook his head with disgust. "The rabbits, or should I say pests, devoured the seedlings year after year leaving the plantation in devastation." The man smoothed his moustache. "Through this, I learned the pines, or the hardwoods rather, made it possible to conquer the erosion of the land. This method is by far the most successful."

The group moved on. Darby had placed so many sign boards he declared he would be doing so in his sleep. Hard as it was, he found himself preoccupied with other thoughts. Thoughts of *her*. Bella.

His heart seemed very much like the forest without the touch of the master. Confusion, guilt, and longing seemed to choke out the true feeling that was still trying to grow. Loneliness stood in the way of companionship. Stubbornness kept the willing heart at bay. He felt unsure what held back his love for Bella. Pride, maybe? But how was he to conquer this erosion, the depletion of the heart, on his own?

Darby's mind went back to Tip One. The trees had been close knit. There was no pruning involved; the trees took care of themselves. Even more so, the lumber produced from such formation was of the highest quality.

Finally, as though a light shined from the outer darkness, Darby concluded that in order to defeat the current emotions swarming inside, he would have to do some major reforestation and allow the floodgates of his heart to open, holding back nothing. Then *that* feeling he shared with Bella could regrow and flourish just like the strong pines among Biltmore Forest had done.

"I just haven't been sleeping well, Fran. I assure you there is nothing wrong." Bella wound her way toward the other end of the room trying to escape her reflection in the mirror.

"Honey, I know a damsel in distress when I see one. Now tell me, what is going on?" Fran followed Bella's every step.

"Nothing." Bella laughed nonchalantly.

Fran took the feather duster from Bella and tossed it aside. "Here, sit. Let's talk."

"There is nothing to talk about. Really, I'm fine." Bella protested.

"Then explain those dark rings around yer eyes, hmmm."

Bella covered her face with her hands. She didn't wish to be in such a shape. She did look terrible but like she had said, sleep had been far from her. "I just need some sleep. That's all." Bella withdrew her hands from her face only to discover Fran ready to pull back the coverlet.

"What are you doing?!" Bella stood to slow the action. "I can't sleep in here!"

Fran froze and rested her fists on her hips. "Then I suggest you talk. If not," she pointed to the bed, "I will pick up your tiny self and deposit you there until you get rest."

Bella sized Fran up once again. Fran could turn her into a pretzel if she wished to do so. Maybe she should talk. A little.

"Fine. I'll talk." Bella huffed.

"Thought so. Now, why can't you sleep at night?" Fran took a seat directly beside where Bella had just sat.

Bella let out a sigh. "It's not that simple of a question."

"I'm good at listening to not so simple answers. Spit it out."

"Good grief, Fran. Are you this way with everybody?"

Fran smiled. "No. I'm only this way with you because I see that there is something robbing you of your happiness and your peace, not to mention your beauty sleep. Your smile has faded and has been replaced with a sadness. There's a distant look in your eyes that prevents you from noticing the blessings at your fingertips. The ring in your voice is no longer there. You are in a prison, Bella, and I just can't stand to see you like this." Fran held her tears in check. "Sometimes when you talk about the things that bother you, it breaks the chains and freedom slips in a little at a time. Then before you know it, the burden is rolled away."

"How do you know? You're always happy."

Fran's aging hand took Bella's. "I know this because I talk to God about my problems all the time."

"Oh." The moment became a hush. Bella didn't want to talk about God right now. It was because of Him that she was in the predicament she was in. If God had not allowed her Papa to die, then she wouldn't have to be here right now. Mama wouldn't be turning to a bottle trying to find what she once had. Ashlynn's physical condition wouldn't be in jeopardy. She wouldn't have met Darby nor Sophia. She wouldn't have known about her other sister. None of this heartache would have existed if God hadn't let her Papa die.

"Bella?"

"Hmmm."

"Tell me what you are thinking." Fran's angelic voice knocked on her hearts door. How did she know Bella was thinking about her problems?

"Well, you already know about my Papa." Bella couldn't stop the tear from rolling down her cheek. It fell to her lap with a thud.

"Yes, now go on."

Bella took a deep breath trying to contain her emotions. "When he passed," Bella swallowed the cry of agony, "everything changed." Her words fell from her lips in a whisper. "I have a sister nine years younger than myself. She suffered from polio when she was five. The disease left her crippled." Another tear fell to her lap.

"I'm so sorry."

Bella shrugged, "My dream was to help her achieve physical strength, so she could walk as well as anybody."

"It can still be. You won't be here forever, Bella."

"Then, once I began working here, I see Ashlynn and Mama very little. When I do see them, Mama is passed out on the couch." Another tear fell to her lap.

Fran offered her handkerchief. Bella accepted. "She needs to see someone strong, like you. If you crumble under the load, then yer Ma will not have any hope."

Bella looked up and found Fran's compassionate eyes. "How do you know?"

"I just do. Now, tell me more."

"Okay. From the first day I arrived here at Biltmore, Sophia has detested me. At first, I didn't understand why. Then one evening, I had finally had enough."

"Why did she hate you? I couldn't imagine anyone feeling that way toward you."

Bella really wanted to keep the reason to herself. It was embarrassing. Humiliating. Bella just shook her head. "I don't know."

"Yes, you do. Now tell me."

Bella remained silent.

"The sooner you talk about it, the better you'll feel."

Another tear rolled down Bella's cheek. "She's my... she's my..."

"She's your what?" Fran spoke softly.

"Sister." The word fell in a whisper, but was powerful enough to mute the entire room. Even the song birds just outside the window had hushed. Even time seemed to stop in reverence of the truth. Bella took a deep breath, "I'm worried for her."

"Why?"

"I haven't seen her. She caused so many problems. I'm afraid she was forced to leave Biltmore." Bella shook her head in disgust.

"So you care for her even though she hates you." It wasn't a question, but it was the spoken truth. Bella did care for the one who detested her so. A daughter of her Papa's. Her sister.

"It seems so." Bella agreed.

"You haven't seen her since that night?"

"No." Bella wiped away another tear.

"That's because she is spending her time ironing countless articles of clothing."

Bella swiftly met Fran's stare. "Really? How do you know?"

"That's why you should start joining us ladies while we sit and sew." She patted Bella's lap, "You learn lots of valuable information."

Bella laughed a little. "Is that so?"

"Yes, now tell me what else weighs heavy on your heart."

How did Fran know that there was something else? Hadn't

she confessed enough to bring the whole world to their knees? Bella decided against sharing her most precious thoughts.

Darby.

As long as breath continued to keep her body alive, she would never forget how he rescued her yesterday. She could have been hurt, or even killed, but he intervened. Bella would never let the memory slip away. How he carried her to a nearby grassy spot and lifted his canteen to her lips. Instantly, her fingertips glided across where the canteen had been. She remembered the sweet taste and wondered if it belonged to Darby. And he had offered her riding lessons! She had declined of course, but deep inside, butterflies hatched from their cocoons and fluttered mercilessly in her tummy. She would love to ride horseback with him. Just like Sophia had done, but it was only a dream. One that could never come true.

"Well, I'm waiting." Fran tapped her foot onto the floor.

"That's all, Fran, and thank you for listening. I feel better already."

"There's more." Fran's keen eye evaluated the distant look in Bella's eyes. "I know a girl in love when I see one."

"In love?" Bella laughed. Could she possibly be *in love*? No. "What in the world makes you think that?" she asked.

Fran took on a painful expression. "Your smile, it doesn't quite make it to your eyes."

"Huh?"

"If he were to walk in this room right now, I wouldn't be able to dust the smile from your face." Fran held up the cleaning instrument. "Not even with this here fox's tail."

Bella just shook her head.

"Who is he?" Fran asked.

"No one. Now let's get to work."

"Not until I know his name and how you met. And the last time you've seen him and the next time you're going to see him." Fran declared.

Bella's mouth stood agape. She quickly clamped her lips together. With folded arms, she quirked her eyebrow and challenged her friend. "What if I don't?"

"Then I shall send word to Humphrey that you request his first dance at the next barn gathering."

Bella gasped. "You wouldn't!"

"There's just one way to find out." Fran smiled triumphantly. She was a winner either way.

Something told Bella that Fran would not hesitate to do so. She took a deep breath, "His name is Darby Pierson. I met him here at Biltmore. I saw him yesterday, and only God knows the next time. Happy now?"

"That's it. You're lovesick." Fran added with a gleam in her eyes.

"Am not." Bella argued.

"Are too." Fran countered.

"Why do you think that?" Bella asked.

"Because your smile reached all the way to your eyes when you mentioned his name."

Bella couldn't help it; her smile broadened.

Fran had been right. She did feel better. The burden was definitely lighter.

"There's just one thing I have to say, Bella," Fran added.

"What's that?"

"You're just gonna have to learn to dance in the rain that your storm brings."

CHAPTER TWENTY TWO

"THANK YOU, HUMPHREY." Bella said as she tucked the tail of her skirts tightly about her legs, careful not to let the carriage door nip at the hems. Her body fell back against the plush seat when the horses pulled forward. Always before, Bella had ridden in the front with Morton. But not with Humphrey.

The sway of the carriage rocked her form from side to side as her gaze remained fastened on the world outside the window. The Approach Road no longer had the luscious appeal of abundant greenery. Instead, the trees had been painted the most beautiful hues of autumn. Peach and orange leaves were intertwined with pink and red. Flecks of yellow were sifted into the artwork of God, balancing in perfect unison.

Bella's hands rung continually in her lap. She tried ignoring the rapid pace of her heart while she rehearsed the words Ashlynn had written in the letter. Bella had found the piece of mail when she returned to her chamber last evening. Inside the wrinkled envelope was the message that stopped Bella in her tracks.

Her Mama was going to church? A place she hadn't been since Ashlynn was diagnosed with polio? And she wanted Bella to be part of it?

Bella took deep, even breaths when the sight of the church filled her vision. This time it would be different. She would sit next to her Mama, and her Papa would not be there.

The carriage came to a halt, bringing Bella back into the present hour. The door opened with ease. Bella accepted the hand Humphrey offered and stepped down. Her eyes took in the image. The church had changed very little, if none at all. The children still played *Ring A-round the Rosie.* Pastor Jimmy Jackson still stood at his post beside the door, greeting all who entered.

"Thank you, Humphrey." Bella said as she stepped away from the safety of the carriage.

"You are very welcome, Bella." The young, chunky fellow blushed.

"We will depart as soon as service is dismissed." Bella said as she pulled the shawl tighter, making timely steps toward the church. She allowed her eyes to roam, finding no sign of her Mama nor Ashlynn. Her steps led her toward the wooden planks that ascended to the tiny porch where the pastor was standing. With each step, the wooden surface gave way, screaking from the force of her feet.

"Bella."

She lifted her gaze to the same set of hazel eyes that were filled with an abundance of love and kindness. "Pastor Jackson."

The smiling minister took Bella by the shoulders and said, "I am overjoyed to see you here today. Ruth Ann was right; you have grown into a lovely young woman."

Bella blushed, "Thank you, Pastor."

"Your Mama will be thrilled to see you here," he said.

Bella followed the direction of his hand and was surprised to find her Mama and Ashlynn sitting two pews up from the back, the same place she and her Papa often sat. Ashlynn's bright blonde ponytail radiated from the sun's light seeping through the window, and her Mama's arm laid gently about Ashlynn's shoulders. The sight made Bella smile.

She proceeded through the door, welcomed by the warmth of the burning coals radiating from the stove. When her Mama caught sight of her figure, she turned and greeted Bella with a smile that had been hiding behind hardened features for years. Bella felt the corners of her mouth lift involuntarily. She met her Mama's embrace with open arms. The heavy scent of cedar testified of her Mama's nearness, her firm arms clasping Bella against her bosom.

She relished the intimate moment for as long as her Mama held to her. She felt the internal walls about her heart crumble under the power of love and disintegrate into tiny pieces of hope. Tears of forgiveness fled down Bella's cheeks, dispersing the bitterness that was once harbored inside her soul. For the first time in a long time, the bond between mother and daughter made itself manifest, building strongholds in desert places.

Bella withdrew herself from her Mama and looked into a set of eyes that had once been desolate, but was now full of solicitude.

"I am so glad ya came, Bella. Here, you sit in the middle," her Mama instructed.

Bella willingly took her place after giving her sister a warm hug.

"I've missed you, Bella." Ashlynn said with a smile.

After placing a kiss on Ashlynn's forehead, Bella said, "I've missed you more."

The sound of the church bell silenced the Sabbath day crowd, making known the stampede of children hurrying to their mamas' sides.

Bella's eyes followed the slow, but steady pastor as he made his way to the Bible stand. "We are glad to have each and every soul present this morning." Pastor Jackson greeted the hushed congregation with a compassionate smile. "Let us all go before the Lord in prayer."

Darby knew where his Ma could be found. Church. He almost decided against the idea of attending Sunday morning worship, yet here he stood anyway. Thankfully he had slipped in without being noticed, taking his place inside the foyer.

Everyone was standing, and the songbooks were opened wide. They were singing his favorite song, *In the Sweet By and By*. Darby joined in. Immediately, Pastor Jackson spotted him. The man laid his book down and cast Darby a wistful smile. Darby watched as the frail man stepped down from the pulpit and made his way toward him. The pastor wrapped his arms around

Darby, embracing him firmly. "Good to have you, boy!"

"Glad to be here, pastor." Darby's gaze followed the elderly man as he made his way back to where he once stood, taking the songbook into his hands again.

Darby allowed his eyes to wander as the group of saints continued to sing. Immediately, his stare fell upon his Ma and Pa. Careful not to distract, Darby stepped past the two pews that separated them, taking his place beside his Ma. She greeted him with a warm smile while her frail hand patted his. On the other hand, his Pa awarded him with a nod and directed his gaze back to the songbook in his hands. Darby swallowed the bitter rejection, lifting his voice in perfect harmony unto The Lord.

A movement to his left begged for Darby's attention. His heart constricted when he saw a very familiar set of hands massaging the lifeless foot of a young girl. He allowed his eyes to venture up her arm and study the twisted braid hanging over her shoulder. He didn't need to see her face. He knew it was Bella. He should have known she was within his vicinity since the scent of cinnamon sugar dominated his senses.

Suddenly, his collar felt tight. Darby willed himself to look away, directing his gaze to where it belonged.

The last words of the hymn were sung, bringing the congregation to take their seats.

"I do have wonderful news for all of us, every sinner." Pastor Jackson retrieved the spectacles from his shirt pocket. "*For God so loved the world that He gave His only begotten Son that whosoever believeth in Him should not perish but have everlasting life. For God sent not His Son into the world to condemn the world but that the world through Him might be saved."*

After wiping his eyes, Pastor Jackson lifted his gaze to the congregation sitting before him. Compassion vibrated from his hazelnut eyes. "That portion of scripture is enough to save the entire world, just forty seven words. Amen."

The congregation echoed, "Amen."

"This morning in prayer, The Lord laid another scripture upon my heart. If you will follow me in your Bible, let us turn to the book of Romans, chapter eight and verse twenty eight."

Darby dared a glance from the corner of his eye and noted that Bella had scooted close to the woman beside her, shuffling the pages of the worn Bible in search of the scripture that seemed to be hidden.

The kind pastor cleared his voice, gaining Darby's attention, and read, "*And we know that all things work together for good to them that love God, to them who are the called according to His purpose.*"

Darby listened intently as Pastor Jackson delivered his heart. "We all know sometimes life does not go as planned. Amen. Oft times we wonder the purpose of those twists and turns that we can't explain. If you'll look at the scripture with me once more, you'll notice that the Word says *all* things." He studied the congregation. "Sometimes we come upon the crossroads of life, a place we had not planned to travel. Friend, let not our hearts be troubled, but let us put our trust in The One who paves the road that leads to eternal life and forget not that all things, whether good or bad, work together for the good."

The congregation echoed, "Amen."

Darby's heart hammered mercilessly inside his chest. How did he know how Darby felt? Did he really mean God controlled all things great and small? Seems as though he had gotten the answer he was in search of without even speaking to his Ma about it. Ma always had an answer for everything, but the pastor's Sunday morning sermon summed it all up.

"It is not by chance that we are here this morning. For God has a plan for every man, woman, boy, and girl. If God seems far away, we can get close to Him right here." The man's finger pointed below, to the altar. "In matter of fact, we can pray anywhere. At home, at work, at school. Wherever we might be, in whatever state we are in, we can talk to The Master."

The preacher flipped through the pages of his Bible, "In God's plan, there are seasons." His eyes observed the saints before him. "In the book of Ecclesiastes, we can learn that there is a time and purpose for everything under the heavens." He cleared his voice. "*A time to be born, and a time to die; a time to plant, and a time to pluck up that which is planted.....*

"*A time to weep, and a time to laugh; a time to mourn, and a time to dance.....*"

Bella tried to swallow, but her throat was too dry. She had never heard such beautiful poetry and found it quite hard to believe the poem had been around for ages. Its words seemed to seep into her soul, her understanding being made manifest.

But as quickly as the words brought peace, Bella was bombarded by the same questions that had been haunting her mind for months. Her eyes darted to her left and to her right. There was no way out except for crossing over Ashlynn's stubborn limb that had finally found comfort.

Instead of remaining seated, Bella tried skirting around her sister's leg. She kept her gaze fastened to the wooden floor until she recognized the large, brown boots across the aisle. Bringing her eyes upward, Bella lost her footing. Her body lunged forward, but before she plummeted to her utter destruction, she caught herself.

Without taking the time to retrieve her shawl that had fallen in the aisle, Bella hurried out of the church. Knowing her face was aflame, Bella rushed to the carriage to hide until Humphrey arrived.

Her hand reached for the handle, but when she yanked its slender form, it didn't budge.

Locked.

Ignoring the bitter taste of humility streaming down her cheeks, Bella ran toward the creek that flowed behind the little church. The chill of autumn enveloped her as the breeze rippled through the air. She hugged herself, perfectly aware of the missing shawl.

Bella's back settled against the rough siding, caring not that it pulled at her hair. She paid no mind to the leaves floating down the stream, nor the squirrel packing nuts. Instead, her eyes drifted closed, trying to erase the *Words of the Preacher*. Darby held the threadbare shawl in his hands. How Bella kept warm from the piece of material, he didn't know. He stepped easily around the side of the church, careful not to startle her. His heart warmed at the sight of Bella leaned comfortably against the church's outer wall, taking note of her closed eyes and rosy cheeks.

As he stepped closer, Darby was able to count the tears dripping from her chin. Her silent cry caused something inside him to ache. He took a deep breath, inhaling the cinnamon wafting in the wind. His hands longed to reach out and take her into his arms, but he refrained.

Instead, his foot stepped on a branch. The snap of the brittle twig immediately opened her eyes. For a moment, he thought she was going to bolt and run. Again.

But to Darby's surprise, she remained perfectly still until he draped the thin shawl around her shoulders. His thumb gently caught the stray tear making swift action down her cheek.

"Do you need to talk?" he asked.

Bella boldly answered, "No." She also refused to look into his eyes. Instead, she was focused on something far away.

He shoved his hands into his pockets and kicked at the fallen acorns. "What are you running from?"

Her gaze collided with his. "You."

His heart faltered. Partly, he believed her. But perhaps she was running from more than just him. She moved away from the church and stepped toward the stream. Thankfully, she didn't protest when he followed.

"What else are you running from, Bella?" Darby asked.

She froze. Again her eyes took on something beyond the stream. "The truth," she whispered.

"The truth? Why run from it?"

"Because it hurts, Darby!"

He flinched at the fierce pitch in her voice, but he understood her feelings entirely. Sometimes the truth was painful. Very painful. He stepped close to her, taking the strand of hair that often fell across her brow and tucking it behind her ear.

"Talk to me, Bella." He whispered against her temple. "Tell me what hurts."

She just shook her head.

Silence proved that her words were muted, so Darby felt for the charm in his pocket. Perhaps it would ignite the flame that had once been blazing.

"Here, let me have your hand," he said.

Bella was hesitant at first, but she finally laid her chilled hand in his. Darby turned her palm upward and pressed the charm into its core. When he removed his hand from hers, he watched the color drain from her cheeks. Slowly her eyes lifted to his.

"*You* stole my heart?" her voice trembled.

Darby smiled as his thumb stroked her cheek gently. "No," he said, "I found it."

CHAPTER TWENTY THREE

BELLA STARED AT THE CHARM in her hand. It seemed as though it shined brighter than it had before. Maybe it was just her, but it also felt much heavier. She fought the urge to ask him where he found it. If her intuition had been correct, Sophia had taken it from the trinket box. But how did it find its way to Darby?

"I would put it in safe keeping if I were you," Darby suggested.

Bella looked up at him. "It was in safe keeping when it vanished." She slid the precious stone into her pocket, patting it gently.

"May I see it?" he asked.

"Huh?" Bella snagged him with a curious gaze.

"The charm. May I see it?" his eyes pleaded.

A tiny smile formed on her lips as her hand felt for the heart. "What are you going to do with it?" she asked as she dropped it into the palm of his large hand.

"You'll see," he said as he withdrew a shiny gold chain from the pocket of his shirt. Bella watched, confused, as he slid the chain through the tiny opening above the crevice of the heart. Her breath caught and held when he closed the gap between them, bringing his hands around her slender neck and connecting the ends of the chain together.

The charm fell against her chest, next to her heart. Instantly, it seemed as though her heartbeat took on a rhythm of its own. Her eyes sought Darby's. The flicker was still there. The gentle breeze fanned the flame. His hand cradled her cheek as he tilted her face upward. His thumb ran along her cheekbone and across her lips. Then he withdrew his hand and stepped back. Bella felt the chill make its way to her bones. Her hand felt for the chain that held the charm, and her palm enclosed about the warm, diamond plated heart. "Thank you, Darby."

He smiled. "You're welcome, Bella. Now I won't have to worry about someone else stealing your heart."

Bella held her tears in check as she climbed inside the carriage, keeping her gaze fastened upon the window that allowed her eyes to absorb the happiness that her Mama felt. There they stood, Mama and Ashlynn, waving their handkerchiefs high.

Bella's heart throbbed. She didn't know when she would see them again. Part of her wanted to forget Biltmore and return home, but the twenty five dollars she earned each month kept the Westbrook house in operation. Perhaps her Mama could make a trip or two to the mercantile to purchase material for a new dress, or maybe Ashlynn could buy stationery with matching envelopes.

Bella knew there was plenty of food in the pantry, especially since her Mama found redemption. No longer would she be left to worry if Ashlynn was fed or exercising her weakened limbs properly. She didn't have to guess if her hard earned wages supported the local tavern. Instead, Bella could see at least ten percent of the money falling into the offering pan on Sunday morning.

Bella waved her hand without ceasing as the carriage pulled away, keeping her tears at bay. The image of the two whom she loved dearly grew smaller and smaller. Finally, she dropped her hand, but it didn't quite make it to her lap. Instead, it paused where the heart laid against her chest. She gripped its form within her palm.

Bella allowed her eyes to close and relish the face of the one who had grown to care for her. The one who placed the chain about her neck. The one who was always there when she needed him. He had departed Sunday service with his Ma and Pa.

Bella released her breath and tried piecing together everything shared between them. Only minutes after he hooked the chain about her neck, a stampede of children invaded the quiet, bringing their tryst to an abrupt halt.

But before he departed with his parents, Darby had whispered something into her ear. He had said, "There is a time of loss and a time to gain back that which was lost."

Bella didn't really understand what he had meant by the statement, and there was no time to ask for an explanation. But she did know that he must have created a proverb of his own. She was certain Pastor Jackson had said no such thing this morning. All she recollected were the words of the preacher and how the message pierced her heart.

Bella allowed her head to fall back against the seat, her lips lifting at the corners. Fran would have a time gaining her undivided attention this evening.

Darby tried to disregard the thick air surrounding him as he took his place at the supper table. His Pa had not muttered a word while they put the horses away. Neither had he shown appreciation when Darby fed every beast and gave them fresh water to drink. But his Ma, on the other hand, had made up for his Pa's short comings.

"And I made yer favorite, son. Peach cobbler with a smidgen of cinnamon."

Darby eyed the steaming dish with golden brown crust peeking over the edges, sprinkled with cinnamon specks. *Cinnamon.* Only the face of the one who had captured his heart came to mind. "My, it sure smells good, Ma. Thank you."

"But ya have to eat yer beans first."

"Don't fret. I have been longing to sit at your dinner table for weeks now," Darby declared as he piled a mountain of fried potatoes onto his plate, right beside the cornbread wedges.

"Hmph!" His Pa gestured before stuffing his mouth with a spoonful of beans.

"Charles," his Ma adjusted the peach cobbler, "only good boys get their share." She quirked an eyebrow before taking her seat beside her husband.

The remainder of the dinner was eaten in silence until his Pa pushed back the plate and placed his folded hands upon his round belly. "Who's the girl?"

Darby nearly choked on the dry pieces of cornbread. He quickly drained his glass of milk, and with a thud, he placed the glass onto the wooden table. Darby brought his watery eyes up toward his Pa who sat boldly, waiting for an answer.

"Her name is Bella." Darby said weakly.

"I think she is very pretty," his Ma complimented.

"I didn't ask you, Odetta. I asked him."

"And he answered you, Charles. I merely gave my opinion."

Darby bit back a grin.

Charles rolled his eyes and asked, "Where does she live?"

"Right now she boards at Biltmore House because she works there."

"Oh, so you've studied more than just the forests?" Charles challenged him.

The chair screaked when Darby scooted it away from the table, his fist still resting beside the empty plate. "Actually, I've learned more than I anticipated."

"Oh? Would ya mind sharin' the whole of it? Can't wait to hear where my money was spent."

Odetta gasped. "Charles Wayne Pierson! Ya know the boy paid his fare. Not a dime of yer money was used!"

"Ma," Darby said calmly, "it's fine, really there is not much to explain." His eyes darted to his Pa. "I found it interesting to know that white pines are the most prosperous trees used to replenish depleted forests, and they are less expensive."

With a huff, Charles rolled his eyes and argued, "There ya go about the forests again. You should know better than anybody that Charles Pierson will not spend a dime more than necessary."

Darby knew that. But Darby also knew that if there was to be a future for his children and his children's children, reforestation had to begin now. Not tomorrow. Not next year. Not during the next century. But it had to begin now.

Darby threw up his hands in protest. "Whatever happened to restoration? Conservation? Did someone unwittingly forget about their seed and their days to come?" Fury shown across Darby's tight brow. "It looks to me as if you don't care if Pierson Enterprises exists or not. You've already lined your pockets and filled your wallet!"

Color filled Charles' bearded face. Immediately, Darby felt convicted for his careless tongue. He opened his mouth to apologize, but it was too late.

Charles arose and withdrew his wallet, opening it with a thrust, revealing its emptiness. "Jus' so you know, Darby, Pierson Enterprises lost its contract las' month. It's goin' under." With that being said, Charles allowed the bare wallet slip through his fingers and fall beside the steaming cobbler.

Darby's gaze locked onto the worn, leather wallet. The screen door slammed shut, leaving only the distant echo of his Pa's footsteps to fade into silence. This couldn't be happening.

Pierson Enterprises had been operating for over fifty years. The thriving lumber business had belonged to Bennett Pierson, Darby's grandfather. Then it was placed into Charles' hands. Then it should have fallen to Darby.

Darby tried swallowing the rush of bile burning his throat. He would just have to find something else. Become a forester maybe. After all, he did have extensive knowledge in the field, and it did interest him more than anything. Well, maybe not everything. Bella was by far the most interesting specimen he had ever studied. *Bella.* What would become of her if he left the Forest School? What if he moved very far away for many, many years?

Darby just stared at the bowl of Peach Cobbler his Ma placed in front of him. The smell of cinnamon danced in the steam. An image of Bella dancing in his arms came to mind. His chest clinched tightly when he imagined her slipping from his grip and dancing alone. That's what would happen if he left. She would have to learn to dance by herself.

"Thank you, Ma." Darby relished the scrumptious bite of cobbler, the taste of cinnamon lingering on his tongue. "It is wonderful."

"You're welcome, son." Odetta took her seat next to him. "I noticed yer foot is doin' good."

Darby nodded. "It is, thanks to Bella."

"Bella? What do ya mean?"

The spoon paused its motion, resting against the side of the bowl. *Bella.* Dear God above, if it had not been for Bella, his life would be in ruins. Had he been dismissed from Biltmore Forest School altogether, then there would be no future for him at all. Instead, the beautiful angel had shared her gift of healing, sacrificing her time. Time that could have been spent with her sister, but instead she spent it with him.

Darby inhaled deeply trying to digest more than just the cobbler. "She has an interest in physiotherapy because her sister suffers a limp, also." He cast his Ma a cautious glance and watched her eyes fill with brightness. The side of Darby's mouth lifted at her approval, "During her spare time, Bella worked with my unsteady gait." He flexed his foot, "As you can see, the girl has a gift."

His Ma's eyes brimmed with tears, "A miracle," she whispered.

"My thoughts exactly."

"How'd ya meet?" she asked.

Here we go, he thought. "Like I said, she works at Biltmore House. She is a maid there." Darby cleared his throat, "She had the book I needed. *The Philosophy of Physiotherapy*."

"Hmmm," she studied him with her keen eye. "So she loaned ya her book, huh?"

"Yes." He shook his head, "I got nowhere with it though." Darby sluggishly met his Ma's gaze, "That's when we started meeting on the terrace."

"Oh, I see."

Did she really see what Darby hoped she would see? Truth was, he had decided to visit his mother because he was confused.

Confused about life. Confused about Bella. Now he was confused about Pierson Enterprises as well.

"So, she is more than just a friend now," his Ma concluded.

Darby directed his gaze toward her. She hadn't asked a question, she had clarified the truth. "I guess it's something like that." He shrugged his shoulder. "It is for me at least."

"It's that way for her, too," she said.

"It is?"

She laughed. "I know a girl in love when I see one. I used to be one, ya know."

Darby felt the heat rising above his collarbone.

"She wouldn't take her eyes off of ya. I watched her."

"You did?" Darby asked.

His Ma nodded her head. "She wasn't the only one doin' the gazin'."

"No, she wasn't. It looks like you are just as guilty as she is." He stood up from his chair, gently patting his Ma on the head. "Thank you for the dinner, Ma. It was heavenly. Now I need to find my Pa."

Darby went to the barn first but only found it occupied with horses. His eyes roamed the hayfields, but they were bare. He felt tempted to call out to him, but there was no use. Darby knew his Pa wouldn't answer.

There was just one place left to look. That was the forest, the place where he and his Pa often went hunting. Perhaps he could find his Pa perched on the same rock that had been there for ages. "The sanctuary," as his Pa would say, "a place I like to jus' go and think."

The shadows swallowed up Darby's form, his head bobbing up and down to dodge the overgrown branches. The worn out path didn't look so ragged anymore. Pods of grass had grown along the way but had now turned the color of brown. The leaves crunched underneath his feet as he drew near rock, the place his Pa might be.

Once the tall trees opened and revealed the rock that was hidden safely within their guard, Darby's gaze collided with his Pa's. The knife in his father's hand froze, as well as Darby's breath. For a moment, Darby thought his Pa would refuse him; instead, he watched his Pa's rough hands close the knife and toss the chunk of cedar to the ground.

"Don't stop whittling because of me," Darby said as he stepped closer.

"Well then, reach me that piece of wood."

Darby stooped down, taking the smooth piece of cedar into his hand. "You've been working on this a while."

"About thirty minutes."

Darby ignored the ill tone in his Pa's voice as well as his short answers and handed him the wooden chunk. Immediately, his Pa went to work, the tiny shavings curling in perfection and dropping to the rock's surface.

Darby just stood there and watched. Finally, his Pa scooted over. Taking that as an invitation, Darby sat down. "Thanks."

Charles mumbled something under his breath and continued working.

"I came to apologize, Pa."

"Fer what?" Charles asked.

Darby sighed. "For how I talked to you."

"Is that all?" his Pa asked, whittling away.

Darby's eyelids slid together. He said a silent prayer asking God to intervene at this present moment. "Yeah, that's all." Darby humbly replied.

"Hmph."

The moment grew silent as the evening grew colder. Darby's insides grew perplexed. Was there really a need to try when the response only caused more pain? If only he could say something...

"I heard there's a possum hunt goin' on at the fair," his Pa said.

"There is." Darby had suggested the idea. It was a favorite sport of his own, and definitely a favorite of his Pa's. For seven straight years, Charles Pierson had been the champion of the Asheville Possum Hunt, taking the grand prize home every time.

"I won't be there," Charles whittled some more. "Got better things to do."

"Since when did anything get better than possum hunting?" Darby asked sarcastically.

Charles paused his motion as if he were searching for a sufficient reason to be absent. "Today."

CHAPTER TWENTY FOUR

SOPHIA WAS GETTING USE TO her new job. Ironing laundry. The transition did not surprise her any at all. Even more so, Sophia had expected to be fired. She knew she had been found out when Mrs. King demanded her presence at once. The Matron had questioned Bella about her serving skills. Immediately, Sophia's sneaky ways had come to light.

She was paying for her behavior now. If she hadn't wiped her brow for the hundredth time, then she hadn't done so once. She ironed for six hours without ceasing. By the end of the sixth hour, Sophia had ironed over one hundred pieces. She had seen enough petticoats, skirts, handkerchiefs, pillow cases, and stockings to make one sick. At least she had the luxury of using an electric iron.

"Well, you put your time in. What's left?" Hannah asked as she took the iron from Sophia.

"That." Sophia pointed to a neat stack of clean laundry ready to be pressed.

"All of that needs ironing? What have you been doing?" Hannah asked unbelieving.

"I've pressed over one hundred pieces. There were two hundred and nineteen articles when I began." Sophia rotated her aching shoulder. Glad that Hannah didn't press further, Sophia was relieved to escape the heat enveloped room. She was surprised to find Mrs. King patiently waiting just outside the door.

"I hear that you are proving well." Was the Matron actually smiling at her?

"Thank you, ma'am."

"I know you are finished with your chores for the day, but I needed a favor of you." Mrs. King explained. "Mrs. Schenck has politely asked for a couple of girls to assist her during the festival. She asked that they be proficient in food preparation, serving, and clean up." Mrs. King took in Sophia's disheveled appearance. "You have enough time to freshen up and to darn a clean uniform. She will be waiting in the Breakfast Room."

Mrs. King turned and walked away. She hadn't give Sophia much of a choice. Not that it would have mattered. Sophia was delighted to assist Mrs. Schenck. Anything to keep her from ironing.

Sophia gleefully skipped to her room and did as Mrs. King had instructed. She even added some powders for a pleasant scent. Her feet were drawing near the Breakfast Room when she heard excessive chattering and laughter. When the massive archway revealed the room and all its elegance, should she have been shocked to discover Mrs. Schenck's company?

Bella.

Bella stood there with the suitcase in hand. She had packed everything she owned, including her book. She and Sophia were to board at the Schenck's home through the duration of the Forest Fair, which was only for three days. Bella feared it would seem like an eternity.

Still, Bella was struggling trying to digest the facts about Sophia. The more she studied Sophia's features, the more confused she became. Nothing about Sophia resembled her Papa at all, but surely if it was true and she really was her sister, something common would make itself known. At least she had three days to figure it out.

Sophia settled herself across from Bella in the carriage. She offered a cold smile; the drudgery was evident. Bella chose to gaze out the window instead of looking upon her dreaded foe. The late fall chill had already taken over. Bella pulled her cloak tighter. If the ride grew any colder, she could possibly freeze to death.

Finally, late that afternoon, they arrived at the Schenck's home nestled in the middle of the Pisgah Forest. Bella bailed out of the carriage without the aid of her uncle. The cottage was plain but nice. A long porch stretched across the entire front of the house. It reminded Bella of her own home, except hers was much smaller.

"May I assist you, madam?"

Bella turned and gasped. "Darby! What are you doing here?"

He cocked his head to the side, "I go to school here, so I believe that gives me the liberty to return the question. What are you doing here?" he asked as he took her suitcase into his hand.

"I will be helping Mrs. Schenck during the festival." Bella tried to ignore the spicy scent wafting in the breeze.

"Really?" Darby smiled.

Bella kept the ripple of excitement at bay. She shouldn't be thrilled, but she was. It seemed as though the further the distance was between them, the more she longed for his nearness, especially since he hooked the chain around her neck. Automatically her hand felt for the charm.

Darby's eyes followed her hand. "I see you haven't lost your heart."

Bella turned three shades of pink. "Nope, haven't lost it."

"Will you stay for the entire weekend?" Darby asked as he led Bella toward the steps.

"Yes." Bella cleared her throat. "Sophia and I are preparing the dinner with Mrs. Schenck."

Darby's countenance fell at the mention of Sophia. He must not have noticed that she had tagged along. But soon his features were filled with excitement, "How about a hike up Mount Pisgah?" His close proximity sent shivers down Bella's spine.

Bella glanced at his foot. "I don't know," she hesitated. "How's your foot?"

"Couldn't be better."

"Good, let's keep it that way."

"But I want to take you," he whispered against her ear. "You deserve it." Darby sat Bella's suitcase beside the door and grasped her hand. "Promise me you'll go if I can arrange it."

Bella tried looking away from his probing gaze, but it was impossible. "But what about your foot?"

"We will go on horseback," his lips curled, "but I'm taking the reins."

"You can't guide two horses, silly." Bella withdrew her hand from his, taking the charm into her palm again.

"I only have one horse, Bella."

"Oh. Right. One horse." She cleared her tight throat.

Darby slipped his fingers around hers, taking hold of her hand once more, the padding of his thumb drawing countless circles. "I really want you to see the world from up there, Bella."

"I-I don't know."

"Please, Bella. For me. For you. We deserve it."

Bella silently searched for another way out, but there was none. Truly, she was delighted to share such an experience with Darby. Finally, she agreed. "Okay, I will."

A deadly smile formed on his handsome face before stooping over and placing his warm lips against her cold hand. Bella felt the heat travel up her wrist and disperse through every fiber inside her heart.

"Until then, my *belle*."

Bella watched him turn away and walk perfectly down the steps. She couldn't help but smile. "Goodbye, Darby," she whispered as she watched him join a group of young men. Before he mounted his horse, he smiled warmly, and then trotted away with the others.

"I do not want to see you near him again." The sudden sound of her uncle's angry voice rang in her ears. She had been so absorbed in Darby's presence that she had forgotten all about Morton and Sophia. Bella turned to her uncle with a new resolve.

"I don't think it is for you to choose whether I see him or not." Bella bit back.

"I believe it is my business. You are my niece, and I made sure you had a job to come to." Morton's dark eyes pierced Bella's. "Stay away from him or you will lose it all."

Tears pricked Bella's eyes. Could Morton not see that she had already lost so much? Did he not know that Darby healed the pain of loss when she was near him? "There's not much more I could lose, Uncle Morton, but I refuse to lose Darby at whatever the cost."

"Even your position? You care more for him than your job?"

"I like my job." Bella's eyes grew distant as if she was in a world of her own. "But I love Darby."

Bella had found comfort at the Schenck's home. Mr. Schenck had left shortly after she and Sophia had arrived, leaving them to prepare the serving schedule with Mrs. Schenck.

"How about a picnic or a luncheon?" Bella suggested.

Mrs. Schenck's eyes lit up. "That's a wonderful idea. Carl mentioned a possum hunt and music with dancing. A luncheon would fit perfectly." She jotted the idea onto her memo. "Who is good at baking bread?"

Bella and Sophia looked at one another. Neither of them moved.

"How about both of you work together on it, and I will prepare the meats?"

Before Bella could protest and offer to help Mrs. Schenck, the lady had already directed them to their post. "Here are the eggs, and there is the milk and flour." Mrs. Schenck turned on her heel, "Please be sure the pan is greased well!" her voice echoed from the far end of the long kitchen.

Bella just stared at the bowl and wooden spoon. As shameful as it was, she had never baked bread before and hadn't the slightest idea of where to begin. "I hope you've done this before," Bella whispered.

"You haven't?" Sophia countered.

Bella tried ignoring the mockery in Sophia's tone. "It doesn't appear that you know what to do either."

"Of course I do. Pass the flour, please."

Before Bella knew it, she was retrieving the third loaf of bread from the oven and inserting the fourth.

"Mmmm. That sure smells good, girls." Mrs. Schenck complimented.

"Thank you." They said in unison.

Bella eased closer to Sophia. "I could eat a whole loaf myself. I'm starving."

"Me too." Sophia agreed. "Next, it's your turn."

"My turn? No thanks. You're doing a great job."

"Five loaves apiece." Sophia grinned. "It's only fair."

Bella felt knots form in her stomach. She had watched Sophia knead the dough. It had formed perfectly. The loaves were flawless. Each of them rounded on top and baked to a golden brown. The sight of them caused Bella's mouth to water. Bella pushed her sleeves past her elbows.

Bella sifted the flour just as Sophia had done. She was ready to add the milk when Sophia intervened. "You forgot the salt. I had it measured right here."

She looked at Sophia with doubt. She hadn't noticed that salt had been added before. What if Sophia was leading her astray again? Sophia smiled. It seemed genuine, but she had been deceitful before. Could she trust her?

"Here." Sophia dashed the contents from the spoon. "If it doesn't rise, then I will take the blame."

Bella was relieved when all five loaves looked just as enticing as Sophia's. Mrs. Schenck didn't have to ask them twice to join her at the table. Together, they shared a loaf of bread with creamy butter. Bella had never tasted something so heavenly. And to think, she baked it.

Finally, after slicing various vegetables that were grown on the estate, Bella and Sophia retired to their room. They were both surprised to find they were sharing a room that housed two twin sized beds. An awkward silence filled the room when they entered.

It had been months since Bella shared a room with someone. Even then, it had been Ashlynn. Not Sophia. Bella placed her suitcase on the bed near the window. Politely turning her back to her company, Bella pulled the curtains together and then retrieved her book. Refusing to look in Sophia's direction, Bella occupied the oak rocking chair. After reading the message written by her father, for the countless time, Bella turned the page trying to imagine Darby doing the same.

"I enjoy reading, too."

Bella lifted her eyes and found Sophia sitting atop her bed with a book in her hand. "What do you read?"

Sophia glanced at the book, "*Anne of Green Gables*."

"Oh."

"It belongs to Mrs. Vanderbilt. She suggested I read it." Sophia shrugged. "I suppose she realized that Anne and I have more in common than just our hair."

"Oh?"

"She's orphaned."

Bella witnessed the unmistakable anguish written on Sophia's features. Living an orphaned life had truly taken its toll on Sophia. She seemed to have little concern for anyone but herself. From an angle, Bella could see where Sophia could be justified by her actions. But then there is such a thing as giving. If Sophia would love, then it wouldn't be such a challenge to love her all the same. If only Sophia could find it inside her heart to forgive, then she could easily be forgiven. If she'd just be kind...

A pang smote Bella's heart. What if she could love Sophia first? The boundless emotion could tear down the broken bridges and build anew. What if Bella could find it in her own heart to forgive first? Perhaps Sophia could learn from being forgiven and do some forgiving of her own.

"Did you hear me?"

"Huh?" Bella asked.

"I said, I see that love found its way back to you."

Bella's hand automatically felt for the charm. Her heart warmed at the genuine expression on Sophia's face. "Yes. I'm glad it did."

CHAPTER TWENTY FIVE

DARBY LED THE ATTENDEES HE had been assigned from the plaza at the Biltmore station. He had been given the privilege of becoming acquainted with many men with the same interest as he. There was one man in particular, Robert S. Conklin, the Commissioner of Forestry from Harrisburg, Pennsylvania, who seemed intrigued by Darby's skills.

"Tell me, Mr. Pierson, how long have you been residing here at Biltmore?" Robert asked above the echoing noise of hoof beats.

"Born and raised here in the Carolina hills, sir. Been acquainted with Biltmore since I enrolled in attendance at the Forest School." Darby explained.

"I hear you are the president of your class. I presume you earned that title. Am I correct?" Robert pressed on.

Darby's chest swelled with pride. "Well, sir, I must admit that my knowledge of tree removal and the drive to see it done orderly was the route to hold such a title."

"So you had prior knowledge concerning logging and reforestation?" Robert questioned.

"Yes, sir." Darby answered. "My father owns Pierson Enterprises, so you could say I've been reared up in the log yard."

The man grew speechless. Darby questioned his reaction.

"Have you heard of Pierson Enterprises before?"

Robert broke out in a smile. "Let's just say that you are the answer to my prayers."

Darby was puzzled. "How so?"

Robert extracted a wad of money from his pocket that was thick enough to gag the horse he was guiding. "All this and more could be yours."

Darby in his confused state said, "I'm afraid I'm not following you."

"I am looking for a strong and knowledgeable young man to join the Pennsylvania Commerce of Forestry with the ideas of Dr. Carl Schenck. And you, Mr. Pierson, are that man."

Join the Commerce of Forestry for the State of Pennsylvania? Darby wasn't quite sure if he heard the man correctly or not. It almost felt like he was suffering from early morning brain fog, and as soon as he woke up he would surely realize it was only a dream.

"Sir, may I ask why you think you have the authority to make me an offer like that?"

Robert grinned at Darby's question. "I am the President. So, therefore, I always make the final decision of whom we hire."

"Oh." Darby was speechless now. The offer had come as a bit of shock. It was a once in a lifetime opportunity, and his Ma would be so proud of him and so would Bella. In this sense, so would his Pa. He would earn enough money to keep Pierson Enterprises afloat.

As the day grew longer and Darby continued leading the

group from Tip to Tip, he couldn't help but look heavenward with a smile. *"All things,"* he could hear Pastor Jackson saying, *"All things work together for good."*

At the close of the first day of the Forest Fair, the adventure ended with an informal banquet at the Battery Park Hotel. Instead of staying, Darby apologized for an early departure, and urged Chestnut as fast as possible toward the Schenck's home.

"Mrs. Schenck?"

The woman's eyes darted from the book in her hand. "Yes, Bella?"

Bella cautiously stepped inside the warm room, the flickering shadows dancing to the rhythm of the popping firewood. "Do you mind if I take a walk?"

"Of course not, dear," Mrs. Schenck glanced at the nearby window. "Do not wander off too far now; the sun will be setting soon."

Bella dipped her head in response. "Yes, ma'am."

The November chill welcomed Bella when she stepped onto the porch. Pulling the shawl tightly about her shoulders, she made her descent. Tomorrow was the big day. Preparing the luncheon for the starving crew of men was going to be exhausting enough. Better to find all means of relaxation now.

The shadows of the tall evergreens swallowed up Bella's figure. The further she stepped into the forest, the colder she became. The pines stole away the rays of the sun's light, only leaving Bella to warm herself. Finally, she paused next to a rippling brook but was startled to hear a continuation of crunching leaves echoing from behind. She turned briskly and was relieved to find Sophia.

Bella's hand fanned her chest. "You scared me to death!"

Sophia only smiled. "Sorry," she shrugged, "Mrs. Scheck sent me to fetch you."

Bella directed her gaze back to the water. So much for an evening alone.

"Well, aren't you coming?" Sophia asked.

Bella kept her gaze fastened onto the white water. "I'll be along in a moment."

Sophia gasped. "Ah, look!" Grabbing skirts and all, Sophia darted up the terrain. "I've never seen a bridge like that before!" she called over her shoulder.

"What?" Bella's eyes followed Sophia. "Where are you going?!"

Sophia pointed. "Up there!"

Bella hesitated for a moment and then darted off in the same direction, her shawl dancing in the wind. The jagged rocks dug into the soles of her feet. She would be sure to buy herself some new shoes for Christmas.

The hill grew steep the further she climbed. Finally, she reached the top, panting every breath.

"This waterfall must feed that creek." Bella followed the motion of Sophia's hand, nodding in agreement. "Are you going?" Sophia skeptically measured Bella's courage.

"Of course, I'm going." Bella took a deep breath and gathered her skirts into her hands, "As a matter of fact, I'm going first."

"Be my guest. I will follow cautiously."

Bella stepped onto the bridge with confidence, ignoring its consistent swaying back and forth. Her palms dug into the fraying rope for security. The rushing of the waterfall called out to her. When she peered beneath her feet, she regretted it. Her stomach flopped with the drumbeat of her heart. She looked back up, calculating that she was already halfway across. Her feet stepped over the broken board and presumed their pace. Glad to feel solid ground beneath her, Bella turned.

"That wasn't so bad, was it?" Sophia asked as she, too, stepped away from the bridge.

Bella swallowed the knot in her throat. "Of course not." She stood there and studied the distance from the swinging bridge to the white water beneath it. She now realized the predicament, "We have to go back across." Her words fell in a whisper as if they were not supposed to have been spoken.

Sophia laughed. "I'll go first this time."

Before Bella had time to gather her bearings, she found herself following Sophia. Again, she ignored the somersaults in her tummy and moved as fast as her feet would let her until she felt herself collide into Sophia's backside.

"What are you doing?" Bella asked impatiently.

Sophia glanced over her shoulder, "Scared?"

"No, I just have a bad case of motion sickness."

"Hmmm, I'm sure." Sophia stepped before she looked, and her foot fell through the open slat. Her hands gripped the worn ropes on either side, pulling them down with her weight.

Bella struggled to keep her balance. "Sophia!"

"Help! My leg! It's caught!"

Bella didn't feel secure when she released her hold on the ropes. The continual bouncing of the contraption had already gotten the best of her, causing every ounce of courage to flee, making it nearly impossible to move. Her shaking hands gripped Sophia underneath her arms and pulled, but she didn't budge.

"Sophia, you have to help me! Pull yourself up!"

"I can't! My leg won't move!"

"You have to, Sophia!"

The bridge shifted from the opposite end. Both of them froze and studied their doom.

A board fell and splintered into pieces upon the jagged rocks from beneath. The next slat dangled. When the rope gave way, it too fell among the boulders.

Color drained from Bella's cheeks. She had to remind herself to breathe and to think logically. "We can't go forward! We have to go back!" Bella pulled on Sophia with strength she didn't know she had. Together, they worked Sophia free of the wedged board and fell back onto the wooden surface. The force of their weight ignited the rush of the falling bridge.

"Sophia! Give me your hand! Hurry!"

The splashing of the slats echoed in Bella's ears as she pulled Sophia to her feet. In her weakened state, Sophia's leg gave way from beneath her. Bella thrust Sophia's arm around her shoulder and guided her with haste toward the other side.

"Hurry." Sophia moaned. "It's falling fast."

"Come on, just a few more feet!"

The falling bridge stole away all the balance Bella possessed. "Jump, Sophia!" Bella lunged toward the earth, planting her hands and knees into the dirt, not sure if Sophia was at her side or not.

CHAPTER TWENTY SIX

"HELP!"
Bella hurried to her feet and followed the plea in Sophia's voice. Her heart faltered. She darted to where the broken bridge dangled from just one rope, where Sophia was hanging on by a thread. "Hold on, Sophia! Don't let go!" Bella scanned the ground for something. A stick. Anything. But found nothing.

"Hurry, Bella!" Sophia screamed when the bridge shifted and dropped several inches.

Bella was paralyzed with fear. She didn't know what to do and she couldn't let Sophia go down. Not without her.

She leapt toward the edge, removing her shawl in the same moment. "Here! Catch!" The length of shawl was barely enough to fill the gap between them. Sophia's shaky hand reached for the threadbare piece of material, gripping it tightly. Her eyes drifted closed for a second before she released her hold on the rope and grasped the shawl with both hands.

"That's it! Now pray!"

Sophia's dark sapphire eyes looked up in fear. "I can't," she groaned breathlessly, "you pray, Bella."

Bella wet her lips, not sure if God would hear her cry or not and whispered, "God, please."

The last thread of rope split, gaining their attention. The bridge finished its fall, collapsing to the white water beneath them.

Bella took a deep breath and pulled on the shawl. "Come on, Sophia." Bella grunted. "Don't let go."

"Hurry..."

"No, Sophia! Hang on!" Bella continued to pull with all her might. Inch by inch, the distance between them grew shorter. "Reach me your hand!"

Sophia weakly allowed her hand to fall free of the shawl and reach upward. Bella grasped onto it. In the same second, the shawl split in two. Both of them screamed. Bella thought sure she had lost Sophia, but she loosed her hold on the material and clasped both hands onto her sister's hand.

"Let go, Bella..."

"No!"

"I can't... hold on... anymore."

"I can't let go, Sophia." Unshed tears broke loose and coursed down Bella's cheeks, salting her lips. "God, please."

From out of nowhere, an arm encircled Bella's waist, pulling her to her feet. Sophia's limp form ascended from the earth's edge, her hand still nestled in the clasp of her sister's. Her toes dug into the dirt leaving her body to collapse lifelessly to the ground.

Bella bravely lifted her eyes and was relieved to find her sister safe. She dashed to Sophia's side, embracing her with open arms. "Sophia?"

Sophia didn't answer.

"Sophia?" Bella gently shook her shoulders, "Sophia, you're safe."

Sophia withdrew herself a bit and whispered, "I am?"

"We are."

Darby watched Bella embrace Sophia. Such a stark difference from before. And just what had happened to get them here? Alone. On a mountain. His gaze scanned the shattered boards and broken pieces that had fallen from what used to be a bridge. His gut clinched. By all means, it looked as though both of them should have gone down with it. His eyes rested on them again. Slowly, he moved to Bella's side and knelt down, grateful to inhale her scent once more.

"Bella?" He whispered her name, but her reaction was fierce. She stared at him wide-eyed and pale stricken. He allowed his finger to dust the dirt from her rosy cheek. "Are you okay?"

Bella only nodded.

Darby shook off his coat and placed it about her shoulders. "You must be freezing."

He felt her smile clear to his gut. "Thank you," she whispered.

He looked from Bella to Sophia. "Let's get you two back to the Schenck's home. It's getting late."

"Right." Bella agreed and accepted his hand. Then she stooped over, pulling Sophia to her feet. "Come on, I'll help you."

Sophia groaned as she tried to rise steadily. Her eyes squeezed shut. Her jaw clinched, biting back the pain.

"Are you okay, Sophia?"

"It's my leg, Bella. It hurts." Sophia moaned.

"Here," Bella took Sophia's arm and gently laid it across her shoulder, "lean against me."

Bella held to Sophia as she hobbled toward the horse that Darby had gone ahead to retrieve. Together, Bella and Darby positioned Sophia comfortably upon the leather saddle.

Bella gasped when Darby slid his hands around her waist. Her reaction made him pause. "What are you doing?" she asked, her eyes searching his fervently.

"You are riding behind her."

She shook her head. "No, it's your horse. I can walk."

He tightened his hold, "I walk. You ride." And with graceful ease, Darby swept Bella up, placing her directly behind Sophia. His hands lingered a bit longer than necessary but regretfully slid away, his warm hand pausing atop Bella's. "Let's get going." With an assuring squeeze, Darby allowed his hand to pull away, grateful to see her palm enclose around the charm that laid against her chest.

"Bella! Sophia!" Mrs. Schenck nearly stumbled down the steps but regained her footing when her husband took hold of her arm firmly.

Bella felt guilty for the woman's pale stricken face and worried expression. Only by the light of the moon was she able to detect the creases across Mrs. Schenck's forehead.

"Not to worry dear. They are safe now." Bella heard Mr. Schenck comfort his wife.

"Good heavens, girls! I have been worried sick." Her hand smoothed her perplexed features, "I should never have allowed either of you to go for a walk unchaperoned."

"I am sorry, Mrs. Schenck. I never meant to cause any harm." Bella solemnly spoke, perfectly aware of Darby's piercing gaze.

"Harm? Who's hurt?" she asked.

"I just have a few cuts is all, ma'am." Sophia explained as she accepted Darby's assistance dismounting the horse. She stood there for a moment dusting her skirts before trying to take a step. "Nothing a little salve and a bandage won't heal."

Mrs. Schenck laid her hand in the bend of Sophia's arm, "Well, come on, dear. I have just what you need. A special salve made from pure minerals, ingredients my grandfather used…"

Bella watched Mrs. Schenck lead Sophia up the steps, followed by the forester, their voices fading into the night.

"Bella?"

She cast her eyes to the voice and smiled as if she had just become aware of her rescuer. "Darby." His big hands encircled her tiny waist and lifted her from the patient horse, placing her merely inches from his stance.

Darby tipped her chin, "Were you on the bridge as well?"

Bella tore her eyes away and nodded before she felt herself being pulled into Darby's embrace. He smoothed her hair, "Thank God, you're all right." He tightened his hold, pressing her ear against the drumming of his heart. "I'm not even going to think of what could have happened."

Bella shuttered, realization dawning like a noonday sun while standing under the light of the moon. She withdrew herself from his hold, his hands still resting on her shoulders. She tried avoiding his gaze. Bella didn't want him to see her cry because that's all she ever did anymore. But still, his calloused thumb slid across her smooth cheek and caught the escaping tear.

"I may have some news that will make you smile and forget everything that happened this evening," Darby said.

Bella's eyes filled with hope as she bravely searched his gaze, "Really?"

He smiled, "Yes, but let me explain as we walk." Darby offered his arm. "You'll be proud of me."

"I'm already proud of you," Bella admitted.

"Thank you, but I believe you'll be even more impressed."

"Out with it then, Darby Pierson."

Darby took a deep breath, "I've been offered a job as a forester in Pennsylvania."

What? Had she heard him correctly? Bella's feet froze. "Excuse me?"

"I have been offered a job as a forester. A forester, Bella!" He took her shoulders. "That's my dream, remember?"

"Oh," she cleared her closing throat, "yes, I remember."

"What's wrong? I thought you'd be happy."

The words seem to stick inside her throat, "I...am."

"I couldn't believe it. That's why I had to see you tonight. I couldn't hold it in any longer." Darby took a deep breath. "Robert Conklin, a forester from Pennsylvania..."

Bella felt her stomach lurch. She had nothing inside to release but remorse, anguish, and bitter shock.

"Bella?"

She quickly swallowed the rising bile. "Hmmm?"

"You didn't hear a word I said, did you?"

"Oh...yes, Darby. I heard everything you said."

"Good because that brings me to my question."

Bella held her breath. What was he going to ask her?

Darby's eyes searched Bella's in the moonlight. His finger pushed back a strand of hair from her forehead and trailed her cheek bone. He braced her chin between his finger and thumb, tilting her face upward. "Will you wait for me?"

His voice sent surging pulses throughout her body. He had asked her to wait. Well, she was definitely going nowhere fast, but how long was he expecting her to sit and yearn for his return? "How long?" she forced herself to ask.

"I don't know. A year, maybe two."

Bella nodded her head while she digested his statement. It would seem like forever, but she would wait. "When are you leaving?"

"April of next year. I have to earn my diploma first."

Relief washed over Bella. At least she could have him for nearly six months. "That's not so bad. Six months from now."

Darby's finger hushed her words. "You will see very little of me during that time span. I will have to study harder than before, and learn all I can from Dr. Schenck to better prepare myself."

"Oh." The pitch in Bella's voice was gone. The moonlight revealed her features. The tears brimming her eyes sparkled like the stars in the night sky.

"Listen, all things work together for good. Just be patient, Bella. Everything will turn out just fine. I promise."

"You can't promise that." A tear trickled down her cheek. "Papa made the same promise, and nothing has gone right since then."

"God has His own time, Bella."

Bella's hand flew up to silence Darby's argument. "Please. Do not mention God." Bella stepped back. "Good night, Darby."

He grabbed her by the arm, pulled her to him, and kissed away her tears. His lips pressed against her forehead. "You go with me."

She stiffened. "I can't."

"Listen, you'll never have to worry about your family. I'll see to it they are taken care of." His hand continued to smooth her hair. "You go with me."

"My sister..." Bella pulled away. Her eyes grew distant. "I can't leave my sister. She needs me." Finally, her eyes reined in on Darby's. "But you know where to find me."

"Bella, don't do this."

"I have to check on Sophia."

"I'll see you tomorrow?"

"Right. Tomorrow." She said as she walked away.

"Good night, Bella."

She turned to get another good look at him before she entered the house. The moonlight outlined his face. His eyes were greener than ever before. Goodness, she loved him. She couldn't bear to see him go; yet, it was his dream. His future. Although her heart was splintered to pieces, Bella allowed a smile to break the forbidden frown on her face. "Good night, Darby." Her hand fanned her heart as she watched him mount his horse and ride off into the night toward his future. Away from her. Chasing the dream that became his driven purpose, the path God had chosen for him to take.

CHAPTER TWENTY SEVEN

THE ORANGE GLOW FROM THE candlelight illuminated Sophia's splintered hands. Bella worked gently removing one splinter at a time.

"Tell me if it hurts." Bella plucked at the tiny piece of wood.

"It stings a little, but they have to come out."

Bella worked a while longer in silence. She replayed the events at the bridge over and over in her mind. An ache settled in her chest. "I will apply some salve and a bandage as soon as I'm through." Bella said as she fought for the last splinter.

"Thank you." Sophia groaned.

"Sorry, it's almost out."

Sophia closed her eyes and waited patiently, careful not to jerk from the sudden prick.

"Mama wouldn't let him see me."

Bella's hands froze. Her eyes lifted only to discover Sophia's eyes closed as if she were imagining her words.

"Finally, he gave up and moved away," Sophia whispered. "When Mama decided to have a change of heart, he had already married your mother." A tear dripped from Sophia's chin. "Mama went downhill after that, and then she took on the wild life." She wiped away another tear. "I was the least of her priorities."

"I'm sorry," Bella whispered.

Sophia opened her reddened eyes and forced her lips to smile.

"No need to be sorry. Just be thankful. If Mrs. Vanderbilt hadn't visited Biltmore Village as often as she did and soon realized that I was a very needy child, there is no telling where I would be tonight."

"Mrs. Vanderbilt took you in?"

"She did." Sophia laughed. "I guess I've given her more problems than Cedric has."

"The dog?" Bella quizzed.

"Yes." Sophia leaned forward and examined her hands. "Guess that's what I get for causing so much pain."

"It could have been worse."

"True." Sophia agreed and then slipped into deep thought.

Bella resumed to her task. "This one is stubborn."

Sophia laughed, "Much like me."

Bella could agree. But she, too, was headstrong. So we do have one thing in common, Bella thought while she applied a thin layer of salve onto the wound.

When she finished, Bella patted the bandage gently and said, "You're all done, sister."

An awkward silence filled the room. Bella briefly smiled when she arose and quietly blew out the candle, and then slid underneath the quilt on her bed. Despite the chill in the air, she felt warm. For whatever reason, she didn't know.

"Bella?"

"Yes?"

"Thank you."

A familiar emotion enveloped Bella. The same sentiment she perceived when she would lie in bed at night and talk to Ashlynn. A smile formed on her lips. "You're welcome, Sophia."

Darby watched the rippling waters of the French Broad River cascade over the rocks. This path led to a walnut plantation that had been reinforced with yellow pines. He directed his crew of men toward their destination where Schenck would explain the importance of fertile soil.

"You see here," Schenck pointed to the seven year old walnuts that stood twenty five feet high and were four inches in diameter, "a heap of manure was distributed about the ground. Now look across the road. Those walnuts are the same stock, the same age, and planted under the same conditions.

"Quite a contrast, huh?" He walked toward the frail growth of timber, "These are about as round as my little finger and only five or six inches high."

Schenck and his guides earned a round of applause. "Now men, these flourishing trees will not meet the ax until they reach maturity." Schenck smiled and said, "Clap now."

He received very little praise for the statement, but most joined in for a good laugh. Before the morning was too far spent, Schenck and the students lined up all the guests along the hillside. Each man stood before a spade hole and had been given his very own white pine seedling to plant.

Darby stood near Mr. Conklin and watched him kneel down

to plant his seedling according to the directions given by Dr. Schenck as each man had made his mark in the Pisgah Forest.

The day progressed on to a luncheon held at the Schenck home where a few picnic tables were tucked away under the branches of an oak tree. The guests along with the students and Dr. Schenck dismounted from their horses, leaving them in the hands of the stable boys.

"This has truly been a success, I do believe." Schenck patted Darby on the shoulder. "I heard about your job prospect."

Darby swelled with enthusiasm, "Thank you, Sir."

"I've passed through Pennsylvania in years gone by. I do not believe you will be disappointed." Schenck stopped his footing, Darby followed step. "Such an open opportunity for a young man like yourself." Schenck stretched forth his hand. "I'm proud of you, Mr. Pierson."

"Thanks to you, Dr. Schenck."

Bella's nerves were frazzled. She had expected a group of men but not an entire army. She carefully observed the food quantity and silently prayed there was enough to satisfy these men. She began to uncover the sliced bread and ham. It smelled delicious. She savored the aroma while she moved down the table to reveal the platter of fresh vegetables. The strong stench of peppers and onions filled her nostrils. She nearly sneezed. Bella tried her best to hold it back. It would by far be the most embarrassing first impression possible.

"What kind of face is that?"

Bella looked up to find a very amused Darby peering at her. She smiled and cringed again. The sneeze almost won. Bella released her breath. "Those onions are so strong." Her eyes were watering uncontrollably.

"Ah. Why not go ahead and slice the pumpkin pie instead?" his eyebrows danced.

"Desserts are for later, Mr. Pierson."

Darby's hands found his pockets. "Why so formal?"

Bella looked up before she uncovered the steamed broccoli. "Why not so formal? You are among professionals, aren't you?"

"Darby will do."

Bella eyed him before she walked back into the house. "Enjoy your lunch, Mr. Pierson."

"Aren't you going to cut the pie?" Darby asked as he followed her to the bottom step.

Bella ascended the steps and then called over shoulder, "Dessert is for later, Mr. Pierson."

Darby watched the plump bow bounce up and down as Bella disappeared through the door. Darby's hand felt for his chin. How did she do it? The sting of rejection smothered the flying sparks, leaving nothing but a hazy fog to dance before him. He shook his head and turned away. He would have his chance. Later.

The men put nothing to waste. Only a few crumbs from the bread slices remained, and a blob of pumpkin filling was left lying in the dish. Bella stacked a tower of dirty dishes and began delivering them to Sophia to wash.

"Where is Mrs. Schenck?" Bella asked.

Sophia pointed toward the hall. "She's getting ready."

"Ready for what?" Bella eased the pile of plates onto the counter.

"The possum hunt."

"The what?!"

"Shhh, she'll hear you."

Bella stepped closer to Sophia. "Is she going on a possum hunt?"

Sophia nodded.

"You jest!"

"I kid you not," Sophia explained, "she and her husband want to win the trophy. I know so because I heard them speak of it last night."

"The trophy? Oh! You mean the competition at the fair."

"Yes, and I can't wait to see it." Sophia's eyes danced.

Bella's eyes darted to Sophia's bandaged ankle. "You're going?"

"Of course. I wouldn't miss it for the world."

Sophia had been right. Mrs. Schenck was participating in the possum hunt. And a tiny twinge of something inside Bella anticipated the event, too. "I did not know that we were to attend the festivities tonight," Bella said as she stepped over a branch in the path.

"I insisted that we were not left out. After all, we did work as hard as any of those men." Mrs. Schenck adjusted her hat. "And there will be a barbeque pit. Delicious, huh?"

Sophia's eyes lit up. "Mmmm, I'm getting hungry already."

"Look," Bella pointed, "there is the trickle of smoke. We must be getting close."

Bella tried to ignore her aching body and her flighty pulse. She hadn't spoken with Darby since the luncheon earlier today, and she knew he would be here tonight.

The sound of yelping dogs filled Bella's ears as the woods opened up. Men stood about on every corner as if they were ready to strike. She had never seen anything like it. She stayed back to watch from a distance. Both Sophia and Mrs. Schenck urged her to follow them; instead she insisted they go on without her. Bella spotted a large rock and stood on top of it. She could see it all from here. Mrs. Schenck paired up with her husband immediately, and as soon as the whistle was blown, hunters and dogs scattered everywhere. The dogs sniffed the ground aggressively, and soon they were onto their own trail. Some even branched out further into the woods leading their owners toward the prize.

Bella stood on the tips of her toes and scanned the dispersing crowd. A tiny twinge of regret pricked her heart when she found no sign of Darby among the hunters. She released a sigh that was soon overtaken by a gasp when two hands encircled her waist. She turned and wiggled herself from his grip. "Darby!" Bella panted for breath and almost lost her footing, but Darby took her waist again. She placed her hands on his shoulders and tried pushing away, but his grip was like a vise. She wasn't going anywhere.

"I kind of like this." Darby's husky tone sent shivers down her spine. Of course, he liked it. He had her exactly where he wanted her, and the rock only aided her to be his height. He was looking directly into her eyes, his smoldering gaze holding her captive.

"I thought you would be hunting," Bella finally managed to say.

"I am." He smiled hot enough to warm her blood. "Or should I say, I was."

Thankful for the settling dusk, Bella knew her face was aflame. "How did you find me?" Bella asked as she tried pulling herself away again, but there was no use. She wasn't going anywhere.

Darby inhaled deeply, "I smelled you."

Bella's jaw dropped. "You're comparing me to a possum?"

Darby smiled, "If a possum smells like sweet cinnamon cloves dipped in vanilla," he took a breath, "then yes, I guess I would be." He moistened his lips, "I just wonder if the taste is similar?"

Bella's heart hammered inside her chest. He surely wouldn't kiss her here, would he? She had to think of something. A diversion of some kind. Bella knew there was no use trying to squirm away; his hold was too tight. But she had to think of something. "Did you enjoy the pumpkin pie?" she asked.

He looked a bit confused as the fire in his eyes extinguished a bit. "Did I what?"

"The pumpkin pie. Did you like it?" Her teeth nervously grazed her bottom lip.

His gaze settled onto her mouth with much appreciation. He managed to say, "It was delicious."

The close proximity weakened Bella's knees as she inhaled the same familiar scent of him. As his eyes slowly left her mouth and met her gaze, the sound of the returning hunters and yelping dogs filtered through the trees.

The hunt was over.

Someone had won the trophy.

Bella released Darby's shoulders and turned to see who had defeated the mob of hunters. It was an older gentleman with a long dark beard, and he was carrying the champion dog under his arm. Others were patting him on the back and congratulating him for his victory. Bella turned back to Darby with a smile and allowed it to slowly melt away when she read the confused look in his eyes.

"Darby?"

Still with his eyes glued to the champ, Darby spoke from a distance, "That's my Pa."

CHAPTER TWENTY EIGHT

DARBY HELD UP A FINGER to Bella and stepped past her without breaking eye contact with his Pa. With lengthy strides, Darby found himself face to face with the one who had tried everything to stop him from chasing his dreams.

"Ol' Barney done it again," Charles said as he patted the dog on its head. "Never failed me yet. Ain't that right, boy?" The dog answered with a howl.

Darby couldn't help it. Although he couldn't remember the last time he had done this, he took his Pa into his arms and hugged him. Darby felt an arm reach around him, and in this moment, the world had stopped spinning. Time stopped ticking. An unbreakable bond was forming, knitting the two together that had been driven so far apart. When Darby withdrew himself he stared into teary eyes.

"I'm proud of ya, boy." His eyes were speaking even more. "I'm rootin' fer ya all the way. Even if yer goin' to Pennsylvania."

Darby was dumbfounded. He must have been dreaming. He would never had expected those words to spill from his Pa's lips. "Thanks, Pa."

"No. Thanks to you, boy. Now let's get in here and celebrate, what do ye say?"

"Sounds good to me," Darby said as he followed his Pa with a smile that couldn't be erased. Had he ever seen a transformation, he saw it now.

Darby caught Bella's gaze several times during the night. He assured her with a smile, and she confirmed it with hers. He couldn't wait until the music started. At the first plucking of the banjo string, he was going to celebrate with whom his heart led him to.

The scholars of Biltmore Forest School began singing, all except Darby. Instead, he was making hasty steps toward her. Bella looked from her left and to her right only to discover she had been left alone. Mrs. Schenck had already joined her husband and Sophia, was she dancing too?

Bella felt Darby's piercing gaze as he approached her boldly. Without saying a word, he took her hand and lifted her to her feet.

Then Bella remembered his foot.

"Your foot." She said as he sent her twirling.

"Let's not worry about that. Let's just worry about us."

Bella knew where he directed that statement. After this weekend, they would see very little of each other, and she knew he wanted to make this precious time count. His eyes penetrated hers as his hand held hers firmly while his arm kept her safe in his grip. She could stay like this forever but it wouldn't last forever. He would be leaving for Pennsylvania in less than six months, and then who knew when she would see him again?

But she would wait.

His head dipped next to hers bringing his mouth close to her ear. "Have I ever told you how beautiful you are?" Bella just nodded her head. He had told her once, and she had hid those words away in her heart.

"Have I ever told you I drown in your eyes whenever you look at me?" Bella shook her head. "Well, I do," he assured her.

Bella allowed her eyes to drift closed and savor those sweet words, to catalogue them in the depths of her heart so she could hear them in her dreams.

Darby inhaled deeply. "You smell so sweet."

By now, Darby had her so flustered she couldn't even speak. She just followed routine and breathed in his spicy cologne, memorizing exactly how he smelled while she was in his arms.

The music took on a different note, a bit slower. Darby drew back and smiled like he never had before, searing her heart like a hot iron. His fingers interlaced with hers, his eyes staying put. "Tell me what you feel."

How does she feel? In love. Confused. Happy. Perplexed. Bella swallowed. Where was she to start? By the way, she wasn't good with words, and she would probably make a fool of herself. She took a deep breath and found his eyes so she could see into his soul. "Besides being a refuge during my stormy life...the stronghold during my weakness..." Her eyes sought his slowly, "the healer of my breaking heart and the giver of all my happiness, you make me smile." She swallowed. "You send my heart into a somersault every time you look into my eyes like you are doing right now." They giggled together. Then her eyes started to fill with unshed tears. "You look past all my faults and believe in me anyway." Bella took a deep breath, "You even dance with me."

"Sounds like you found true love," he said in a whisper as he kissed away the tears slowly trailing down her cheeks. Truth was, she had found it, but her greatest fear was professing it to him. What if it shattered what they had?

Soon, not only tears dripped from her chin but the chilled raindrops falling from the dark sky. Her feet froze. She was dancing, and she didn't mind it, but there was only one person she danced in the rain with, and he was looking down on her now from the heavens above. Darby looked at Bella curiously but said nothing. He pulled off his coat, wrapped it around her shoulders, and led her to a nearby tree for shelter. The steady rain extinguished the campfire leaving only the smoke to dance toward the sky.

Soon everyone started taking his or her leave. Everyone but them. She held up a finger toward Sophia meaning for her to wait, but Darby encouraged her to go on and he would see that Bella return safely.

Together, they walked arm in arm in the rain toward the Schenck's home. "Can I see you tomorrow?" Darby asked as Bella neared the steps.

She allowed his coat to fall from her shoulders and into his hands. "I don't know. We are leaving early. Uncle Morton will be here with the carriage."

"Ah, Uncle Morton."

Bella smiled apologetically and said, "He likes you, Darby."

His hearty laughter filled the air. "Bella, there's no need to lie."

"Okay, maybe he is just concerned for me and a bit leery of you."

"Leery of me?" his hand fanned his heart.

"Because we are two totally different people who are travelling in opposite directions."

"Whoa!" Darby caught Bella's wrist and spun her around to face him fully. "Do you really believe that?"

Bella swallowed and barely nodded.

"Clarify that please because I am a bit confused."

Bella cleared her throat. "Well, you are going to Pennsylvania. Aren't you?"

Darby nodded. "Soon enough, but that still doesn't explain what makes us so different from one another."

"Well... you're a man and I'm a woman?"

Darby cocked his head to the side, "No kidding." The moment grew silent, only the consistent raindrops falling to the ground. "Why does your uncle not trust me?"

Bella bit her lip. "Darby, it's raining. Can we talk about this another time?"

"Just tell me now so I will have at least six months to prove him wrong."

Bella watched the drops of rain drizzle down his cheekbones and drip from his chin. He refused to loosen his grip on her hand to wipe away the droplets on his lashes. "Because you..." Bella looked away, "Because you are wealthy."

She tasted the salty tears mixed with rain. His finger tilted her chin upward. Instead of rendering unto his gaze, she closed her eyes.

"Bella?"

"Hmmm."

"Look at me."

She surrendered to his gentle coaxing.

"Listen to me. Open your heart and let these words pour straight into your soul. There is nothing, not Biltmore, not Pennsylvania, not even Pierson Enterprises...there's nothing on this earth as dear to me as you are."

Bella's eyes fluttered closed. She trusted him even if no one else did.

"Do you believe me?" he whispered.

Bella nodded.

"Good. Now it's time for you to get inside and warm up."

Bella had ascended a couple steps leaving them to stand eye to eye. His hand took her jaw, leaving his thumb to caress her cheek. He inclined his mouth unto hers, allowing his lips to brush hers lightly. "Good night, Bella."

Her fingertips instinctively went to rest upon her lips. "Good night, Darby," she said as she watched him leave. She just couldn't help it. She twirled herself around countless times before entering the home, knowing tonight that sleep would be hard to come by.

Ping!

Bella raised straight up in her bed. Had she been dreaming, or did she hear something?

Ping!

The sound came from the window. She peered over at Sophia, but she still slumbered. Bella's heartbeat drummed in her ears as she scooted near the curtain. She was about to peep out when again, Ping! She jumped. Beads of sweat formed along her forehead. Maybe I should wake Mr. Schenck, she thought.

Instead of using good sense, Bella slid her finger behind the curtain and pulled it only by an inch. Her eye roamed the outside. The dusky dawn made it hard to see. Then a figure erupted from the gray. Quickly, Bella replaced the curtain. Nervous flutters set off inside her. She needed to wake the man of the house, so she easily removed the blanket and placed her bare feet onto the cold, wooden floor when she heard her name being said in a loud whisper.

She swallowed. Surely she was dreaming and would wake at any moment.

"Bella!" Again the thunderous whisper nearly took her to her knees.

"It's me. Darby!"

Darby? What was he doing here? She bounced back onto her bed and barely pulled the curtain. Confusion marked her features. She knew something must be terribly wrong for him to call on her before sunrise.

"What's wrong?" she whispered.

"Meet me on the porch."

Bella barely nodded her head and let the curtain fall. She quickly put on the dress she had worn last evening, thankful that it had dried, and put on her shoes without socks. She tiptoed through the house, careful not to wake anyone, and stepped onto the porch as she finished the end of her braid. Darby was already there waiting but he appeared calm, not at all flustered as she was.

"What's wrong, Darby?" she asked.

"Nothing, I just wanted to introduce you to Chestnut."

"At six o'clock in the morning?" Bella yawned.

"Yes, and where is your cloak?" Darby offered his hand.

"I don't have one," she shivered.

She watched him retrieve a blanket that had been rolled up. He gently shook it loose and laid it across her shoulders.

"What are you doing?" she asked curiously when he offered his hand.

"Taking you riding."

Bella withdrew her hand. "Darby! No one will know where I am."

"I have that arranged," he assured her.

"You do?"

"I do," he answered confidently.

"But I've not had breakfast," she argued.

"Not to worry," Darby patted the saddlebags, "I have that taken care of as well." He smiled. "Are you ready?"

Bella hesitated. "I don't know."

Darby looked up to the lightening sky. "We best leave now if you want to see the sunrise."

"The sunrise?"

"Just get on the horse, Bella."

She smiled and willingly complied. He took his place behind her, his arms wrapping around her waist and taking the reins. With a little flip and a kissing sound, they were off.

"Where are you taking me exactly?" Bella wondered.

Darby pointed although it was still too dim to clearly see. "Up there. I want you to see the sunrise from the top of Mount Pisgah."

Bella's breath caught. She wasn't sure if it was because of where he was taking her or because of the chills going down her spine from the close proximity.

"My Papa and I were supposed to hike Mount Pisgah this fall."

Darby leaned in closer, "I remembered."

Bella smiled and allowed her head to fall back against the crook of his neck. "Will we make it before the sun comes up?" she questioned.

"Yep. Just hang on."

The early morning fog prevented the exposure of her surroundings, but Bella was enjoying it anyway. Finally, she said, "My tummy is growling."

"We're almost there, and you can indulge in your favorite breakfast; biscuits and bacon with fried apples on the side."

She gasped. "How did you know?"

"I know more about you than what you think." He smiled victoriously.

"Obviously so. What have you done? Stalked me for the past several months?"

He let out a sigh. "Just give thanks to Bessie."

"Bessie?!"

"Let's just say, I've been up for a while." His words echoed in her ear. She shivered. Then he wrapped his arms around her a bit tighter. "Cold?"

She nodded her head. "A little."

"We're almost there."

Bella had grown too comfortable in Darby's embrace. When they topped the mount, the fog had begun to lift. The horse slowed to a mere trot, coming to a stop on top of the knoll.

Darby dismounted first. "Give me your hand."

She tugged the blanket tightly about her shoulders. "Thank you."

Darby extracted another blanket and spread it on the ground. Then he withdrew a small basket from the saddlebag and his canteen. Bella had already seated herself, waiting patiently for him to share the food.

Darby took his seat across from Bella and took her hands in his. "Let us ask the blessing." Bella nodded and bowed her head.

Never before had she heard a man pray so beautifully. Her heart swelled with delight as she took in every word.

"Dear heavenly Father, we thank You for the daily bread You have given. We thank You for allowing our paths to cross and our hearts to bind as if You created them in Your likeness. Father, we know You will guide our every step and work all things together for good. In Jesus name we pray, Amen."

"Amen." Bella agreed. "You mustn't have slept much last night."

"Why do you say that?" Darby asked as he opened the basket's lid and allowed her to take first.

Bella removed a biscuit and the bowl of fried apples. "You've chased down breakfast before sunrise."

"I wanted you to remember this day for the rest of your life, so I had to stay awake all night to plan it out."

"Oh?"

Darby smiled. "Just eat, Bella."

He didn't have to tell her twice. She was famished. She'd have to thank Bessie for being so kind and allowing Darby to swindle away some breakfast food. Together, they shared the canteen that held crisp, cool water.

"Thank you, Darby."

"You are very welcome. Now come, I want to show you something." He took her by the hand and led her to the fog's edge. It was lying in the valley like a fluffy blanket.

"Wow." Bella examined the peaks of the Blue Ridge Mountains peeking from above the fog. An orange sun ball was beginning to illuminate the entire creation. "I see now why they call it Blue Ridge. It's beautiful."

"Not near as beautiful as you," Darby whispered, taking her chin and staring deep into her eyes. "Now, every time you see the sunrise, you'll think of me."

Bella just nodded. She most certainly would. She would remember him when it was autumn, she would think of him in the summer. He would dominate her thoughts when it rained. He would be her snowflakes when it snowed. He'd be her blooming flower in the spring and her sparkling stars at night. He'd be her sunrise in the morning and her sunset in the evening.

Bella silently wondered if she would be all those things to him, even in the state of Pennsylvania.

CHAPTER TWENTY NINE

KNOCK. KNOCK. KNOCK.
Bella barely tapped her knuckles against the old wooden door before twisting the rusty knob. The warmth of the tiny cottage enveloped Bella when she stepped inside. "Hello, Mama." Bella whispered, glad to find her mother hovering over the old cook stove.

Ruth Ann straightened, letting out a sigh of relief, "Ah, Bella, so glad to see ya." As the rag in her hand fell into the sink with a thud, the woman took Bella into her arms, "I was specting you'd show up today."

"Is Ashlynn expecting me as well?" Bella whispered as she placed the package next to her worn out boots.

Ruth Ann shook her head, "I don't think so. She was looking for you at church this morn."

Bella frowned. "I'm sorry. I had to work half a day and practically begged Uncle Morton to bring me. He is seeing to the horses."

Ruth Ann's eyes lit up. "Ashlynn's in her room. Go get her. The soup's bout ready."

Bella stepped quietly and peered into the room that used to belong to her. There Ashlynn sat at a makeshift desk in an old wooden chair. The candlelight flickered when Bella stepped into the room. "Hey, birthday girl."

Ashlynn turned from the piece of paper lying in front of her and gasped. "Bella! I knew you would come! I just knew it!" She arose gracefully, an action that froze Bella's heart in place.

"Ashlynn," Bella whispered.

Ashlynn's face lit up. "Look!" She took a step. A rather even step. And then another. And then another. "Mama has been workin' real hard, Bella."

Bella's glassy eyes shined brighter than they had in months. "I can see that."

Ashlynn giggled and clapped her hands. "I got my wish."

"You did, didn't you?"

"And you are smiling too! It must be that man." Ashlynn batted her eyelashes against her blushing cheeks.

"What man?" Bella asked as she pulled on Ashlynn's braid.

"You know, the cute one from church. He was there again this morning."

"He was?" Bella asked.

Ashlynn nodded her head and clasped her hands against her stomach. "He even shook my hand."

"Soup's ready, girls!" Ruth Ann called from the kitchen.

"Come on, Ashlynn, you go first. It's your birthday."

Bella followed close behind her sister and evaluated her steps. "Your left side has definitely become stronger."

Ashlynn paused and turned her face. "Do you really think so?"

"I know so."

Ashlynn smiled and turned back. "Uncle Morton!" She grasped him. "Good to see ya."

"It's good to see you, pretty girl. Happy birthday."

"Thank you."

Bella's eyes scanned the room as they each found a seat. She was glad to see food on the table. Her favorite potato soup, especially. A pile of cornbread wedges and sliced onions were placed directly beside the steaming soup. She was pleased to find the lamps filled with oil and the glowing embers on the hearth. She was happy to be home.

Bella rested her spoon in the bowl and observed Ashlynn. Bella smiled and said, "I like your new bow."

"Thank you, Bella. Mama bought it for me. She is even going to make me a blue dress to match it."

Bella smiled. "You will be pretty in blue. It will match your eyes."

"That's what I said, Bella!" Ruth Ann exclaimed.

"Good. I'm glad you like blue." Morton withdrew a small package from his coat pocket and laid it near Ashlynn's plate.

"Can I open it?" she asked.

"Of course."

Ashlynn took the small package into her hands, tearing the paper easily. She gasped. "Gloves! Blue gloves!" She slid her fingers into their confines, admiring the handiwork of the knitter.

"Thank you, Uncle Morton! Who made them?" Ashlynn asked.

For a moment, they could have heard a pin drop. Morton tapped his fingers against the crevice of the table, his dark eyes matching Bella's. "Sophia made them."

Bella hadn't meant to clear her throat when he spoke of her other sister. The one Ashlynn knew nothing about. Instead of reading the expression on her Mama's face, she took the spoon and stirred the bowl of soup as if she were in search of the right words to say.

"Tell Sophia she did a great job. They just fit." Ashlynn stretched her hands out before her and studied her palm, again turning them over to view the other side.

"Well," Bella stood and retrieved the package she had laid beside her boots. "Here, sister. Happy birthday."

Ashlynn's eyes lit up again. She took her gloved fingers and tore the paper apart from the object. "Bella." Ashlynn's curious gaze met her sisters. "I can't." Ashlynn handed the gift back to Bella. "Papa bought this for you."

"But you need it now." Bella slightly pushed the book back toward Ashlynn. "Since you are doing so well, it would be a good time to increase the exercises."

"But Papa..."

Bella's hand rested on her sisters. "Please. Papa would want this."

Ashlynn stared at the book. She opened its cover and smiled. "Thank you, Bella. I promise I will take good care of it."

"I know you will."

Ruth Ann stood up from the table and found her way to an old wooden box that sat on the fireplace mantel. She took it into her hands, gaining the attention from the others. For a moment, Bella thought she was going to return it to its place. Instead, she made slow steps back to the kitchen table. "I finally had the nerve to look at some of Walt's stuff." Her eyes brimmed with tears, avoiding all eye contact. "I fergot he even had this."

She opened its lid, the contents unable to be seen. In silence, Ruth Ann withdrew a pocket watch and laid it on the table. "He wore that everywhere he went."

Bella reached to grab it, thankful that no one objected. It's cold, metal chain fell against her wrist. She opened it, her thumb caressing the face. The glass was no longer clear but foggy, yet the numbers were still able to be seen. She could still hear it jangling while Papa danced in the rain with her, it sounded like chimes in the wind. She learned to tell time by looking into this watch while it laid in the center of his palm.

"Take it, Bella."

Bella looked up at her Mama. "Take it?"

Ruth Ann smiled. "Better put it in yer pocket before I change my mind."

Bella smiled. "Thank you, Mama." She slid it into her pocket, securing its form with her hand.

Then Ruth Ann had pulled out a few other things that used to belong to her husband. A knife. A fishing hook. A nail. A button that had fallen from his favorite shirt. She smiled, "I fergot to sew it back on."

The button fell to the table, its sound as loud as thunder. "Well, I'll be. I plum fergot about these."

She withdrew two little pink booties tied together with a white ribbon. Tears filled her eyes as she fingered their softness.

"May I see them?" Bella asked.

"Of course."

Bella took the tiny pink knitted socks into her hands and smiled. She enclosed her fingers around them, hiding their form in her palm. She allowed her fingers to fan out. "It's hard to believe my feet used to be this small."

When no one remarked on the statement, she looked up. Ruth Ann was studying something very far away. Ashlynn was lost in *The Philosophy of Physiotherapy*. Morton was eyeing her suspiciously.

"What is it?" she asked.

Ruth Ann turned her painful gaze to Bella. "Those weren't yers, honey."

"Oh, I suppose they used to fit your tiny feet, Ashlynn."

"They weren't hers either," her Mama admitted.

Bella caught her Mama's gaze. As if all the world came crashing down, the pressure inside her chest needed relief. She pierced the pink socks with her gaze as if she was expecting an answer from them. Finally, her eyes lifted to her uncle's. A softness resided there like never before. He knew.

Bella brought them close to her face. They smelled musty. They were old. They were older than she was. They belonged to Sophia.

"What is his name?" Ashlynn asked.

Bella looked up from the weight that was lying in her hand. "Huh?"

"The man," Ashlynn blushed, "you know, the one from church?"

"Oh! That man." Bella laid the booties onto the table next to the wooden box.

"A man?" her Mama asked.

Immediately, Bella's gaze collided with her uncle's. The softness that was there just moments ago had vanished. She looked to her Mama, surprised to find a hopeful expression. Bella cleared her closing throat. "His name is Darby."

"Darby?" she asked. "Why, that's a mighty handsome name."

"His name ain't the handsomest thing about him, Mama," Ashlynn admitted.

"Ashlynn!" Bella and Ruth Ann said in unison.

She held up her palms, "He's got really pretty eyes, and he likes Bella."

Bella was praying the floor would open up and swallow her. Chair and all.

"Is this true, Bella?"

Bella looked at her Mama and shrugged. "I can't even remember what his eyes look like."

"I don't see how you could forget."

Bella looked at her Uncle Morton in disbelief. Had he really just made that comment?

"What do ya mean, Morton?" Ruth Ann asked.

"What do I mean, Bella?" Morton's probing gaze made her grow more uncomfortable by the minute.

"I have no idea. And if you'll excuse me, I'm going to wash the dishes."

Bella heard her uncle's words as she arose. "He's a scholar at Biltmore Forest School..."

She ignored the rest of his speech, fully aware of her flaming cheeks. Surely, he wouldn't tell everything. Would he?

Bella finally dried the last plate and put it away. Other than worrying about what Morton might reveal, the image of the booties remained in the forefront thoughts of her mind. She wondered how Sophia would feel to know that Papa had kept her baby socks all these years. Perhaps he had hopes of giving them to her himself. Maybe he looked at them every night before going to bed. Or he might have carried them in his pocket. The items in the box did come from his pocket...

"Bella?"

At the sound of her Mama's voice, Bella turned.

"Here, I want you to have these."

Bella dried her hands on her skirt and took the booties into her hands again.

"Maybe you can give 'em to Sophia when the time's right."

Bella nodded and smiled before sliding them into her pocket. "Thanks, Mama."

Ruth Ann smiled. "Now, tell me 'bout this Darby fellow."

Bella shook her head. "There is really nothing to say."

Ruth Ann folded her arms. "Bella?"

She sighed. "Okay, he is leaving for Pennsylvania when he graduates from the Forest School."

"Why's he goin' all the way up there?" she asked.

Bella sighed. "A once in a lifetime opportunity to be a forester."

"Hmmm."

Bella turned to walk away, but Ruth Ann caught her arm. "What about you?"

"What about me?" Bella asked.

"What does he say about leavin' you?"

Tears brimmed Bella's eyes. Immediately, her mind went back to the mountain. Her sunrise. "I promised I would wait."

"You love him."

Bella smiled. "I do."

Ruth Ann took Bella into her arms. "Goodness, child. Love hurts sometimes."

Bella knew all too well that heartache grew hand in hand with love.

"Would yer Papa like him?"

Bella withdrew herself and found her Mama's eyes. An image of dancing in the rain with Papa came to mind, but the taller she grew, the more the figure in the rain changed. She no longer danced with Papa but with Darby.

Bella smiled. "Papa would love Darby."

CHAPTER THIRTY

BELLA HAD NEVER BEHELD SUCH beautiful Christmas trees in all her life. And never had she stood before one so enormous. Her eyes roamed up...up...up.

"Little Christmas tree, isn't it?"

Bella spun around and was glad to see Darby looming over her much like the tall evergreen. "I would hardly call it little," she said as she directed her gaze back toward the Fraser fir.

"It's just as heavy as it is tall," Darby said as he took his place beside her. "All forty feet of it."

"Hmph, how would you know?" Bella asked as she noted just how taut the white material of his shirt fit his biceps. She swallowed and looked away.

"I know because I cut it down."

Darby won her full attention. "You did?" Bella felt her chest swell with delight as she imagined Darby slinging an ax or working a saw, the ending result being the tree on the ground.

"I did." The golden flecks in his eyes had returned like so many other times before. "It's good to see you again," he said as his finger slid along her jawline.

"It's been so long," Bella whispered, perfectly aware of her racing heart.

Darby cocked his head to the side. "It's been a month."

Yes, Bella knew it had been a month. She had relived the stolen moments she had shared with him through the duration of the Forest Fair and the beauty of the sunset he was sure to let her see. But still, it seemed like it happened an eternity ago.

"I didn't know you were invited to the Christmas party," she murmured.

The side of Darby's mouth lifted, drawing far too much to the fullness of his lips. "The entire host of scholars was invited."

"Oh, I didn't know." Bella couldn't keep from smiling all over herself. "Christmas just keeps getting better and better."

Darby offered his arm. "I know and I can't wait until the party's over."

Bella's eyebrows drew together in horror. "Why?"

Darby leaned close to her ear and breathed, "You'll see."

Bella firmly placed her hand into the crook of his arm and allowed him to guide her toward the Banquet Hall's table. Bright red poinsettias spilled over shiny brass churns, intertwined with golden ribbons and holly stems. Each setting consisted of sliced oranges and spiced cider. The scent of cinnamon mixed with evergreen was pure heaven.

She took note how steady Darby's steps were. Relief flooded her soul. "I see that you have been taking care of yourself," Bella whispered as she took her seat.

"Of course. I can't afford to lose sight of my goal at this point," Darby said as he took the seat next to her.

Bella tried ignoring the pang that smote her heart when the she heard the undeniable ring in his voice. It was Christmas.

Only good tidings of joy was supposed to be felt, not a sense of dreaded fear or devastation. She inhaled deeply and picked up an orange slice silently thanking God for a first Christmas spent with the man she loved.

"You look beautiful," Darby whispered entirely too close. Bella stiffened. "You should wear that dress more often. Red is definitely your color."

Bella forced herself to swallow the piece of orange in her mouth. Her eyes flitted toward him cautiously. "Thank you. My Mama made it."

"I know."

She looked him full on. "How did you know?"

"Because I chose the material."

Her eyes grew large, nearly choking on her own words. "You what?"

Darby's teeth shined bright, radiating through his smile. He fingered the cuff of her sleeve. "I knew you wouldn't use any spare time for yourself, so I asked your mother to make it."

Bella swallowed the knot that had suddenly formed thick inside her throat. She wiggled her toes that rested so peacefully in her new boots and wondered if he, too, had purchased them. "Thank you, Darby." The nauseous feeling gnawing at the pits of her stomach nearly made her swoon. She had nothing to give in return.

With a reassuring squeeze, Darby said, "My pleasure."

Just then, the bell rang loudly silencing the merry chit chat. Mrs. Vanderbilt smiled. "Merry Christmas, everyone!"

"Merry Christmas!" the crowd echoed.

"First of all, I want to say thank you to all of you who make Biltmore what it is supposed to be."

The statement earned an applause.

"I also want to say thank you to Mr. Carl Schenck and to the forestry scholars for their endless labor."

Again, the statement was awarded by the applause of many.

Mrs. Vanderbilt smiled warmly at her husband and lifted the goblet in her hand. "Here's to Mr. George Vanderbilt, the man with an undying vision."

"Hear! Hear!"

The fiddler struck his chord hastily, the bass swiftly following suit. Cheerful shouts of glee erupted from the merry makers as they stood to their feet taking a dance partner by the hand. Bella felt Darby's gaze only a second before she found her hand safely in his.

"I've never danced to *Joy to the World* before!" Bella blurted out.

"Neither have I!" Darby answered louder than the host of strumming instruments.

"Where are we going?!" Bella shouted while trying hard to keep up with Darby's hasty steps.

"The Winter Garden!"

"What?!"

Bella could no longer protest when Darby's hands enclosed around her waist like a vise. She had no choice but to place her palms onto his shoulders.

"Merry Christmas, Bella," he said as he slipped his hand into hers, spinning her form in a bound spiral while the bright red skirts moved in unison. Then his hand paused her motion, her eyes fastening boldly onto his. The bright winter sun poured from the dome above, beaming on the pair as if only they existed.

Bella's hand rested firmly in his, the other on his shoulder. His large palm fanned the small of her back, drawing her close. Their feet moved gracefully, her skirts sashaying about their ankles. In perfect time, each step coherent leading them around the circumference of the garden.

Bella's heartbeat drummed in her ears because of the rapid pace of the music. The heat she felt was not generated from her hand being in Darby's or his other hand positioned on her back. The shortness of breath was only caused from being tired and had nothing to do with drowning in the deep pools of emerald or the close proximity to his broad chest. His charming smile stole away all the moisture inside her mouth making it difficult to swallow. She was enjoying this dance far too much. It would end soon. Christmas would end soon. Spring would chase winter to the other side of the earth. And Darby would be in Pennsylvania.

Darby noted the look of terror that crossed Bella's features. He regretfully slowed his pace although the music was still going strong. Maybe she hadn't broken in her new boots and her feet were hurting. The dance came to a brief pause before its initial stop, but the room and its vibrant plants kept dancing around them.

"Bella?"

"Huh?"

He took her rosy cheek into his palm. A slow but steady smile made its way to his lips. "Thirsty?"

Bella only shook her head. He cupped her hand, firmly placing it in the bend of his arm only to be alarmed by the lurking crowd of Biltmore employees and forestry scholars. An abundance of whistlers declared their approval as well as those applauding.

Darby barely dipped his head in reverence before dispersing the crowd. He led Bella through the throng of people, briskly making their way to the table. He took her cider and placed it in her spare hand and then took his own. Together both drank in silence until each goblet was empty.

The music took on a drastic change. *O Come, O Come Emmanuel.*

Darby was pleased to see her look of distress replaced with comfort. "I'm sorry, we shouldn't have danced so long," he apologized.

"So long?" Bella quizzed. "It was hardly long enough."

"Hmmm. Perhaps I shall ask for the next dance." His eyebrows danced with delight as he took her hand and placed a chaste kiss atop it. "May I have the honor of enjoying your presence on the terrace, Miss Westbrook?"

The corners of her mouth lifted. "It's cold outside." Bella glanced to the window. "And it's snowing."

Darby leaned close to her ear, "Hmmm, another reason to hold you close." He heard her gasp. He withdrew himself and offered his arm. "Shall we?"

Bella hesitantly took his arm and whispered, "Hurry before my Uncle Morton sees us."

The chill of a white Christmas welcomed them as they stepped onto the terrace. Bella leaned in close to Darby as he placed his arm around her shoulder, pulling her to his side. "This is the best Christmas I've ever had," he said.

Bella looked up and smiled. "Me too."

"Are you cold?"

"A little," she answered as the fog lifted from her lips.

"Come here." Darby led Bella to the bench where he often sat. There laid a beautifully wrapped package with a large red bow. He took the gift into his hands and placed it into hers. "Merry Christmas from me."

Water filled the corners of her eyes. "Darby, you shouldn't have."

"I wanted to."

Bella fingered the bow. Finally, she slipped her finger within a loop and pulled. The ribbon fell freely to the ground. She easily tore the paper only to find a box. She paused and lifted her eyes.

"Go on." Darby coaxed her.

Bella smiled and returned to the task at hand. "You distract me sometimes."

"You distract me all the time."

She batted her eyelashes daringly. She lifted the lid of the box and pulled back the paper that hid the gift. Her lips parted when her hands brought the lovely shawl into sight. The box, along with its lid, fell to the ground. "It's beautiful," she whispered as she studied the craftsmanship of the embroidery. Tiny red flowers travelled along the edge of the black wool, and a shiny red ribbon made a perfect bow at the collar.

"Put it on," he said.

Bella willingly complied and untied the bow.

"Here, allow me?"

Bella was met with both a determined and passionate gaze. Without protest, she allowed him to take the shawl and drape it across her shoulders. She watched his big hands work as he tied the two pieces of ribbon together, although his fingers lingered a bit longer than necessary. Her eyes lifted only to discover that his were already reined in on hers.

"Darby," she whispered.

His Adam's apple bobbed before whispering her name. "Bella."

His hands slid from the ribbon to the slenderness of her neck. Tilting her face upward, his lips found hers. With a heavenly softness, the kiss deepened. For a moment, he withdrew only to find her eyes dazed much like his felt. Again, his lips met hers. She tasted of sweet orange mixed with spiced cider. Her pulse vibrated through his palm, matching the heartbeat of his own. While cherishing the taste of perfect love and bliss, Darby thanked God for being the recipient of such a perfect and unspeakable gift.

CHAPTER THIRTY ONE

BELLA JUST KNEW SOMEONE HAD surely spied them. If they hadn't, then her flaming cheeks would truly reveal any hidden secrets. She was glad Darby had at least excused himself and joined the guys for a moment.

"Is this seat taken?"

Bella lifted her gaze and smiled. "Of course not. Sit down, Sophia."

Sophia gasped when she noticed Bella's new wool shawl. "That's beautiful." Her fingers slid across the numerous stitches. "Let me guess. Darby gave it to you."

Bella smiled. "How did you know?"

"Because it matches your dress too well."

"How did you know about my dress?"

Sophia chuckled. "Did you think I was really measuring you for a new uniform?"

Bella's eyebrow lifted. "That's how he did it. I wondered how Mama got it so perfect. But how did Darby manage to arrange that with you?"

"At Sunday service."

"Oh, I see."

"Why is your face all flushed?" Sophia felt Bella's forehead. "You aren't feverish."

Bella swallowed the lie, but it quickly resurfaced. "I think it's warm in here. Maybe I'll just take this off."

"That's a good idea. Here, let me have it. I will hang it on your chair."

"Ladies and gentlemen, it's time for gifts!" At the sound of Mrs. Vanderbilt's voice, a herd of employees passed by the long table making their way to the tree.

"Come on," Sophia nudged Bella, "let's hurry."

Bella followed quickly behind Sophia but still ended up near the back.

"Mrs. Vanderbilt went to Paris to buy our gifts," Sophia whispered.

"Really?"

"Yes, and I hope I get perfume."

Bella pinched her nose and said, "I hope you do, too."

Sophia nudged Bella. "Silly girl. Maybe she got you something to help with that ailment you've come down with."

"An ailment?"

Sophia arched her eyebrow. "Yes, the one that causes your lips to swell and your face to blush uncontrollably."

Bella's mouth dropped. "What are you talking about?"

Sophia's eyes darted toward Darby. "Hmmm, Bella. I wonder."

Bella didn't have to search for Darby's gaze. Neither did she have to wonder what ailment she suffered. The molten look in his eyes still remained. She looked away hoping that no one else noticed the connection between them.

"Merry Christmas, Sophia," Mrs. Vanderbilt greeted.

Bella watched as her sister opened the lid to her gift. Sophia gasped. "Thank you, Mrs. Vanderbilt!" Then she withdrew a fancy glass bottle that held a precious perfume.

"Merry Christmas, Bella," Mrs. Vanderbilt smiled as she presented Bella her gift.

Bella lifted the lid to her gift. Curiosity furrowed her brow. The little ball of greenery was bathed with ribbons and fine beads. She looped her finger through its ribbon, lifting it from its confines. It danced to its own beat while the charm descending from its form glistened in the light.

"A mistletoe!" someone shouted from behind her.

Immediately, her gaze snagged Darby's. His appreciative scrutiny fanned the flame. Redness crept up her neck and flooded her face. A nagging feeling told Bella that there was most definitely no cure for being lovesick.

Finally, the last gift was given, or so Bella thought. Then Mr. Vanderbilt entered the Banquet Hall toting along a long, slim box, and she watched as he approached Darby with the package.

"Ladies and gentlemen, to the president of the class and future forester in the state of Pennsylvania, Darby Pierson!" The room filled with an applause. Bella's chest swelled with delight as she watched Darby accept the gift. She wondered what was inside such an extraordinary box. It wasn't long before he slid his pocket knife along the box's edge and revealed a brand new shot gun.

"If you are wondering why Mr. Pierson is receiving such a gift, it is *not* because of his honorable achievements!" The crowd hushed at Mr. Vanderbilt's statement. "Mrs. Vanderbilt has been in a frenzy since she heard the news that Darby did not participate in the possum hunt during the festival!" Mr. Vanderbilt chuckled, "She didn't want him traveling all the way to Pennsylvania without a gun."

Bella watched as the color drained from Darby's cheeks, yet she felt certain her face heated a great deal. She knew why he didn't join the game of fun. He had other *things* on his mind.

Darby cleared his voice, "I appreciate the amount of concern and the trouble you have gone through, Mrs. Vanderbilt." Darby smiled at the Mistress of the house and said, "But I had chosen to study that particular evening." His eyes darted to Bella. She felt the need to squirm away from his sight as his green eyes bore into hers. "My most favorite subject to be exact."

Bella knew that every other set of eyes present was now looking upon her as well. She silently prayed to be a snowman so she could melt to the floor and cease to exist.

Mrs. Vanderbilt smiled and said, "If I had known that I would have given you a hammer and a nail instead of the shotgun!"

Thankfully, everyone turned to the very amused Mrs. Vanderbilt. "At least you could hang her mistletoe!"

The room filled with laughter, and soon the music struck again. Darby started in Bella's direction not taking his eyes off her. He stopped just a mere hair-breadth away and said, "You got a mistletoe?"

Bella just nodded.

Slowly a smile crept onto his gorgeous face. "Christmas just keeps getting better and better."

Soon Bella found herself latched onto Darby's arm once more. She shivered. "Are you cold?" he asked.

"No," she whispered. "Just a little flustered. I've never ridden in a sleigh before."

"There's no need to be afraid. I'll be right beside you."

She looked up at him. "That's what scares me most."

The gleam in his eyes caused her heart to trip. Why did he seem to find satisfaction in her statement?

"I'm glad to share your first sleigh ride," he said as he pushed back the stray hair that so often fell about her brow. Finally, he looked up. "Ah, here it comes."

Darby assisted Bella into the beautiful white sleigh. The glistening gold accents were breathtaking. She had truly underestimated its image. Instead of a wooden bench like she had imagined, it was plush. She sank into its softness, gently trailing her fingertips along the cushions edge.

Darby took his place close beside her. Really close beside her. She felt the urge to move a little closer to the edge but refrained.

The clicking sound of Humphrey's tongue urged the Belgians to move forward.

"Are you cold?" Darby asked.

"I'm fine," she answered.

"Let me see your hands."

She hesitantly removed them from underneath the shawl and was surprised to find him retrieving gloves from his pocket. Very feminine looking gloves. She instantly withdrew her hands in shock.

"Give me your hands, Bella."

"Whose gloves are those?"

"They are yours."

She eyed Darby curiously, "Who did they used to belong to?"

He arched his brow. "Bella, do you think I actually make a habit of carrying another woman's gloves in my pocket?"

She smiled. "I would hope not. If so, then maybe Mrs. Vanderbilt should have given the shot gun to me instead of you."

He tweaked her nose. "The only woman's gloves I would even think about touching would be yours. Now give me your hands."

Bella stretched her chilled hands. His warm grasp held one hand in place while he slipped the glove onto each finger. He repeated the same for the other hand. She stared at them in awe. The same person who made her shawl made the gloves. The same little red flowers trailed the cuffs.

"Who made them?" she whispered.

"My Ma."

"Wow."

"And she also made this." Darby stretched a matching toboggan and slipped it over the crown of her head, her braid left hanging from beneath it.

Bella didn't know what to say. Thank you seemed too mild. "I don't know what to say."

He took her chin and tilted her face upward. "Oh, I think you do." His eyes were burning into her soul. The rosy blotches on his cheek beckoned for her touch. The windy chill and dancing snowflakes couldn't quench this fire.

Bella swallowed the dryness in her throat. Her eyes searched his frantically hoping to find some sort of clue that he wasn't insinuating what she thought he meant. But there was none to be found. She knew the words he was longing to hear. The same ones she was chanting over and over and over.

I love you. I love you. I love you.

Her teeth grazed her bottom lip. Instantly, his gaze was drawn to her mouth. Perhaps the words would have to wait.

CHAPTER THIRTY TWO

SNOW CRUNCHED UNDERNEATH BELLA'S FEET as she followed Darby's lead. Silver light shined from above calling out to the glittery blanket of snowflakes on the ground. "Where are you taking me?" Bella asked.

"Is there any need to guess?" Darby said as he squeezed her hand gently.

"Probably not," she smiled.

As they stepped onto the terrace Bella felt an urgent need to beg him not to go. To forget Pennsylvania and share the rest of his life with her. She knew tonight would most likely be the last night she would get to see him. Really see him. Stare into the bottomless emeralds. Enjoy the warmth of his fingers grazing her skin. Struggling to keep even breaths.

She was surprised when he abruptly spun around to face her, taking hold of her waist with his free hand. "I want to dance with you," he said, his voice warm and husky. "I want to dance for only you."

Bella's breath hitched when he moved his hand from her waist and took the side of her face. "I know you won't dance in the rain with me," the dip in his tone evident. But he cleared his throat and said, "How about dancing in the snow?"

Bella searched his eyes in wonder. Although she was unwilling to give him that special place in her heart, he was humble enough to accept less than the best. She cleared her swelling throat. "Of course."

His face lit up with a deadly smile. "Good. Because I wasn't taking no for an answer."

Bella giggled and fell into step. Their eyes locked into place. Each of them fell into the deepest, hidden parts of the heart as their feet moved accordingly the length of the terrace.

"Do you remember the first time we met here?" he whispered.

"How could I forget?"

"You held my hand while I limped along." His expression was full of unbound appreciation.

"You got frustrated, and I ran away." Bella shook her head. "I should have never run from you." If only he felt the same about her and decided to stay in Asheville.

Darby arched his eyebrow. "And you regret doing so, Miss Westbrook?"

Bella swallowed and tried concentrating on her next step, but the tiny circles he was drawing on her wrist nearly stole away her next breath. "At least I only stayed away for a few days."

He cocked his head to the side, "And what might you be insinuating, Bella?"

"I think you already know." She tried masking the hurt and pain and longing and dread, but the tears refused to stay put. Darby's feet ceased to move. His countenance fell. "I thought you understood."

Bella looked away. She couldn't bear to look at him. She didn't wish to unleash the harbored feelings. She didn't want to understand his decision. She wanted him. She wanted him more than anything. More than Biltmore. More than dreams. More than life itself. And she wanted him to want her unconditionally as well.

"Bella, look at me."

She gradually lifted her gaze.

"I will only be gone for a year," he reminded her.

"You don't understand, Darby." Bella shook her head. "So much can change in a year."

The moment fell silent as if he was trying to understand her. Neither moved. They just stood there. Her hand still rested in his. Finally, his forehead fell against hers, and her eyes drifted closed. "Look at me." Hot breath fanned her face. She allowed her eyes to open only to discover the trueness in his gaze. "My heart will not change."

"You can't make that kind of promise. The heart is deceitful. You should know that."

He smiled. "So you have been listening to what the preacher has to say."

"I've heard exactly what I have wanted to hear."

Darby squeezed her like a vise. "Why does that not surprise me, Bella?"

She shrugged.

"Come on," he said, "let's dance in the snow."

"Wait. I want to give you something." She searched her pocket and withdrew her greatest possession. "I want you to have this. Merry Christmas."

Darby stared at the aged pocket watch lying in his hand. "Where did you get this?"

"It used to belong to my Papa."

He lifted his eyes. "You want me to have it?"

Bella barely nodded her head. "I know it's not much."

"Bella, it's more than enough." His free hand hooked around her waist and pulled her close. His lips softly found hers. "Thank you," he muttered.

"You're welcome. I hope you like it."

"I love it." He whispered against her lips. "There's not enough money in the world to purchase it."

Bella smiled and withdrew another item from her pocket. "I thought you were going to hang this for me." Lying in her palm was the mistletoe.

Darby smiled warmly, his eyes transitioning from emerald to evergreen. "I hang the mistletoe; you dance in the snow. Deal?"

"Deal."

Bella's steps were slow as she found her way to her quarters. Her heart was still hammering uncontrollably. She had never danced so much in her entire life. Especially in the snow. That had definitely been a first. And it was with Darby. Despite the falling snowflakes, she remained warm in his embrace.

Once she was in the confines of her room, she allowed her arms to enfold around her waist. Her form spun once more while envisioning Darby and his disarming smile. He had reassured her countless times that his heart would never change even though he never confessed the three words she longed to hear. Yet his random kisses told her as much.

Her heart ached when she thought about how long it might be before they could see each other again. She knew he had lots of studying to do. Above all of his expectations, Darby was going to be taking a trip to Pennsylvania in January. He would be gone for an entire week. Still that didn't compare to a year.

But she trusted him.

He trusted her.

Together, he had promised her there was nothing they couldn't accomplish.

A light tapping on her door caused her to yelp. "Yes?"

"Bella, it's me."

Relief flooded through her as she stepped toward the door and twisted the knob. "Sophia, you scared me to death." Her hand fanned her heart.

"Sorry," she smiled. "May I come in?"

"Sure."

Sophia stepped inside the small room dimly glowing by the lamplight. "I see you have not been cured of your ailment."

The tips of Bella's fingers grazed her puffy lips. She smiled. "I hope I am never healed of being lovesick."

Together they giggled. "So he's really leaving, huh?" Sophia asked.

Bella took a deep breath and nodded. "I want to support him in every way, but when he leaves," Bella just shook her head, "the better half of me will die."

"Well, here." Sophia stretched out her hand revealing a package that Bella hadn't even noticed. "Maybe this will help."

Bella nervously took the package into her hands. "You bought something for me?"

Sophia smiled. "Just open it."

Bella took her fingers and tore the brown paper gently. It fell to the floor. In her hands was a beautiful stationery. Cream colored paper with light pink accents and matching envelopes. "Thank you, Sophia. It looks romantic."

Sophia giggled. "I thought so, too. Now you can write to him every week, and maybe the time will pass more swiftly."

"I hope you're right."

"Well, I am exhausted." Sophia yawned. "I waited for hours to hear your footsteps."

Unbidden heat flushed Bella's cheeks.

Sophia held up her hand. "You do not have to enlighten me."

"We danced in the snow."

Sophia's eyes smiled. "That must have been wonderful."

"It was." Bella looked down at the gift in her hands.

Sophia stepped forward and embraced Bella. "Merry Christmas, Bella."

"Wait. Don't go yet. I have something I want to give to you." Bella laid the paper and envelopes onto her bed and stepped over to the chest of drawers. The top drawer stubbornly opened. Her chest tightened when she laid her eyes on them. She had refused to look at them ever since her Mama gave them to her. She took the pink booties into her hand. Even their weight seemed to be far too heavy than necessary.

She turned and stretched out her palm. "Merry Christmas."

Sophia took the booties into her own hands. Her fingertips caressed the stitching. Water brimmed her eyes. She knew. "He loved me."

"Obviously so. They were in a box of *very* important things."

Tears rolled down Sophia's cheeks and fell to the floor with a thud. She brought the tiny booties to her face and inhaled. "Cedar. I always wondered what he smelled like."

Now, both sisters were releasing tears of joy mixed with an unknown longing. They fell into each other's arms cherishing the warmth of Christmas while the flakes of snow danced in the moonlight.

CHAPTER THIRTY THREE

WINTER HAD COME AND GONE. The trees surrounding Biltmore Estate were starting to bud and bring forth new life. The chirping birds were glad to be returning home. The day lilies were showing off their blooms. Everything seemed as it should be. Except for Bella.

Darby had stood true to his word. She had seen very little of him. But she would see him today. At the graduation ceremony of Biltmore Forest School.

The Courtyard was filled with a host of people. Bella's eyes scanned the crowd, and finally her gaze landed on her Mama and Ashlynn. She stepped cautiously down the steps, careful not to step on the hem of her new dress. A pink one. One she had actually made herself, although she hated to sew. A hand gripped her bicep. She turned briskly and suddenly had to concentrate on breathing. "Darby," she whispered.

He inhaled deeply. "You smell like honeysuckle today." He stepped back and drank in her image. "And you look absolutely divine in pink."

Redness crept up her neck. "Thank you."

He fingered the sleeve. "Did you make this?"

"I did. I had to do something during the winter besides mooning over someone."

"So you didn't moon over me?" he teased.

Bella smiled. "Only in my dreams."

He tweaked her nose. "At least I haunted your sleep much like you did mine." He took her elbow, "Come on, the ceremony is ready to begin." He inclined his mouth to her ear. "And I shall meet you on the terrace afterwards."

Bella's heart skipped a beat, and instantly she knew the ailment from which she suffered greatly while in Darby's presence would weaken her resolve today. He propelled her toward where her Mama and sisters were seated. "Until then, my *belle*." Bella took seat beside her Mama after giving her a warm hug. Her hand reached toward Ashlynn. She gave her a gentle squeeze and turned her attention toward Mr. Schenck.

"Good afternoon, everyone. We want to thank each and every one of you for attending the graduation ceremony. We also want to thank these young men for their appreciation of the school and for making it what it is." His hand fanned the standing men behind him. "These are the men of our future." The crowd applauded.

"Also, we wish to thank George Vanderbilt, the man with a vision. Had it not been for his undying desire to see the depleted forests be transformed into vast, nourishing farmland, then we would not be standing here today." Again, the crowd applauded.

"Mr. Vanderbilt, if you will." Carl Schenck nodded toward the stack of leather backed binders. "When I say your name, scholars of Biltmore Forest School, please come forward. Lyle Asher." The crowd applauded as Mr. Asher took his diploma into his left hand, his right hand joining Mr. Vanderbilt's.

"Joshua Crider... Brent Frasier... Patrick Hunts... David Loving... Hunter Morris..."

Bella watched as each young man proudly stepped forward and accepted his well-deserved diploma. She noticed Darby's name was not called. Her eyes carefully roamed toward his masculine form. He was already looking at her. Butterflies unleashed when he winked at her. She hurriedly looked away, silently chiding him for being so bold.

"Ladies and gentlemen, due to his God-given talent for forestry and his drive to achieve his goals, I wish to present to you the president of the class of 1908-1909, Mr. Darby Pierson!"

Bella leapt to her feet. Forbidden tears of happiness and sudden dread streamed down her cheeks. She cheered him on as he took his post before the crowd. He held his head high, his shoulders broad and squared. His smile was deadly, and his eyes locked onto hers. Suddenly her weakened knees were begging to be supported. She took her seat along with the rest of the crowd, her heart pounding in her ears.

"Thank you Dr. Schenck and Mr. Vanderbilt. I truly appreciate your confidence." His eyes finally roamed the crowd. "Since I was just a child, I had a dream to stand exactly where I am standing right now."

Bella's chest tightened.

"An internal Voice has called me to a higher ground. In order for my children, your children and their children to enjoy the fullness of Mother Nature, we must begin conserving our forests today." His statement earned an applause. "The term here at

Biltmore Forest School has not only taught me how to replenish depleted forests, but it has enlightened my heart."

The crowd hushed, and Bella had begun to squirm under his scrutinizing gaze. "Sometimes life turns upside down, and when it does, there is usually no warning. It's during those times when we find out who we really are. Our weaknesses come to surface. Our strongholds come to light. But oft times instead of working through our problems, we allow bitterness to take over our hearts much like a vine of thorns, choking out all rays of hope."

Bella swallowed and tried tearing her eyes away, but the magnitude was too strong. "To overcome the sting of disappointment, I've learned to plant seeds of hope and water them with care. The ending result is nothing less than the unspeakable gift of true love." Darby smiled and redirected his gaze. "Learning how to dance was not on the agenda of becoming a forestry scholar either." His eyes darted back to Bella. "But I've learned to dance in the worst of storms. Even if I had to dance alone."

A man that had been seated on the front row stood up in reverence to Darby's speech and was wiping his eyes with his handkerchief. Everyone else followed suit. Finally, the echo of applause filled the air while the scholars took Darby, lifted his masculine form from the ground, and paraded him around the courtyard.

A firm grip took hold of Bella's arm. She turned and was surprised to see Morton.

"Uncle Morton," she smiled, "thank you for bringing Mama and Ashlynn."

"No need to thank me," he waved his hand. His countenance was softened a bit more than usual. "Bella, I'm proud of you."

Her eyebrows raised. "Really? What for?"

"It looks to me like you have a very good judge of character. I was wrong. Darby is a good man."

Bella smiled. "I could have told you that."

A saddened smile crossed his features. "I know, but I wouldn't have listened. Forgive me?"

"Forgiven." She smiled and embraced her uncle.

He held her at arms-length, "You're one of the strongest young women I know." His eyes darted to where Sophia was standing.

"Thank you," Bella whispered.

With a gentle squeeze, he released her and strode away. Bella turned to her Mama and two sisters. "Come on, I want you to see the terrace."

Darby was relieved when the boys finally put him down. He hurried to find his Ma and Pa before they departed. His gut clenched when he found them in conversation with Morton. He approached them and hooked his arm around his Ma's shoulder.

"Darby! You sure know how to make a mama proud."

"Thank you, Ma."

"I will let you visit," Morton stretched out his hand toward Darby, "I enjoyed your speech. It was very true. Good luck in Pennsylvania."

Darby's hand gripped Morton's in unusual unity. "Thank you, Morton."

Morton turned and walked away. Before he was out of sight, he turned and hollered, "Don't forget about my niece!"

Darby smiled victoriously. "Not a chance!"

Darby turned to his parents. Surprisingly, his Pa stepped toward him with open arms. He felt the strength in his Pa's embrace. He withdrew his face. "I'm proud of ya, boy. Couldn't be happier."

"Thanks, Pa."

Charles buried his fists in his pockets and studied his feet. "So yer goin' to Pennsylvania?"

Darby nodded. "I'm leaving in the morning."

Charles lifted his eyes and withdrew an envelope from his shirt pocket. "This might change yer mind."

Darby took the envelope into his large hands and extracted a letter. His eyes scanned its contents. His throat went completely dry. Were the words really there or was he hallucinating? He tried swallowing the shocking news. "I can't believe this," he whispered.

"Well, b'lieve it cause it's true. Pierson Enterprises is yers."

Darby lifted his eyes. "Are you sure?"

"More sure than I'll ever be."

"What about the contracts?" Darby asked.

"Signed one this mornin'. Best contract Pierson Enterprises has ever had."

Darby swallowed the large lump in his throat and shifted his gaze to the man striding toward him. It was none other than Robert Conklin.

"Hello, Mr. Pierson! Such a heart-warming speech."

Darby folded the letter and slid it into the envelope. "Thank you, sir. Meet my parents, Charles and Odetta Pierson."

Mr. Conklin stretched out his hand. "Nice to meet both of you. You have a fine son. One to be very proud of." He directed his gaze back to Darby. "I guess you're packed and ready."

Darby gritted his teeth. "Everything is packed and waiting beside the door, sir."

"Good. I will pick you up at nine in the morning." He nodded his head. "Good day."

They stood in silence as Robert Conklin walked away.

A gentle touch on his arm pulled Darby out of the trance. "What are ya gonna do, son?"

"Oh, Ma, I don't know. It's like I'm standing at a crossroad, and the arrow is pointing in both directions."

"You'll know in the morning, son." Charles said as he patted Darby's chest. "You'll feel it right here."

"He's right, Darby," his Ma said. "Jus' follow yer heart."

As Bella stepped onto the terrace to meet Darby for the last time, her emotions almost got the best of her. She took in the purple specks of Wisteria hanging over her head and the abundance of greenery creating a vast amount of shade. Even today the Blue Ridge Mountains seemed bluer.

When she felt she was no longer alone, she turned. There he was. Handsome as ever. Darby's eyes connected with hers as he strode toward her with confidence. There was no need to speak. Their actions said it all. Bella took step to meet him in the middle underneath nature's canopy.

The closer they drew to one another, the more beckoned Bella felt to run and jump into his arms and never let go. And she did. Darby took her by the waist and spun her until she felt dizzy. Her braid had unwound leaving an abundance of golden waves for Darby to bury his face in as he had always dreamed of doing. He inhaled her sweet scent and kissed her cheek, her forehead, and her eyelids. Finally, his mouth found hers.

Bella pulled back as her eyes drifted open. She had never seen the intensity that was in his eyes now. "I don't want to leave you." She heard him say. "Never," he said. Bella wanted to agree but she was supposed to be supporting him not hindering him. "You'll be back soon," she whispered.

"Not soon enough. I'll go crazy without you." He held onto her petite form. "Go with me." He leaned back and found her eyes. "We'll be married today and leave in the morning." He smiled as if he had the most genius idea.

"Is that a proposal?" Bella's eyebrow raised in question. "Because that's not quite how I had it pictured."

His brow lifted. "Should I get down on one knee?"

She laughed. "And we will live with Robert Conklin. I'm sure he would be thrilled."

"Oh. I never thought of that."

"Just wait a year, Darby. Next spring." She acted nonchalantly but deep inside Bella didn't know if she, too, could stay sane without him near.

"Next spring?" He digested the thought. He took Bella's hands into his and found her eyes. "Promise me that you, Bella Westbrook, will await my return and become my wife."

Bella's pulse quickened. He was asking her to be his wife! "Tell me, Darby Pierson, what makes you think you deserve the title of being my husband?"

The side of his mouth lifted. He knew why he deserved her to be his wife. "Besides the fact that you are my refuge in the storm and the stronghold during weakness," his finger trailed her cheek bone, "you make my sun rise and my sun set. I love you, Bella."

"You-you love me?" Bella's voice grew hoarse. She had longed to hear him say those words over and over without end.

"I love you more than life itself." He touched her forehead with his. "I hope the feeling is mutual."

Bella's eyes lit up as only Darby could make them do. "Yes!"

"Yes as in you will be my wife, or yes as in you love me?" Darby jested.

"Darby Pierson, I love you with my entire heart! And yes, I dream of being your wife!"

"That's what I was hoping for." His lips barely grazed hers.

"By the way, I brought you something. It'll keep you busy until I return."

Darby pulled away and walked to the nearby bench where a package laid. Bella hadn't even noticed he had brought it along. He gestured for her to sit. The package was neither large nor small. It was wrapped in brown paper and tied with a red bow. Her fingers pulled the bow loose, and she gently uncovered the gift. Her breath caught. "Darby," she whispered his name, "where did you find this?"

Bella was staring at an all new edition of *The Philosophy of Physiotherapy*. She fingered its glossy cover as she awaited his answer.

"Do you like it?" he asked.

Bella swiftly turned her face to him. "I love it, Darby, but it must have cost a fortune."

"It's been bought and paid in full; no need to worry about it." He watched her as she removed it from the paper. He watched her eyes light up when it popped and squeaked when she opened its cover. Her eyes drifted closed when she inhaled the scent of a new book.

"Darby, I don't know what to say." Her eyes focused on him. "Thank you."

"You're welcome, beautiful." His finger touched the tip of her nose.

As embarrassing as it was, Bella didn't have anything to give Darby in return. She couldn't afford to buy something new, and she certainly didn't possess anything of much value. "I'm sorry I don't have anything to give you."

"You've given me everything I ever wanted. You've given me your heart."

Bella stopped him. "The heart!" She wound her hands behind her neck and fingered the golden latch. The charm dangled, the diamonds glistening in the sunlight. "Here, take this."

Darby took the tiny jewel into his hand and examined it carefully and then slid it into the pocket on his shirt. He patted it gently, "It'll keep my heart beating with your love while I'm away." He took her hand. "Dance with me one last time."

Together their feet moved along the length of the terrace and back. He placed his forehead onto hers, relishing the moment. Finally, their steps slowed, and Darby took Bella into his arms for the last time before letting go. His finger trailed the course of her lips. "I have to go," he choked.

"Don't go," she whispered.

"Oh, Bella." And for the first time, Bella tasted his tears. "I love you," he whispered.

"I love you, too, Darby. More than you will be able to think or imagine."

"Don't ever forget how much I love you, and I promise you my heart." Darby placed another kiss onto her lips. "Until then, my *belle*."

Bella stood on the terrace alone and watched him walk away. He waved his hand in the air until he was out of sight. She stood there clutching the book to her chest. She refused to cry. He would return soon, if she could picture a year being soon. Finally after what seemed like forever, Bella retired to her room. When she heard the door click, she could hold it no longer. A sob erupted from way down deep. She collapsed onto her bed and let her heart cry.

Bella had been crying so hard she hadn't even heard the thunder, and she thought the drops on her cheeks were just tears, but they weren't. Rain drops were falling steadily from the clouds above. How she had gotten outside in the midst of the Spring Garden, Bella didn't know. But here she stood. She was surrounded by beauty. And vibrant color. And life. Yet, why did she feel so sad? So alone? So broken?

Then Bella was reminded of Darby's departure. That's what was wrong. She turned and began to walk back toward the house when a loud clap of thunder shook the ground beneath her feet. She collapsed to her knees and buried her face in her hands. She had begun weeping again as the heavy drops of rain fell from the heavens. Suddenly, she heard someone say, "Just dance, Bella."

She looked up expecting to find someone there, but she was alone. Bella was certain what she heard was audible, not something that just darted through her mind. The rain slacked so she stood with haste trying to ignore her rapid heartbeat and jogged toward her exit when a lightning bolt splintered a tree causing it to fall in her path. Bella screamed and turned to run in the opposite direction when the waters had swiftly risen blocking her escape. Bella turned in a circle, not sure what she should do when she heard the voice again say, "Just dance, Bella." She turned another circle looking for the owner of the voice but found no one. Rain was steadily dripping from her chin. She had to blink away the droplets just to be able to see her surroundings. She was drenched. She had to get out of here, but there was no way out.

Bella spotted a bush large enough to give her shelter. She ran to it and hunkered down on her knees trying to hide herself under its branches when she heard the voice speak for the third time. "Just dance, Bella."

Bella lifted her eyes to the sky. A gentle ray of light fought the stormy horizon. She watched it as it peeked its way between the dark clouds. Then with great strength, the light pushed through and drew the most beautiful rainbow in the sky. The rain drops were nothing more than a drizzle, the thunder had been silenced and the lightning had been driven far away.

Bella scooted out from underneath her sanctuary and stood. Still, her eyes were focused on the light that was now shining more vibrantly than before. Was it the light speaking, encouraging her to dance? Or was it the rain? Or could it possibly have been Papa?

CHAPTER THIRTY FOUR

THE HOUR HAD GROWN LATE. Bella could tell that much. She obviously had cried herself to sleep because her pillow was still wet with tears. She raised up in her bed while her gaze landed upon the book Darby had given her. Already she felt the ache start to come alive again. She took the book into her hands and opened its front cover. Her heart jolted when she noticed Darby had written something inside. His script was flawless. Much like him.

My Dearest Bella,

Had it not been for you, my life would not have taken this wonderful turn. Had you not helped me when I was crippled, I would have been forced to limp away from my dream. But you were there.
Sometimes life takes these twists and turns and that's what makes us who we are. Either we stand defeated or we learn to weather the storm. You have taught me so much. You've learned to handle whatever life throws your way. You stand strong and I want you to know that I stand amazed.

There is just one tiny part of your heart you will not open unto me. It's a special place you hold dear to your Papa. As I recall, he told you God would send you someone to dance in the rain with when he is gone. Remember? I want to slip off my shoes and take your hands in mine and dance in the rain like there's no tomorrow. Together we could fight any storm. I am willing to take that step if you'll unlock that sacred place in your heart.

Bella, if you begin to miss me while I'm gone, just dance.

With all my love,
Darby

Bella's heartbeat echoed in her ears. Now she remembered the dream she had what little time she slept. Odd that he used the same words that had been spoken to her. *Just dance.*

She pondered if that was what God was waiting for. She remembered in her dream the tree had fallen in her way, water had risen beyond escape, and then finally, she was driven to her knees. Perhaps that was what God wanted.

Bella pondered Darby's words as she recalled the many times as a child that she danced in the rain. Although she didn't understand the fullness of its purpose, she truly enjoyed it. It felt exhilarating. She was free. Nothing stood in her way. The storm didn't frighten her. She didn't notice the thunder. The lightning didn't blind her.

Like a rushing water of life, Bella realized just what to do. If she'd just dance now, she would be free. Nothing could stand in her way. The storm couldn't be strong enough to frighten her nor the lightning bright enough to blind her.

Bella slid from her bed and onto her knees. She figured this was as good a place to start as any.

Morning came just as it always did, but Bella was different. She awoke with a smile. She hadn't forgotten that Darby was leaving today; neither had she forgotten her last moments with him. She was reminded of her dream when she heard the rain drops falling. Bella bit her lip. Dare she even think it, but wouldn't it feel nice just to get a little wet?

Bella escaped the house without being noticed and bypassed the terrace. This time she didn't allow it to intimidate her. She paused before the Courtyard. No, the area was too open. Then her eyes traveled the length of the Pergola. The bountiful Wisteria was in full bloom; it seemed to beckon her presence. She took slow, steady steps the entire length of the arbor. Her feet drew near the open end of the Pergola. It was a perfect place to be alone. The raindrops had begun to fall a bit harder. Flashbacks of her as a child dancing with Papa froze her in place. She could hear him. She could hear herself giggling as any child would. Bella had to close her eyes to silence the moment.

She could do this.

She knew she could do this.

When she reopened her eyes, Bella was aware of the light peeking from behind the clouds. It took her breath away as she stretched her hands out, and opened her palms unto the heavens. The cool drops of rain rolled from her skin and fell to the earth. It was in that moment the same voice in her dream spoke, *"Just dance."*

Bella turned thinking surely she was not alone. But she was. Her attention was drawn back to the light. It had opened a little further. Her heart pulsated so strongly she could feel it in her hands. She knew deep down that the voice came from the light. But who was it?

"Papa?" Bella whispered as she observed the storm, but the voice didn't answer.

She swallowed the knot in her throat. She could do this.

She took one foot and slipped off one shoe. And then the other. Her fingers peeled off her socks. She lifted the hem of her skirt and observed her bare feet. Feet that used to dance in the rain without being told. Her eyes lifted to the rain and then fluttered closed as she stepped out from underneath the shelter of Wisteria. Cool drops of rain rolled down her cheeks. Her neck. Her hands. Her ankles. Her head tilted back and her eyes opened. The light had become even greater; so had the rain. Again, the voice spoke, but this time she heard her name. *"Just dance, Bella."* A smile formed on her lips. She knew who the voice belonged to.

The Light.

Bella dropped the hem of her skirt and opened her palms. Soon they were filled with water. A bounce started to form in her feet. She took a deep breath. Her body turned in a circle. And another. And another. The bounce in her feet became greater. Greater. Greater. A giggle erupted as she smiled into *The Light*.

She was dancing.

Darby loaded his last suitcase onto the carriage. His peers stood by to wave him off, but for some reason, he didn't feel as excited about this as they did.

Robert Conklin had already taken his seat and called, "Come on! It's raining!"

Raining.

He knew that.

Immediately, his thoughts were filled with someone he held dear to his heart.

Bella.

He wished she were here to wave him off, but she wasn't. She had duties to fill. With one last goodbye to the scholars and his mentor, Darby took his seat beside Conklin and closed the carriage door.

The coachman called, "Are we ready?"

"Ready!" Conklin answered.

Darby felt the carriage urge forward. He broke out into a cold sweat, almost feeling suffocated. What was wrong with him? He had rode in a carriage many times without being sick.

Images of a beautiful young woman filled his mind's eye. The way she smiled at him that caused his heart to flop. The way he drowned in her lovely eyes. The way her braid laid gently across her shoulder. The way she felt so perfect in his arms. Her hand in his hand. What was he doing walking away from a love like that?

"Stop!" Darby yelled. The carriage came to a halt.

"Did you forget something?" Conklin asked curiously.

Darby looked to the man who was giving him an opportunity of a lifetime. "I most certainly did, Mr. Conklin. I'm afraid my possession cannot come along with me, so therefore, I mustn't go." He held up his hand, "If you'll excuse me."

Darby bailed out of the carriage and made straightaway to the barn leaving his belongings behind. He didn't care what happened to them. All he needed right now was Bella.

He mounted Chestnut, caring not about the rain. He urged the beast forward. Even Chestnut sensed the importance to get moving. When Darby rounded the last curve and the extravagant house came into view, his heels dug deeper into Chestnut's side. The horse came to an abrupt stop in front of the house, and Darby dismounted. He entered the mansion without permission caring not how soaked he was. The butler just dropped his jaw, and a nearby maid screamed when he trampled on her freshly polished floors. Darby apologized and continued moving. He racked his mind trying to think of where Bella would be right now. He didn't know, but he knew someone who did.

Darby darted through the door just past the Grand Staircase and descended the steps. He made his way down the stone hallway and past the pool. Finally, he could see the view of the kitchen. Just as he was about to storm into it, Sophia made her exit. Her eyes grew large when his form nearly crushed her.

Darby gripped Sophia's shoulders to steady her. "Where's Bella?" he asked breathlessly.

"I don't know. We've searched for her all morning." A worried expression filled her eyes.

Darby put his hand over his face. Think Darby! Think! He finally caught his breath.

"The terrace!" Sophia exclaimed. "We've not looked on the terrace!"

Relief melted over Darby. Of course, that's where she was! Why had he not thought of that?

"Thank you." Darby broke off into a swift jog back the way he came.

Sophia couldn't help but smile and thank the Lord that Darby had changed his mind. Not caring if anyone noticed, she turned in a circle and bounced a bit on the tips of her toes. God really does answer prayer.

The maid had just gotten the last muddy footprint removed from the shiny floor when Darby came barreling back through the foyer again and out the front door. She sat back on her heels and shook her head. Men.

Darby slowed his pace when he approached the terrace. His eyes searched the area frantically. She wasn't there. He felt beckoned to call her name as his heart beat mercilessly inside his chest. Where could she be?

Instinct drew him down the steps. The beating rain blurred his vision. He lifted his hands to wipe away the water droplets from his eyes. Just then a movement from the opposite end of the Pergola stole his attention.

He had to blink again.

No.

It was impossible.

Darby stepped underneath the shelter of Wisteria to get a better view, and never before had looked upon something so beautiful.

Oh, but yes.

It was Bella.

In the rain.

And she was dancing.

Bella had never felt freer. She just couldn't stop dancing. Despite everything that had gone wrong in her life, she refused to let it steal her desire to dance in the rain. Her eyes blinked back Mother Nature's tears. Thankfully, this time the tears were not her own. It felt so good. Revitalizing.

Bella's feet had grown a bit tired and had slowed a great deal. She was soaked through and through. She was new through and through. She was-

Bella's breath caught when she caught sight of the man making confident and even strides down the length of the Pergola. She froze, her palms still facing upward catching every droplet of rain possible. Was it just a mirage? She blinked several times, but the mirage never faded. Instead, she detected a fierce gaze. One that caused her heart to race. His green irises penetrated into her very soul like always before. She felt like she was swiftly falling into a bottomless vortex.

It was him.

Darby.

He stepped from beneath the natural canopy, his eyes still reined in on hers. Bella had to force herself to breathe as she watched the rain roll down his face and fall to the ground. He was as drenched as she.

His fingers gripped her wrists slightly and turned her palms over. Together, their fingers interlaced. His thumbs caressed her wrists. Surely he felt her undying pulse.

Darby took her hands and hooked them around his neck as his hands encircled her waist. His gaze had taken on a different note as his eyes pierced hers. Bella's eyelids drifted closed as his face drew near. His lips sought Bella's. They were warm and sweet even in the rain. Darby drew back and moved his hands to her face. This time he held nothing back. His kissed her with a fervent love, one that he hoped she wouldn't forget. When he opened his eyes, he found Bella smiling. He kissed her smile. He kissed her cheek. Her forehead. Finally, he rested his forehead against hers. A love sparked between them that even the rain had not the power to extinguish.

"I thought you were leaving," Bella whispered.

Darby smiled. "I thought I was, too."

"You mean you've- you've changed your mind?" Bella tried blinking away the salty tears mixed with rain.

Darby held her face in the palms of his hands and pressed his lips firmly against hers. "I can't believe I considered walking away from this," he confessed before their lips met again.

"So, you're staying in Asheville?" Bella asked in between kisses.

"Yes, I'm staying."

"Really?"

"Just dance, Bella." Darby's husky tone reverberated throughout her veins as he placed another kiss on her lips. He took her hand and spun her. Not once. Not twice. But many times.

Together, they shared an undying love as they danced in the rain in the midst of their storm.

CHAPTER THIRTY FIVE

Six months later

BOTH SOPHIA AND RUTH ANN fussed over the heaping curls that were deliberately piled atop Bella's head. "Sophia, hand me one more pin. That outta do it," Ruth Ann said as she held her hand on the mass of hair she intended to stay put. Sophia just shook her head with a smile. The same statement had been made twenty pins ago.

"Here." The ruffles of Sophia's dress swished as she stepped around Bella. She playfully tugged at the curl lying against Bella's face. "You're the most beautiful bride a man could ask for."

"Until you put on this dress, dear sister," Bella countered. "You'll have so many forestry scholars nipping at your heels today you'll know not what to do." A smile formed on Bella's face. Just months ago, she had feared she could never come to love Sophia as a sister, but now she couldn't imagine life without her.

"All right, Bella," Ruth Ann's voice called out, "stand up easy." Bella obeyed and barely moved the upper portion of her body as she stood.

"It couldn't look more beautiful, Bella!" Ashlynn's blue eyes sparkled as she took in her sister's abundance of hair.

"Thank you," she said stepping in front of the mirror, the same mirror Mrs. Vanderbilt stood before each day. The kind woman insisted that Bella make use of the luxuries while she was away, and that wasn't even the best of it. During their absence, the Vanderbilts insisted Bella and Darby were to retreat to Biltmore House for their honeymoon and accommodate themselves however they pleased.

Ruth Ann stepped in front of Bella and pressed down on her hair for the hundredth time. "Hold still again."

"Mama, don't worry with it. It'll be a mess in a bit anyhow." Bella glanced at the window, "It looks like rain."

Ruth Ann stepped back and inspected Bella for the last time, "All right, baby girl," her face lit up with a smile, "this is it."

"Yes," Bella took a deep breath, "this is it."

Bella followed her Mama, Sophia, and Ashlynn down the corridor and watched them step onto the elevator. They would be waiting in the foyer along with the rest of the guests. Bella took another deep breath although the attempt failed to keep her heart from racing. Her eyes shifted toward the window. The smile on her face indicated that today was the happiest day of her life, and she felt confident that growing old with Darby was the next best thing to serving God.

Her hand took hold of the stair railing while the other hand held her bouquet; then she began to make her descent down the Grand Staircase.

Bella took only one step at a time careful not to trip over the excessive material dancing about her feet while the train followed close behind hushing the crowd below as it slid from step to step.

Darby could not tear his eyes away from the most beautiful woman he had ever beheld. He took note of the abundance of honey colored curls, delicate creamy skin, her full rose colored lips, and her chocolate coated eyes. His heart constricted as he tried to slowly calm himself. Her eyes were burning into the innermost parts of his soul as she descended the staircase like a queen. Finally, he swallowed the massive knot that had formed in his throat and stepped to the bottom step where she took his arm. For a moment, Darby forgot exactly what he was supposed to do until he was reminded by the preacher.

"Ladies and gentlemen," Pastor Jimmy Jackson spoke clearly, "if you'll please step aside and allow the bride and groom their exit."

The crowd split evenly down the middle and waited reverently as Darby escorted Bella through the foyer and out the door. Once they were outside, Darby leaned close, "You're beautiful, Bella."

Her pink cheeks turned a shade deeper, "Thank you," she whispered.

Darby led the bride onto the terrace, the place they had met so many times. They were to exchange their vows here where the Blue Ridge Mountains created a perfect backdrop for the couple. Bella released her bouquet unto Sophia and planted both her hands into Darby's.

"Dearly beloved," Pastor Jackson began, "we are gathered here today..."

Bella stared into the eyes of the man God had created for her. A strong, godly man who could see directly through her eyes and into her heart. He would be a tremendous husband to her and a wonderful father to her children. Together they would share their lives, through good times and the bad. Bella couldn't help but wonder if they would dance in the rain quite a bit, too.

"And I now pronounce you Mr. and Mrs. Darby Pierson," Pastor Jackson declared. "You may kiss the bride."

Darby gently loosed his hands from hers and lifted the veil with ease. His gaze awarded her silently with praise and promise as he slid one hand around her waist and took her chin in the other. Bella hooked her hands around his neck and inclined her face unto his. Together, their eyes fluttered closed, and their lips met softly.

The crowd cheered and whistled, and then the kiss deepened. Finally, Darby pulled his mouth away from hers and scooped Bella up, fluffy dress and all, and carried her away from the terrace.

Bella planted her feet onto the ground once Darby lowered her body. She called for Sophia to bring her bouquet. "Get ready girls!" All the unmarried women gathered around as Bella turned her back.

Bessie was on the front line; so was Fran. Then there were Grace, Sophia, Ashlynn, and...Ruth Ann?

Bella started counting. "One! Two! Three!"

The bundle of flowers soared into the air and landed right in the middle of some determined maidens. And a widow. Finally, after a few tugs, Sophia arose. Her eyes darted down to the bouquet as if to say, "Uh-oh."

Thunder rolled in the distance causing the crowd to disperse. The Banquet Hall was prepared with the finest foods prepared by Chef, not to mention the cake with a hidden charm.

Darby held out his arm, "Shall we?"

Bella folded her arm in his, but instead of allowing him to lead her inside, she pulled him toward the green grass.

"What are you doing, Bella Pierson?" Darby questioned with an infectious smile.

White clouds full of rain had settled above them. Behind the clouds was a silver lining.

The Light.

Bella withdrew her arm from Darby's and opened her palms toward the heavens. A drop or two rain fell from the sky and bounced in the core of her hands. They stood closely enough for her to return his smile with a kiss while she stared into the depths of his heart as the rain came down.

Bella interlaced her fingers with his and said, "Just dance, Darby."

EPILOGUE

Six Years Later

BELLA STOOD BEFORE THE SINK full of dirty breakfast dishes, her protruding stomach nestled in between. Her hand fished for a plate as she studied the gray horizon while she scrubbed.

"Haven't you been washing that plate long enough?" Darby said as he slipped his arms around her, nuzzling her neck.

She squirmed a bit. "I hadn't realized."

"Your thoughts were somewhere very far away."

"And you could probably guess where," she said.

Darby withdrew himself and took his place at her side. "Sophia," he said bluntly.

Bella just nodded her head in silence.

"You can't help what she does, honey."

Bella turned a fierce gaze toward Darby. "Didn't you see her?"

"Not as good as you but I did notice the bruises."

Bella just stood there staring out the window in search of an answer that could not be found. Darby's big hands turned her body. He pressed her firmly against him, caressing her back with the palm of his hand. "Listen, I'll stop by her house after meeting with Grayson & Sons Lumber Company. Maybe she will come stay with us."

Bella gasped as she tilted her head back. "You would do that for me?"

"Anything for you." His finger trailed her chin. "Besides, you need to be more concerned for the little life inside your womb."

She nodded in agreement, "And Bayla."

"Yes," Darby agreed, "and Bayla. Where is she anyway?"

"Getting her boots on."

An alarming smile spread across his face just before his lips softly caressed Bella's. "Just like her mother," he mumbled.

"Daddy! I'm ready!"

Both Darby and Bella turned at the sound of Bayla's voice. There she stood in her blue gingham dress, the same shade as her eyes. Its hem barely teased the tops of her boots. "Hurry! It's starting to rain!" Bayla pointed toward the window.

Darby chuckled as he knelt down before his five year old daughter. "Sweetheart, Daddy has a real important meeting in a little bit; maybe Mommy can dance with you this time."

Bayla dropped her head and shrugged her shoulders. "But you're more fun. She just waddles."

Darby bit the inside of his jaw to keep from smiling. "Okay, maybe just for a few minutes." Bayla's eyes lit up. "But I'm only dancing if Mommy does."

Bayla started jumping up and down pulling at Bella's apron. "Please! Mommy, please!"

"Okay, maybe just for a few minutes," Bella said as she glanced toward the sink full of dishes. They could wait.

Bella's bare feet stepped onto the concrete porch, the cool crisp feeling traveling up her ankles. She watched as Darby took Bayla's hands and twirled her little body around and around. She placed her palm on the tiny foot pushing at her side. "Are you going to be born dancing, too?" Bella whispered.

"Come on, Mommy!" Bayla cheered.

Bella's heart swelled with pure bliss as she descended the steps, the rain beating upon the tops of her feet. Her eyes drank in the image of Darby and Bayla. So much like her and her Papa. Her eyes was drawn to *The Light* peeking through the clouds. Her heart hummed a prayer of thanks as she joined hands with her husband and daughter. Suddenly a loud clap of thunder ceased their dance, and they hurried to the porch, Bella lagging behind a bit.

"I don't like it when it thunders." Bayla whined as she wiped away the raindrops sliding down her forehead.

"Don't worry, baby," Darby took his daughter into his arms. "It's just God talking to the wind."

"Really?"

Darby tweaked her nose. "Yep."

"What's he saying?"

Bella just stood there with her palm resting firmly upon the roundness of her belly and studied Darby, the perfect father and husband. The president of Pierson Enterprises. The man she loved with her entire heart. The man she danced in the rain with...

"Do you hear that whistling sound the wind is making?" she heard him ask.

Bayla just nodded her head.

"God is telling the wind that it's time to sing."

AUTHOR'S NOTE

In 1895, George Vanderbilt built what we call America's Castle, known as Biltmore Estate near Asheville, North Carolina. Biltmore Forest School, the first practical forestry school in America, was founded in 1898 by German forester, Carl A. Schenck. In November 1908, the Biltmore Forest Fair was held to demonstrate practical forestry methods, and to celebrate the tenth anniversary of the Forestry School.

A fun fact about Cornelia Vanderbilt's birthday party is the charms were really hidden in the cake. All except the heart; it was purely fictitious. The dime was the one all children hoped for, and the one Mrs. Vanderbilt feared had been swallowed by a child.

Research states that a maid had been astounded by the beauty of the Banquet Hall and dropped the serving tray. Mr. Vanderbilt got down on his hands and knees to help clean up, and then promoted her to chambermaid.

The Matron, Mrs. King, was the head of command and was paid more than the butler, and she was known for the constant jangling of her keys.

For Christmas, Mrs. Vanderbilt hosted a party for the employees and the scholars. It was then she presented them with gifts she purchased in Paris.

Pierson Enterprises is entirely fictitious, as well as the *Philosophy of Physiotherapy*, the book that changed the story.

Janie Jackson Beeler, thank you for traveling every step of this journey with me. Thank you, Lucy Ewing, Tammie Reed, Tonja Saylor, and Danessa Saylor for your constructive criticism and support. Thank you, Helen Wilder, for your support, guidance, and editing services. Thank you, Danielle Saylor and Jake Alred, for posing as fictional characters; Bella & Darby. Thank you, Lifetime Portraits by Samantha Blondell, for making the cover awesome!

Most importantly, I give thanks to *The One* who placed the words in my heart and directed the path that led to *Dancing in the Rain*. Sometimes the storms of life dim my vision, but I'm thankful *The Light* kept calling me.

Book Two

Singing in the Storm

Coming in Fall 2015

PROLOGUE

August, 1915
Asheville, North Carolina

The blow had come as a bit of a shock. And then another and another. Sophia thought that Curt had changed. He had promised to never lay a hand on her again, but his actions proved his statement a lie. She bit back the cry of agony as her body weakened under his violent force. Her mind begun to swirl. Slowly she was slipping into the unknown.

Curt would apologize tomorrow and cry about his stupidity in a drunken stupor. He'd pull her close and try kissing away the bruises, promising her that he would a perfect husband if she would only give him a chance. But Sophia had already given him so many chances. She had already decided there was no more mercy when she questioned the scent of whiskey on his breath.

Sophia's limp form sank to the old wooden floor beneath her with a thump while Curt staggered to the bedroom where his lifeless body fell onto the bed made of feathers.

Neither of them were aware of their surroundings.

Not even the smoke dancing above the cigar that had fallen to the floor.

The sodden ashes gave way as her feet stepped closer to the place she used to call home. Immediately, Sophia's hand went to her cheek. It still stung from the bruise. Her eyes took in what used to belong to her. And Curt.

But it was gone. Everything. Even Curt.

How she escaped without a burn, Sophia would never know. All she remembered was waking in Bella's living room begging for a sip of water. No one knows how she crawled out of the burning three room house and made it to safety.

All she knows is she's alive.

And Curt is dead.

A pang smote her heart. Sophia cared deeply for her husband of less than a year. Curt had been nothing short of one surprise after another. She had remained in the dark about his drinking habits until their wedding night when she found a half-pint hidden beneath his pillow. That was the same night his fist had struck her for the first time.

She wiped away a stray tear. It seemed to be one gigantic nightmare, and she should awaken soon. Except the dawning never came. Instead, the echoes of Curt screaming at her bombarded her mind. His ruthless hands seemed to reach from beneath and enclose about her neck.

"Sophia?"

She felt a gentle hand rest on her shoulder. She turned. "Bella," she whispered. Arms of love reached around her, embracing her, although Bella's protruding stomach stood in the way. "Why does life take me down these crooked and vile paths?"

Bella stroked Sophia's back. "It's not always going to be like this."

Sophia withdrew herself and wiped away the bitter tears streaming down her cheeks. "No peace. No happiness. No home," a sob erupted from the deepest parts of Sophia's soul. "The only things life has offered me have been pain and loss." She ground her teeth together. "And hate."

"That's not true, Sophia."

Sophia stormed away from Bella. "I don't want to hear it! Your life is perfect! My life is a mess!"

Bella followed Sophia, stepping across the splintered boards. "Sophia, stop! You don't have to live the life you have been living." Bella pleaded. "There is freedom. There is hope. There is love…"

"Not for me."

"You can stay with us and try to forget what happened."

Sophia turned and faced Bella boldly. "Do you really think that's possible? No, wait. Don't answer me. I think it's absolutely ridiculous to allow someone like me under your roof."

"You're my sister."

Sophia's sapphire eyes froze Bella in place. "I am a vile person. A wretched, adulterous woman!"

Bella stepped toward Sophia. "Listen, we are here to help you, Sophia."

"You know I don't do church."

"You used to."

Sophia turned away and studied the tiny trickle of smoke dancing above the remains of her home. Suddenly, she realized how cold she was inside. "I'm leaving."

"Where are you going?" Bella asked full of concern.

"I don't know. I'll go as far as my money allows me," Sophia said as she started to walk away.

"Then what?" Bella sobbed.

"I don't know. I guess I'll cross that bridge when I come to it." Almost immediately, thoughts of just a few days ago filled her mind. She tried so hard to silence the evil remarks she had received from Curt. *Go ahead, Sophia! You need a little money; you know what to sell!*

And that was exactly how she earned the few dollars that was safely tucked away against her bosom.

Sophia shook her head and ignored the churning in her stomach. That was one way she would *not* earn money. In the new place, wherever that might be, no one would know what her past consisted of. She could be a new person, even though something inside her mocked her conscience.

Sophia started toward the borrowed buggy when her gaze collided with the tarnished, silver band. Then she remembered. She had taken it off and thrown it at Curt when he was late coming home that dreadful evening. For a moment, she thought she would walk away from the only item that survived the flames. But instead, she stooped down and took it into the palm of her hand. At least she could use it to ward off unwanted male attention. Then again she pondered throwing it far from her and forgetting about the man who had slid it onto her finger.

Instead, she slid the band into her pocket.

At least she wouldn't be on the train alone.

Made in the USA
Charleston, SC
04 February 2015